PENGUIN

McGARR ON THE

Bartholomew Gill, Irish-American in descent, has
received an M. Litt. degree from Trinity College in
Dublin and presently lives in New York State. His
other novels include *Little Augie's Lament*, *Lucky
Shuffles*, *McGarr and the Politician's Wife* (also
published by Penguin Books), and *McGarr and the
Sienese Conspiracy*.

McGarr
on the Cliffs
of Moher

by
Bartholomew Gill

PENGUIN BOOKS

Penguin Books Ltd, Harmondsworth,
Middlesex, England
Penguin Books, 625 Madison Avenue,
New York, New York 10022, U.S.A.
Penguin Books Australia Ltd, Ringwood,
Victoria, Australia
Penguin Books Canada Limited, 2801 John Street,
Markham, Ontario, Canada L3R 1B4
Penguin Books (N.Z.) Ltd, 182–190 Wairau Road,
Auckland 10, New Zealand

First published in the United States of America and Canada by
Charles Scribner's Sons 1978
Published in Penguin Books 1982

LIBRARY OF CONGRESS CATALOGING IN PUBLICATION DATA
Gill, Bartholomew, 1943–
McGarr on the Cliffs of Moher.
I. Title.
PS3563.A296M34 1982   813'.54   82-506
ISBN 0 14 00.6197 5   AACR2

Printed in the United States of America by
George Banta Co., Inc., Harrisonburg, Virginia
Set in Caledonia

CONTENTS

MC GARR ON THE CLIFFS OF MOHER

1

ON THE CLIFFS NEAR THE WIDE OCEAN

"I was after having a bit of a gargle, sir. Truth is, I was under the gaff. I thought I'd pull the car in off the road and put the public out of danger. I tried to get in close to the wall. I guess I was worse off than I thought." He pointed to the left side of the new Jaguar sedan. The paint was torn down the length, showing bright sheet metal below the cream-colored lacquer. The rear fender was crushed.

"Then I felt a need."

McGarr glanced at the man. The euphemism seemed odd coming from him. He was a Dublin dance hall owner, but McGarr knew better. Barry Hanly was a type—he'd trade in anything that promised a fast profit. He had said he was forty-two. To McGarr, Hanly looked fifty-two. He was fat and pasty. The only chins that he had were unnecessary. Even the expensive three-piece blue suit and cashmere chesterfield coat couldn't hide the collapse of his upper body. McGarr had grown up with and, later, had had to arrest dozens of men like Hanly. They had spent so much energy trying to avoid real work they were used up before their time. And Hanly was nervous now, puffing a little as he tried to explain to McGarr how he had come to stumble across the body of a young woman out here in a pasture near the Cliffs of Moher.

She was propped against the other side of the wall, dressed in a stylish full-length leather coat. Her legs were crossed casually. Through her violet-tinted glasses her eyes seemed to be focused on a point distant in the Atlantic. She had four punctures where somebody had jabbed a pitchfork through her upper chest.

"I don't know what it was," Hanly continued. "Either me being 'locked,' like I told youse, or just being a city boy or what . . ." He glanced up at Garda Superintendent O'Shaughnessy. The tall Galwayman's face was impassive, his eyes seemingly disinterested in anything Hanly might say. "Ach—what's the use? You'd never believe it anyhow. I must have fell over the wall, hit me head on a rock. When I woke up, I was sprawled on her lap." The right side of his forehead was a large blue bruise with a pink center that was scabbing. "And she as dead as a post." Hanly turned away from McGarr and O'Shaughnessy and kicked a stone. His feet bulged from loafers made of glove leather. They were Italian, and McGarr had seen them in a Grafton Street shop for thirty-five pounds a pair. "Well—would I have flagged down a car and told the driver to get the Garda if I had killed her?" he implored. "Cripes, I haven't touched a thing. I know you boys'll get me out of this one."

"Here's what Bernie could dig up on him." Hughie Ward handed McGarr the facts that had been relayed over the police radio in the Rover. It was parked back on the road to avoid marring the tire impressions in the soft ground. "All old stuff. One case of aggravated assault, though."

"In 1957, for God's sake!" Hanly said. He turned to McGarr. "And it was dismissed. Just some little gouger I had to chuck out of the dance hall. He kept coming back in. I had to settle him." Hanly's face, once handsome in a rough way—nose upturned and thick, beard black and heavy, hair wavy—was livid, and he seemed to have a slight case of the shakes.

McGarr knew what it was. Hanly was indeed hung over.

"Take it easy, Barry. May I call you that?" asked McGarr. He took Hanly by the arm and walked him away from O'Shaughnessy.

After several paces, McGarr stopped and removed a small flask of whiskey from the liner pocket of his raincoat. He took a nip himself and handed the bottle to Hanly. "The situation calls for courage, my friend."

"Ah, thanks, Super. You're a right man." Even the sight of the flask cheered Hanly. "I thought I was drowning in a sea of thirst, so I did."

He took a long pull on the flask, nearly finishing it. When he could speak again, he said, "Remember, now—I owe you one." The whites of his eyeballs were laced with red veins. His nose was running. "Which reminds me." He turned from McGarr and peeked over the wall. He had still not handed McGarr back the flask. His pinky finger protruded daintily. On it was a fat gold ring with a red stone. "I could have sworn I had a bottle of Canadian Club in me jacket. I brought it along for companionship, just in case I got lost on the way to the jakes." He winked.

McGarr motioned to the stile and followed Hanly over it. "What can you tell me about her?" he asked.

"Nothing. Never saw her before, and that's the God's honest truth, I swear it, Superintendent." Hanly then finished the flask as though he believed he wouldn't get another chance now that the questions had begun anew. "You can check for yourself down in the town." He meant Lahinch, about five miles away. "If you can trace me movements." Again he winked at McGarr. The whiskey had hit him fast. McGarr imagined booze generated much of whatever trouble Barry Hanly currently experienced.

3

In front of them for several hundred yards lay pastures which walls of narrow stones divided. Then, suddenly, the land stopped. It was as though whatever force was responsible for Ireland had become contrary and quit its work of island making peremptorily. The cliffs of black basalt fell six hundred feet into the sea.

As usual, the wind that swept in from the Atlantic seemed to collect below the cliffs and, with a blast that could stagger a man, raged over the bluff and across Ireland. But today the breeze was warm, even hot almost. The ocean was white and glary and shrouded in mist.

McGarr nudged the brim of his straw hat so it would shade his eyes. He turned toward the land. Below him and stretching for miles into the hinterland was a sloping expanse of green meadow tinged yellow now in late July. It had been the hottest and driest summer on record. For the past two weeks it had rained but once, and for an hour only. The tourist industry was ecstatic, the farmers complaining. McGarr could see some of them about a half mile distant. Using pitchforks taller than two men, they were piling sweet dry hay into a large cart. This two draft horses pulled. The field was too rocky for a tractor.

Turning to Hanly, he said, "She looks like a city girl, doesn't she?"

Hanly cocked his head. "That she does." He studied the empty flask for a moment, then handed it back to McGarr. "But not Dublin. More like London, by the look of her. She's too . . ." He couldn't find the right word. He looked away.

But McGarr had understood what he meant. She was a bit too totally stylish for an Irish girl. Her platform shoe was just slightly too tall and impractical for walking. One was missing. Her glasses were immense and ludicrous. The lenses alone were the size of McGarr's palms.

4

McGarr reached down and removed them. They were heavy, too. Prescription lenses, the sort that shaded in direct sunlight, the frames made in Italy.

McGarr guessed she was thirty or thereabouts. She wasn't exactly a beauty—her face seemed drawn and not just in death—but her build was ample, legs well shaped. Her hair was black and worn in a windswept fashion that seemed redundant here. Her mouth was just slightly open, as though she was expecting somebody out there in the ocean where her gaze was directed. McGarr could see that her front teeth had been capped. In all, she moved McGarr to pity her—to have tried to be so chic, only to have died in the crotch of a country wall in the West of Ireland by means of an instrument as rude as a pitchfork.

McGarr tried to remove her right hand from the coat pocket. He had to use both hands.

Hanly bent to help him but jumped back when her hand jerked free with an automatic pistol locked in it.

It was a Mauser, a small but powerful gun. This, McGarr could see, was an old one, an antique of sorts. It went with her other things. McGarr removed it from her grasp and smelled the barrel. It had been fired since its last cleaning, and recently, too. He checked the clip. One bullet was missing. He scanned the area for the shell casing but couldn't see it.

"Radical chic," said Ward, who was now standing in back of McGarr waiting to give his boss a hand.

In her other pocket McGarr found a leather case. It contained two passports—Irish and American—a driver's license issued by the state of New York, and $27,000 in American currency. The bills were large—five $5,000 and two $1,000 notes—but so new and thin they fit into a back pocket of the case. McGarr found them only after having rummaged through everything else.

When Hanly realized what they were, he staggered a bit.

"You certainly picked a pillow for your head, Mr. Hanly," Ward said.

McGarr handed him the driver's license. It read May Quirk, 638 West 71st Street, New York, N.Y. The American passport gave a different Manhattan address, and the Irish passport said she was born and still lived as of December 29, 1967, in Lahinch.

McGarr turned and motioned to Dan O'Malley, the Lahinch Garda superintendent. An older man, O'Malley carefully negotiated the stile. McGarr showed him the Irish passport. "Do you know the family?"

At first O'Malley didn't say a word, only squinted into the dim photograph of a considerably younger person, no more than a girl. He held it at different distances from his eyes, turning it until he got the page in focus. He then read the name aloud. "Quirk. Quirk." His eyes suddenly cleared and his mouth dropped open. "Oh—God, no. It can't be." He glanced down at the dead woman. "But it is. It's John and Aggie Quirk's only child. May, she was. Went to the States about ten years ago and only just returned for a visit. They hired a cab, too, you know, to fetch her from Shannon. They'd been living alone since she left." He looked down at the passport again and then back at May Quirk. He closed the little green book and handed it to McGarr. He looked beyond the pastures, toward the sea, as though following her gaze. "I think I'll retire. They give you the option now, you know."

McGarr well knew. It had been he who had convinced the commissioner of police that the early retirement of senior-most Garda officers would free up many of the higher-paying posts to younger men whom police work still regaled.

"I've seen too much—" O'Malley's voice broke. "—tragedy in

6

my time. And now this. I grew up with her father and mother. We went to school together. They weren't married until late, you know. He had to wait for the farm. I went to their wedding. And her—" He pointed to the dead woman. "—christening. And even to the party they threw before she left for the States. They didn't want her to emigrate, you see. Thought something might happen to her over there in the concrete jungle. And then to have this happen to her here, after she went and became a lovely worldly woman and all." He shook his head. "I'm sick of it. How can I tell her folks." In no way did his face, which was shaved so close it shone, betray the emotion he was expressing. His eyes were very blue and clear. His Garda uniform fit him snug, but McGarr noticed, as O'Malley turned and walked back toward the stile, he had the step of a tired man.

McGarr called to his back, "Don't worry about that, Superintendent. I'll tell them, if you prefer."

O'Malley shook his head. "That's my job, thanking you just the same, Peter." He paused at the top of the wall. "And then tomorrow, I'll be after sending you my badge and so forth, if you don't mind."

"Why don't you take some time and think about it first, Danny," said McGarr.

"Cripes, I've had fifty years to think about it. Enough is enough."

O'Shaughnessy offered the old superintendent his hand and helped him down the other side of the wall.

O'Malley said, "It's high time I left the job to a younger man. New blood and all that."

McGarr turned to Hanly. "You know, Barry, I'm half tempted to believe your story, wild as it is. You can't fake a hangover the way you're doing now, but how in the name of hell you managed to pass out in a dead woman's lap with a ten-thousand-quid pillow for your head is something that requires a definite explanation.

"Now then, did you meet her in Lahinch, and did she then agree to accompany you up here?"

"No. At least I don't think so, Super. Like I told youse before." He turned to O'Shaughnessy and Ward as though pleading with them. "I was under the gaff. Jarred, I was. And I don't rightly remember much of anything. And that's the long and short of it, I swear." He passed a hand over his face, which was greasy. He needed more whiskey. "That happens to me sometimes. Once I woke up in Belfast, another time in a motel outside Manchester. I guess I've got the failing, *but* I do remember most of last night—I think!—and I can tell you I never saw this girl before this morning. Honest. I'll swear to it." His bloated face was running with sweat now.

"But how did your head come to rest on her lap?" Ward asked.

Hanly just looked at him and blinked. His eyes were bulging and McGarr could almost feel the pain throbbing behind them.

The wind off the cliffs had increased now and wailed through the chinks in the pasture walls, sounding to McGarr like the keening of women at wakes.

Finally Hanly said, "I remember Lahinch. I stopped in two—no, three bars. All of them right there in the middle of town. In the last I bought the C. C."

"Why C. C.?" O'Shaughnessy asked. It wasn't something a person with Hanly's background would usually order.

"I don't know. A whim, I suspect. Maybe I was just putting on the dog for all the locals. You know—big car, the expensive clothes. I get to playing the fool when—" He broke off and passed his tongue over his upper lip, which was parched. He then pulled off the heavy coat. The light, tan cashmere was soiled and matted where he had slept on it.

8

"What do you usually drink?" asked Ward.

"Anything with a punch in it, but I think I might have ordered Scotch first. Just by way of getting a rise out of the barman, you know."

In his mind's eye McGarr could see the drunken Hanly bashing the wall with the Jaguar, then getting out to relieve himself. The wall proved too much for him, though, and he conked his sconce. He staggered up and, seeing May Quirk sitting against the wall, went to her for solace or companionship or whatever. The moment he got his head on her lap, he passed out. All this hinged upon Hanly's having told them the truth, that is, and May Quirk's being dead at the time. Where, then, was Hanly's bottle of whiskey? For a man of Hanly's preoccupations, that would be the one thing he'd remember. He probably hit his head while protecting the bottle as he fell.

Another possibility was that May Quirk had come along after Hanly had passed out and, seeing his car, had poked about to find him. She discovered Hanly and tried to help him. Then Hanly himself or somebody else killed her. But then where was her car? Why was she down this laneway at least a mile from the road and carrying so much money on her person? At whom might she have fired the Mauser? And, of course, why was she killed?

McGarr said, "What time did you leave Lahinch?" The pathologist could place the time of May Quirk's death within reasonable parameters.

"Closing, I think. It must have been closing. I never leave the last pub before closing."

"Which was what time?" O'Shaughnessy asked. On Friday nights in the country, greedy publicans' clocks sometimes ran very slow indeed.

Superintendent O'Malley said, "Half eleven. I run a tight town. That's one thing they'll never take away from me."

9

McGarr turned to Ward. "Take him down to the barracks in Lahinch. I want to know every intimate detail of Barry Hanly's life from birth through the concatenation of misadventures that have led him to this sad pass. Specifically, since I'm sure it's a question of near-criminal interest, what windfall has put him in the way of that Jaguar, these clothes, and this wallet." McGarr had another wallet in his pocket. Hanly's contained items of personal interest along with a roll of currency from various countries that totaled over twenty thousand pounds. It was as thick as the Dublin phone directory.

"That's just the receipts from the dance I put on."

"In Dublin?" McGarr asked.

"No. The one last night was in Ennis. It's the only way to make money in this business anymore. You've got to bring the talent to the people now. I'm even thinking of closing down the dance hall in Dublin. There's nothing but headaches in it." Just the mention of the word seemed to bring one on for Hanly. His hand went up to his brow.

McGarr turned to Ward, who nodded. Hanly had staged a dance that night. "But how big can your dances be? What do you charge for admission? And why so much foreign money?" At least a thousand pounds of it was South African. There were Australian and Canadian dollars, some gilder notes from Holland, greenbacks from the States, and New Zealand currency as well.

"It's the tourist season. I don't like to exchange me money out here in these country banks. I've got a little deal with the manager of the Provincial Bank on Pearse Street in town." He meant Dublin. "He gives me commercial rates."

"What's his name?"

"Scannell."

"Check that," McGarr said to Ward. Then he asked Hanly,

"What were your immediate plans, say, for today, tomorrow, and the coming week?"

Hanly began scratching the balding crown of his head. Not once during the interview had he looked directly at McGarr, who had put it down to Hanly's former brushes with the law and his background in the Dublin slums where anybody interested in an easy living learned early to avoid the police. But now McGarr detected a new attitude. Hanly was gloating—his ears pulled back just slightly, and McGarr could have sworn he flashed a drunken smile—as though he had pulled off a slick caper, and right under the nose of Ireland's top cop. "Don't know, Super. I suppose—" He straightened up. "I'll try to pull meself together and go on with affairs. Got another dance to-night."

"Where?"

"Salthill. And then there's the car. Haven't had it but a week."

McGarr handed him back his wallet. "I wonder how many Irish South Africans return every summer. I'm sure we can find that out."

" 'T weren't Irish at all," said Hanly, staggering toward the stile in the wall. "South Africans pure and simple. Ruggers on tour."

"But they paid over a thousand pounds to dance?"

"And drink. I run that concession too, of course. And all legally." He nearly fell on the top of the stile. "I followed them through three towns—Wexford, Waterford, and Youghal. They made crowds, which love to dance. Which is my business."

"And mine is to ask you to accompany us to the barracks in Lahinch. You want to help the police in the investigation of this murder, don't you?" said O'Shaughnessy. Under Irish law the police could hold for two days a man who was "helping" them.

After that he must be cautioned and arrested or released. Under the Offenses Against the State Act, which deals with terrorist groups like the I.R.A. and lists a schedule of offenses such as the possession of firearms, explosives, and gathering in groups for the purpose of overthrowing the state, the suspect might be held indefinitely.

"But how long am I going to be held?"

"Depends on how much and how quickly you help us."

"But my dance. It's my livelihood, my life's blood! I thought the super . . ."

"My title is Chief Inspector of Detectives," said McGarr. It was a classification that had been made especially for him when he left Interpol to join the Garda Soichana. McGarr's only superiors were the commissioner of police and the minister of justice, who was an elected official. Unofficially, McGarr was being groomed for the top job. The commissioner was only a few years from retirement. "And I'm just the pretty face in the crowd, Barry. I carry the flask." McGarr wiggled the little bottle at Hanly. "A few drinks, some pleasant conversation. It's all in a day's work." McGarr looked down at May Quirk. She was still looking out over the far ocean, as she had, he imagined, before she left for America—expectantly, almost hopefully. McGarr wondered what she had found there. He wondered also about the money and the ugly way she had died. "And make sure he's as clean as a whistle. I'd prefer to have him handy."

"But my *business*, McGarr!"

"To hell with your business," said O'Malley. "In my book it's just trash anyhow, and you're the dirty bastard what done this thing to poor May. And if I have my way we'll get it out of you by noon. By the old methods, too. The ones we used on liars."

"Don't you have a partner who can step in for you?" O'Shaughnessy asked. "Or are you too concerned with your profits?"

12

Hanly glanced up at the Garda superintendent. "Profit? There's no way I could keep tabs on anybody else. They'd rob me blind."

McGarr said, "But the dance will go on."

Hanly hunched his shoulders. "I suppose."

O'Shaughnessy said, "Anyhow, you're agreeing to help the police in our investigation of this murder, aren't you, Mr. Hanly?"

"The last time I agreed to that I spent a couple of days in the can and then got arrested on trumped-up charges."

"But this time you're not guilty of anything, or so you've said."

Hanly said nothing, only allowed himself to be led toward the Rover.

O'Shaughnessy closed the door.

McGarr was saying to Ward, "Autopsy, of course. And a thorough job on that car. I want to know if May Quirk was ever in it. Then the area around this field. I want to know where the shell casing is. Also, get a wire out to New York to see what they know or can learn about her there. Tell them about the money and ask if they can find out where she did her banking and if the funds were her own. I don't have to tell you to leave no avenue open on him." McGarr meant Hanly. "Call up Bernie and have him personally look up our contacts in town. I want any rumors he can get on Hanly."

"You mean you don't believe him about the money?"

"Would you get drunk with that much cash on you if it was your own?"

Ward wrinkled his forehead.

"And Hanly, despite his plush appearance, is *not* your average happy-go-lucky bowsey. You can bet he keeps a tight grip on a thrupenny bit. Early poverty like his must have been is memorable." McGarr himself was speaking from experience.

13

Ward, O'Shaughnessy, and O'Malley drove off with Hanly. McGarr's own private car was parked out by the road, but he decided he'd wait until the Technical Bureau arrived. And, in a vague way, he wanted to keep May Quirk company.

He started across the pastures toward the cliffs and the ocean beyond. The mist had begun to lift now. A bright red trawler was lurching in the silver sea. There was a vivid band of sunlight just above the horizon where the clouds began, and the breeze off the water carried the steady knock of the vessel's diesel shoreward. Clumps of witches'-broom with tiny yellow flowers and the purple blossoms of thistle dotted the fields. A solitary and old cow turned her head to McGarr as he hopped over another wall into her pasture. She followed him with her eyes, her jaw swirling on her cud.

McGarr felt almost giddy as he approached the edge of the cliff. Below he could see heavy ocean rollers rushing shoreward, the water so deep here that none crested before slamming into the basalt cliffs. Each clapped through the backwash of the preceding wave and broke full on the cliffs, giving off a rumble that seemed to quake the ground beneath McGarr's feet.

Having heard about slides off the Cliffs of Moher in which cattle and farmers had plunged to their deaths below, McGarr looked in back of him to make sure the technical crew's van had not yet arrived and then got down on his hands and knees to belly himself up to the edge of the cliffs. He removed his Panama hat and began edging himself forward.

McGarr was a small man with a thick build and red hair gone bald on top. His features were regular, but his nose was perhaps a trifle overlong. His eyes were gray. He was forty-nine years old and today wore a short-sleeved white shirt, tan slacks, and dark brown brogues.

Nearly seven hundred feet below him the surf boiled against the black cliff face. Sea gulls whirled at various levels,

14

none having to flap its wings in the blast that pushed up from the sea and over the land. McGarr knew there were caves below there. During the eighteenth century they had been used as keeps for smugglers who in wood and tarred-canvas curraghs braved surf and rock and perhaps an enraged bull seal within the cave to avoid paying the king his tax.

Off to McGarr's right was O'Brien's Folly. It was a granite turret that the foolish Irish M. P. Corny O'Brien had built in 1835 as a teahouse and observatory. If anything, it marred the clear sweep of the cliffs. McGarr could see tourists struggling against the breeze up the pathway toward the edifice. Others were, as he, crawling over a rock escarpment to peer below.

That was when he saw the small amber-colored cap snagged in the gorse near his face. Using his handkerchief he picked it up, holding as little of its surface as possible. He held it to his nose—rye whiskey, no doubt about it. The proximity of this object to the cliff face made him wonder if May Quirk's killer might have chucked the pitchfork off the cliffs. It seemed the handiest place. If so, it might be recovered, and, if recovered, it might reveal important details. But the project of descending from this eminence and then putting divers into the frigid waters was a tall order and a dangerous task. He'd have to word his request tactfully, pointing up the advantages such a massive undertaking might mean for the Technical Bureau.

He heard a door slam and, looking behind him, saw that the technical crew had arrived. Easing himself away from the cliff, he stood and walked toward them.

Chief Superintendent Tom McAnulty himself was in charge of this van. "Just keeping myself in touch with my boys," he told McGarr. McAnulty headed the Technical Bureau (ballistics, photography, fingerprints, and mapping) and was usually lodged behind a desk at Kilmainham in Dublin.

"But on Sunday?" McGarr asked.

"Got the wife and kids in the car in Lahinch. We were just on the way to the folks' place in Kilbaha."

"On holidays?"

"Have been for a week."

McGarr could tell from the way his men were glancing at McAnulty that he was the last person they had expected to see. McAnulty was also a short man, but he had a thick shock of black hair and a busy manner. He was known for keeping tabs on the slightest move his men made. They respected him for being a gifted professional, but they grumbled whenever he tried to do their jobs for them.

McGarr showed him the cap, and McAnulty called a sergeant over to take it away. McGarr then posed the question of a search effort below the Cliffs of Moher.

"Now *that's* a challenge," said McAnulty.

His men, who had been listening with half an ear as they went about their duties, swapped glances.

"Plenty of publicity for the Technical Bureau in it, too, I should think." McAnulty's small dark eyes were alight now. He liked the idea. "You know, we'll get Des Moore from the Sunday *Independent*. Have his cameraman Hogan get some pics of my men rappeling down the side of the cliff. Lovely stuff that is. You know—dramatic."

One of the detectives swore. When McAnulty turned, he pretended he had been clearing his throat. McAnulty knew what was best for the Technical Bureau and himself, even if they didn't.

When McGarr climbed into his Mini Cooper, he called the Lahinch Garda barracks and asked Superintendent O'Malley if he would have his men canvass the area, asking local farmers if they were missing a pitchfork.

"Half of them haven't looked for one in years, I trust," said

O'Malley. "Hate the sight of them, they do." He was in a foul mood still. "Hardly more than a dozen of them farm much more than the dole. They put a few cattle out to God and then pray the postman will bring them social insurance from Dublin and the price of a pint from wherever their kids have fled to abroad."

"Have you been to see the Quirks yet?"

"Just going now."

"I'm thinking I should be going with you."

"Funny they haven't called me already to report May missing."

McGarr now wondered about that too. "I'll be along shortly. We can go in my car."

2

A PUB MORNING IN A MARKET TOWN

Lahinch was a bright, crossroads market town that Saturday morning. The streets and sidewalks were thronged with shoppers. Not a door was closed. Some shop owners had carried their wares out into bins on the sidewalks, and street vendors had set up stalls in the square. Rubber boots, summer-weight clothes, a van the back of which was loaded with live chickens were offered, as were pyramids of purple cabbage, tomatoes, blond heads of cauliflower, and the <u>sempiternal</u> potato, the mainstay of the Irish diet. These last were new, with fine pinky skins. McGarr could tell they'd taste sweet with unsalted butter or sour cream. He was getting hungry.

He found an illegal parking place not far from the square, hesitated to pull down the visor with his Dublin Municipal Police pass on it, and finally, at least ten minutes later, parked the Cooper in a safe, regular spot back the way he had come on the road to the Cliffs of Moher.

Seeing the yellow-and-green kiosk of a public telephone outside the first pub he came to, McGarr stepped into the bar to get some change. It was so dark in there after the sunlit street that the damp, smoky air felt almost cold on McGarr's bare arms. The place was packed with men who, in spite of the fine

18

weather, were wearing wool coats over their shirts and even, some of them, vests below. Only one other man in the bar was without a soft cloth cap. McGarr had left his Panama in the car.

McGarr changed two pounds, ordered a large glass of Canadian Club, and took the glass out to the kiosk. The operator said the lines were jammed and he'd call back. McGarr had the luck of finding an open stool at the end of the bar closest to the street and the kiosk. Another man had meant to have that seat, though, and he said to McGarr, "The drink has no goodness in it today, has it, mister? It's as weak as sow's milk. The farmer, sure there's no contentment for him today. Pleasant weather, wouldn't you say?"

McGarr smiled and tilted his head. He took a drink of the Canadian Club. He was trying to keep half an ear to the telephone. He had called his wife, Noreen, since he believed he'd be spending at least several more days out here in Clare and wanted her with him.

"Well, mister," the man continued, "g' luck." He raised his pint, which was nearly full, and the black, frothy liquid seemed to slip down his throat with nary a swallow. Under his cap the man had the face of a bony steer, all nose and chin. His eyes were brown, soft, and gentle.

McGarr finished his whiskey and placed the glass on the bar. The man said, "I've got that," and laid a fiver on the bar.

This was, McGarr well knew, extraordinary behavior for a West-country man. Although in recent years Lahinch had become something of a resort town, with a fine golf course and a long, sandy beach, McGarr supposed that the gesture and all the convivial talk he could hear in the tight-packed barroom were remnants of the summer feeling that used to suffuse country society when relatives returned to bring in the hay or cut turf, or fish for lobster and mackerel. Few emigrees returned now, but

McGarr knew the bonhomie sometimes surfaced. For a few weeks in the summer the men spoke to strangers like McGarr. They even sang songs, and the very brave might buy a foreign woman a drink and flirt with her a bit.

"Thank you kindly. You're a good man. My name is McGarr. Peter McGarr."

"Michael Daly is mine." The man's hand engulfed McGarr's. "Stranger here?"

McGarr nodded and reached into his shirt pocket for his smokes.

Daly tried to beat him to it, though, and, in pulling his packet of cigarettes from his jacket, opened the top, and they spilled all over McGarr and the wet top of the bar. "Jesus, I'm an oaf," he said.

McGarr started picking them out of his lap.

Daly bent for the others that were on the floor. "Well, have one anyhow." When he straightened up, he said, "Have two."

The bartender was picking the others off the bar. He chucked them into the bin in back and gave Daly a reproving look.

McGarr said, "I can only smoke one at a time."

"Take two," Daly insisted. "Go ahead."

"But I've got my own." McGarr slapped his shirt pocket.

"No—I insist. Take another." He pushed his large hand at McGarr. It was bristling with cigarettes.

McGarr smiled and said, "All right." He placed the second cigarette behind his ear where the man could see it.

The man stuffed the other cigarettes in his coat pocket and struggled to pull out a box of matches.

McGarr already had a match lit.

As did the bartender, who held the light to the end of McGarr's cigarette. Again he gave Daly an admonitory glance.

"Where's yours?" McGarr asked before he put out his match.

"Oh—I don't really smoke myself. I found them in the booth." He jerked his thumb over his shoulder. "Last night. Just before closing." To conceal his embarrassment, he asked, "Are you married?"

That made McGarr remember he should be listening for the telephone.

"I hope you're not thinking of proposing, Michael," the bartender said, and several of the men close by laughed.

Daly turned red.

McGarr smiled and considered Daly closely. Only then did he realize that he and the man were roughly the same age. If anything, Daly was younger, but given his dress and manner he might well have been mistaken for a pensioner. The battered cap, the dark woolen jacket, the vest below, and the wide pants and brogans made him seem like a nineteenth century man stranded in the twentieth. The society that had sustained the simplicity of good men like the Michael Dalys of the past had now vanished. "Yes, I'm married. And you?"

Daly shook his head. He was now looking into the foamy head of his pint of porter. "Any nippers?"

"Not yet. We've only been married a few years."

"Keep trying," said Daly. "You've got to work at it."

The bartender had had enough of him. "And how would you know, Mick? The most you've ever seen of a woman was the scabby legs of a tinker wench on a wagon."

Again the other men laughed.

Daly reddened.

The phone was ringing outside in the kiosk. McGarr said, "That's the missus now," and rushed out to answer it.

"What's up?" asked Noreen, in a voice so faint and squawky McGarr could barely hear her.

"You sound like you're halfway around the world."

"What? I didn't catch that." The connection was bad at the Dublin end too.

"Can you come out here?"

"What?"

"Can you come out here?" He had to shout.

"Where are you? What happened?"

McGarr didn't want to explain his presence in Lahinch there where half the people on the street might hear. "Lahinch. The weather is beautiful. You can meet me at the usual place." He meant the Garda barracks.

"But where are you?"

"Lahinch, County Clare."

Noreen had heard "Lynch." She repeated it.

"No, no. *La*-hinch." McGarr spelled it out.

She got it that time.

They shouted their good-byes and rang off.

When McGarr got back into the pub he found that Michael Daly had bought him another whiskey. Daly said, "How can she meet you in the regular place when she didn't recognize the name?"

McGarr raised his glass, over the lip of which he said, "You didn't tell me you were a detective."

"Nor did you, though I'm not."

McGarr had underestimated the farmer.

"What did you say your last name is?"

The bartender and several patrons nearby had pricked up their ears.

"McGarr."

Daly nodded, then glanced at the others. "*Peter* McGarr," he said in a loud voice, as though he had announced a race winner.

Talk had quieted considerably in the pub now. McGarr was well known to most of his countrymen, the reputation he had developed while working for Interpol and, earlier, Criminal Justice in Paris having preceded him to Ireland. Since assuming the post of Chief Inspector of Detectives with the Garda Soichana, McGarr had hardly passed a week without his picture being in at least one of the national newspapers or on the telly.

Now that they knew who he was, McGarr decided he'd pursue the business at hand. "Who else drinks Canadian Club?" he asked the bartender.

He didn't even have to look around. "You're the only man, and I'll advise you to go slow on it, for that's the only bottle I got."

There was hardly a drink left in it.

"That's because a short, fat man dressed in a tan cashmere overcoat and blue suit put a dent in it last night," said McGarr.

The bartender raised an eyebrow.

Somebody at the other end of the now quiet bar said, "I told you that fellow was a bit of a chancer."

McGarr had lucked out. The men who were here this morning were sure to have been present last night. That the pub was like a social club for them McGarr didn't doubt.

Said Michael Daly, "That's not all that he put a dent in, neither. Jasus, he nearly run me down last night, and I noticed he had hit something with that beautiful new car of his. It was a darling machine, so it was."

"A Jaguar XJ12L, cream in color."

"The very same," said Daly. "But he'd bashed the back fender all to blazes."

The pub was so quiet now McGarr could hear water dripping from a tap onto sheet metal in back of the bar. "Are you sure?"

"It makes it the more tragic having that happen to a big white machine with such lovely lines. That's the sort of car on which a small scratch stands out like a mortal sin. But a folded fender! It makes you want to curse the owner."

"And he was a man you could curse, too," said another man.

When everybody turned to him, he added, "Flashy and bloated. Had a way of speaking that put me in mind of the bawl of an ass."

"How many drinks did he have?"

"Three quick ones," said the bartender. "He was half seas over as it was. And he tried to con a fourth out of me as well. And him with that coat and car and all. I told him his trade wasn't wanted, and if he hadn't been so quick with his glass I would have taken that from him too."

The men in the barroom agreed with him. The flashy Dublin fellow had been pretty much of a bad type. They then quieted again and waited for McGarr to ask the next question.

"Was he alone?"

"Yes."

"And in the car, too," Daly added. "I only saw one head. His. Sort of neckless and piggy, if you know what I mean."

"He didn't happen to buy a full bottle of Canadian Club from you before he left, did he now?"

"He did not!" The bartender straightened up and smoothed down his white apron that was stained from heading pints of stout.

"Could he have bought a bottle of Canadian Club in some other public house in Lahinch?"

"Indeed he might have. But not here."

"Could he have stopped at another pub on his way out of Lahinch?"

"No, sir. This is the last stop in Lahinch."

Daly added, "And he didn't, anyhow. I saw him stagger to the Jaguar, fumble around with the keys, and after a couple of minutes he roared away. The way he shifted that luvely machine was enough to make you cringe. Like he was grinding coffee."

McGarr thought for a moment, taking a sip from his glass. He was getting a little tight, which—he checked his wristwatch, 11:45—did not augur well for the rest of a day that undoubtedly would be filled with many details. "Does May Quirk come in here?"

The men looked at each other. "Do you mean John Quirk's young daughter? Is that what all the police business is about?" asked a man sitting on a bench along a wall. He set his glass on the table and stood. "I saw Dan O'Malley go out early this morning. She's my niece, she is."

McGarr was still looking at the bartender, who asked in a low voice, "What's this all about?"

"Does May Quirk come in here?" he asked again, this time staring the man straight in the eye. He had always believed that the only real advantage he had over other policemen was that people always seemed willing to talk to him. For a long time McGarr had thought this was because he looked harmless and gentle, but his wife, Noreen, had told him it was his eyes. When he stared at somebody, she had said, he looked as though he could see right into them and knew their secret thoughts. His eyes were the palest of gray and unblinking.

The bartender looked away and arranged a few of the glasses that were drying below the bar. "Yes," he said with a sigh. "She's been popping in here regular since she's returned, *and*, I might add, all over town too. There's not a licensed premises in the area that she hasn't been in and out of at least once a night." And before May Quirk's uncle could object, he turned to him and said, "Well—it's true, Billy. You know so yourself."

"Is she a drinker?" McGarr asked, restraining his own urge to sip from the whiskey glass.

"Not a bit of it!" roared the old man, her uncle. "Just like her mother and father, she is. Oh—she'll buy herself a drink, just to please certain parties." He meant the publican, McGarr supposed. "But she never drinks it, does she now? And you never cry seeing her come through the door, do you, Edward? Not a bit of it! She's always got half a dozen thirsty friends trailing in her wake. And who buys every time? May—that's who."

"Ah, g'wan wid you," said another man. "She's an American now and probably makes more in a month than we do in a year."

"I'll not have her dragged down in the muck by the likes of you ungrateful bowsies!" the old man roared.

McGarr asked Daly, "What is she like?"

Daly tilted his head slightly and said over the lip of his nearly empty pint, "Ah—May's a great one for a laugh. And she's got jokes. A codder, she is. She could wheedle a song from a stone, or make any man in this room blush and run."

McGarr pulled out his wallet and placed a ten-pound note on the bar. He then gestured his hand in a way that meant he intended to buy everybody a drink. He put his hand over his own glass, though, and said, "But not me, please."

Another man said, "And a finer pair of legs I've never seen in Lahinch!" He was an old gaffer with a stain of tobacco juice running into his white chin bristles. He then cackled a bit and clapped up his toothless jaw. He rocked back and forth in his seat and studiously avoided May Quirk's uncle's eyes.

"That's not all that's fine on her, neither," Daly whispered to McGarr.

"You fancy her, do you?"

Daly was a bit tight himself. He leaned close to McGarr and said in a rush, "God, I'd cut off my—" he paused, "—toes, if she'd have me just for a night. A woman like that . . ." His voice trailed off and there was a faraway look in his eyes.

"Have you approached her, I wonder?" asked McGarr.

"Me?" Daly rocked back on his heels, his long chin upon his chest.

"Why not? She sounds like a jolly girl to me. There's no harm in trying."

Daly shook his head. "She's jolly, all right, but there's them that have tried. And I'll say no more about that." He glanced down the bar.

"Hey, there!" May Quirk's uncle roared. He began shuffling toward them with the aid of a cane. He was a tall, stout man with a red porous nose and blond hair that was turning white so that it looked dirty.

"It's none of your damn business," said the bartender.

"It's not, is it?"

"No. You're not in this company." He meant the group around McGarr at the bar.

"May Quirk is my niece and I'll not have you talking low about her in my presence." He reached over Daly, grabbed McGarr by the shoulder, and spun him around. McGarr nearly fell off the stool and his drink sloshed against his chest, wetting his shirt and pants.

"Christ!" said the publican, reaching for a bar rag.

"What's happened to May Quirk, little man?" the uncle roared. "And why are you asking all these questions? You'll answer up fast or I'll know why not!"

Daly attempted to step between them, but the man shoved him out of the way like he was a bit of fluff. In spite of his years, he was still a strong man.

McGarr looked up from his wet shirt and fixed the man with his gaze. He said, "You can best show your concern for May Quirk now by keeping your voice down and your hands to yourself. If you'll wait for me outside, I'll talk to you in private in a minute."

The old man blinked several times, then turned and shambled out the door.

McGarr stepped off the stool.

"Here, have your drink first, Inspector," said the bartender, rushing to fill his glass.

McGarr shook his head. "I can't. Much as I'd like to. I've got a full day's work ahead of me. What do I owe you?"

The publican stepped away from the bar. "Not a thing," he said in a louder voice. "The round is on me. It's been our pleasure to have a drink with you."

"Please," McGarr objected.

"No." He shook his head. "I insist. And I wish you luck with whatever you're about, here in Lahinch."

Nobody was talking. They all sensed McGarr's business was serious. What was more, McGarr guessed, it had been a month of Sundays since the publican had been so generous.

He turned, shook hands with Michael Daly once again, and started for the door.

"You forgot your note," said the publican. He pointed to the bank note on the bar.

"That's for the next round," McGarr said and waved going out the door.

Outside, McGarr directed the old man into the shadows of a doorway and told him what had happened to May Quirk. He then advised him to do what he thought best, after Dan O'Malley had been to the Quirk house. He had to grab hold of the big man to keep him from falling. Old Quirk's eyes gushed as though his tear ducts had burst, but he didn't make a sound. McGarr took his arm and walked him slowly to his Cooper, where he eased him into the passenger seat.

Climbing behind the wheel, McGarr called the Technical Bureau van on his police radio. When Chief Superintendent McAnulty came on, McGarr said, "Can you ascertain if that car really hit the wall alongside it, Tom?"

"Already have and it did but it didn't." McAnulty's voice was excited, like that of a child playing a particularly enjoyable game. "Although somebody has taken great pains to see that it looks that way. The stone, you see, is somewhat porous, and if the car had struck these particular pieces, some of its paint would have become lodged in them. Well, that's happened, but all the stones that contain the paint don't conform to all the striations on the body of the car.

"And the rear fender has just a little more rust on the bared metal than the scratches along the side. None of it is visible to the naked eye, but it's there, all right.

"Now then, as for the scratches themselves. The ones that were made up here and recently—I'd say sometime last night— were put there by a sharp instrument, which had substances on it that we're betting are dirt or earth or animal slurry."

"Like a pitchfork."

"You're a smart man, Chief Inspector."

"Are you going to search below the cliffs?"

"You can bet your bonnet we are. And I've got another little something for you. It's not certain, but the doctor guesses she was pregnant."

Her uncle turned and looked at McGarr, wide-eyed. He then slowly rolled down the window and looked out.

"Anything else?"

"Just one thing. You'll see a Wolsey parked near the green-grocer's on a corner near the church. It's black and kind of battered. My missus and the kids are in it. Can you tell her to go on without me? Tell her I'll catch a lift later."

"How much later?" McGarr speculated that telling Tom McAnulty's wife what he wished would be a trying experience. "I thought you were on holiday?"

"Well—I am and I'm not. You know how it is, Peter. At least I'm away from my desk, amn't I?"

But McGarr knew how it would be, and it was. Mrs. Mc-

Anulty said, "You mean to tell me he's had us waiting here in this heat for hours now and all along he had no intention of returning?"

McGarr was leaning in the window of the car. Four little children in back were looking at him shyly. One little girl couldn't keep from giggling. McGarr said, "I wouldn't presume to know his intentions, Mary."

"Well then, where's your wife?"

McGarr had been afraid of this. Without McAnulty to abuse she was going to seize upon the man nearest at hand, but McGarr didn't want to make McAnulty's position with her worse than it was. "Dublin, of course." That was a lie.

"I suppose you're as much of a demon for the job as his nibs."

McGarr reached back and tousled the little girl's blond locks. "He's a real professional, your Tom is. He doesn't get half the credit he deserves. There's not a man who could take his place."

She slid behind the wheel and started the car. "Perhaps not in the Technical Bureau," she said. "Perhaps not there." She roared away.

McGarr drove May Quirk's uncle to the Garda barracks, where he asked one of the officers to see the old man home and stay with him for a while. He was, McGarr had learned, a widower and without family.

McGarr then strolled over to a cafe in the middle of Lahinch, where he tried to ignore the purported Veal Cordon Bleu on the menu, knowing that it would be in some major way a disappointment. Long ago McGarr had learned to avoid the pretensions of most Irish country restaurants, but the rest of the fare seemed to be only mixed grill, mutton, fried fish and chips, Irish boiled dinner, or round steak, and after debate he succumbed to the temptation.

Sun poured in the window onto a spanking linen tablecloth

and the open window of the dining room allowed him to hear the talk of the passersby on the sidewalk. After all the whiskey he had drunk, the tea was refreshing, which was the most that could be said for the meal. How the cook could have allowed such fine scallops of milk-fed veal to scorch amazed McGarr. It was such a moment that made McGarr regret his decision to quit the European continent and take his present job with the Garda. On the Continent McGarr had grown accustomed to thinking of each meal as an event to be anticipated with no little joy. When his expectations had been met in full, McGarr was suffused with a sense of well-being. Such a moment made him feel very fortunate to number among those of the species who were so elect as to share his time and place, in particular a choice table in whatever restaurant, inn, trattoria, cafe, bistro, or gasthaus that had pleased him.

These other moments, however, plunged him into a funk.

In such a mood, McGarr climbed into the Cooper, collected Dan O'Malley at the Garda barracks, and drove toward the Quirk farmhouse.

3

IN THE IRISH COUNTRYSIDE

The Quirk farm lay along the road between Lahinch and Ki-shanny, up a winding, hilly road between tall earthen banks and hedgerows. McGarr had to slow at each turn to make sure the car didn't slam into the side of a cow or clip through a flock of sheep. He waited twice while farmers waved their arms and directed their dogs after errant sheep. The farmers only smiled and tilted their heads to the side, a form of silent hello all over Ireland. Superintendent O'Malley, who was sitting beside McGarr, waved to them all.

The Quirk property ran up the side of a steep hill. The garden by the road became in turn a potato patch, a pasture, rough forage, and finally, like much of the terrain in this part of Clare, a bald summit of rough gray rock. Near the top McGarr could see the odd white patch—sheep that had been left out to God and were collected twice a year for shearing, dipping, or sale. In all, the Quirks had little more than forty acres. Had they tried to farm it all, they could barely wrest subsistence from this poor land.

Like many farm families, they had two houses. The smaller, its lime now fading back to mortar, was doubtless the house John Quirk had been born in. It was now used as a stable. The new house was, to McGarr's way of thinking, one of the finest accomplishments of the Republic. For the last thirty years the government, through low-interest loans, subsidies, and direct grants, had been helping farmers build new houses with modern facilities. McGarr had visited other English-speaking countries in which no planning was evident in the selection of dwelling styles, and the tastes of the builders who had raised whole square miles of tight-packed oddities—some mere boxes with roofs, others grotesqueries conceived by addled brains—were suspect, to say the least. The new Irish farmhouse was no work of art, mind you, but it was pleasant to look at. The structure blended with the landscape and was built to last generations, if not centuries. Even the interior walls were either poured concrete or cinder block. The rooms were spacious and well lit by casement windows. Each house had at least a full bath and water closet. Most roofs were tiled. In short, the government had provided its people with a house any European peasant could be proud of.

McGarr suffered no delusions about Ireland. The base of his country's economy was agriculture, and most of his countrymen were farmers. As one who had lived with the effects of industrialization in other countries, McGarr wouldn't have Ireland any other way than what it had been since recorded time—perhaps the finest bit of natural pasturage in all Europe. Certainly there was a hot demand for the products such a country could supply on a grand scale, given certain improvements in farming methods. Many of the Continental countries even now couldn't feed their populations.

But Clare was another story. Clare was rock, albeit picturesque rock. Stepping out of the Cooper, McGarr remembered what an old woman in Lisdoonvarna had once told him when he had remarked about vistas in that rugged terrain: "Ah, lad—could we but eat that beauty, things would be grand."

Superintendent O'Malley said, "I'd prefer to do the telling alone, if you don't mind."

"I'll take a gander out back, then," said McGarr.

An old man was standing in the doorway now. "Is it about May that you've come?" he asked O'Malley.

O'Malley removed his blue Garda cap. "Maybe we better go inside, John. The news isn't good."

McGarr walked around the outbuildings: an old barn in which cows were once kept before the new house was built, a three-bay hayrick, the old house, in the main room of which a Massey-Ferguson tractor now sat—and stopped at the garden. The cabbages were big but withering, as were the cauliflower, squash, and turnip plants. However, the quarter acre of potatoes farther up the hill seemed to be reveling in the hot, dry weather. In other fields McGarr could see corrugated folds of earth that marked former potato beds.

He reached down and plucked a bright red tomato from the shadows of a plant. The vines were loaded with them, nobody seeming to care that they had fruited, grown prime, and now were beginning to rot back. He bit into it. The flavor was as sweet as anything he could ever hope to taste. A mere second it had been from vine to mouth. And no chemical fertilizer or insecticide had ever touched this land, he didn't doubt.

At that moment, looking down the valley toward Lahinch and the ocean beyond, McGarr wished fervently that he had taken his uncle's farm in Monaghan when it had been offered to him twenty-five years ago, that he had become a farmer and raised a tribe and followed his country's footballers into Croke Park of a Sunday afternoon to cheer for his boys. In Rathmines, where McGarr now lived, he hardly knew more than a half-dozen people who lived on his street.

But, he supposed, there was another side to this idyllic picture before him. The urban world had so intruded on the Clares and Donegals of Ireland that few young people chose to remain. Television, the press, movies, and magazines had made so many other places seem so much more glamorous that the young people were off as soon as they were old enough to scrape up the money. And few returned.

McGarr thought of May Quirk and New York, and he knew what would greet him when he entered the house: two old people who had been forced into a sort of isolation in a farmhouse with nobody but themselves and some neighbors like them; in short, no real reason to have more than a small garden, a couple of chickens, and two dozen sheep. McGarr only hoped they were strong, for the death of their daughter would hit them doubly hard.

McGarr didn't bother to knock. He opened the front door and stepped into a hallway. The parlor door was open. The room was filled with two stuffed chairs, a divan, and a thick rug, all in some red color, and a sideboard with Waterford crystal on top. The mantel of the glazed-brick fireplace held an eight-day clock made in Japan and a gilded-frame picture of their only and now dead daughter, May. But something else on the sideboard caught McGarr's eye—a half-empty, open bottle of Canadian Club.

Superintendent O'Malley seemed lost, both in the immensity of the divan and in his own thoughts. His blue eyes had clouded. He was gently touching his fingers to the plush of the upholstery. The balls of the clock spun in its vacuum. McGarr could hear a woman crying somewhere within the house and the low voice of an old man trying to soothe her. McGarr poured himself a very large whiskey, drank that off, and poured himself another. He filled a second glass and handed it to O'Malley. He then made a cursory search for the cap to the Canadian Club.

He could find it neither in the parlor dustbin nor in the kitchen.

After a while, John Quirk appeared in the doorway. He was a very tall man who had once carried a heavy frame. Now his neck was thin, his head skull-like, eyes sunken. His jawbone was visible right back to his ears, which were large and hairy. His face, however, like his daughter's, was long and regular. His hand, which McGarr took, was massive and had once been heavily calloused. He wore a green woolen shirt and gray pants held up by leather suspenders. His socks were black.

McGarr poured him a drink.

"You're from Dublin, are you?" John Quirk asked McGarr when he handed the old man the glass.

McGarr nodded.

"Are you going to catch the villain who did this to my May?"

McGarr nodded again.

"How can you be so sure?" The old man set the glass on a small table next to the stuffed chair in which he now sat. White doilies covered the back and arms of it.

"I won't stop until I do."

"That's easy to say," said Quirk.

"He's the best, John," said O'Malley. "He'll find the bastard. For my money, we got him already. Like I told you."

Quirk wasn't listening to O'Malley. "And what will you do when you find him?"

"I'll try to make it so he'll get hanged," said McGarr without hesitating. He knew what Quirk wanted to hear, and in fact it was the way he was feeling then too.

Quirk nodded his head. He then turned and looked at the picture of his daughter on the mantel.

From where he sat, McGarr couldn't tell if the photographer had added the blush to May Quirk's young cheeks, but she looked fresh and innocent, with a happy smile and a big space between her two front teeth, which then had not been capped. Knowing how she had been murdered was enough to mist the eyes of even McGarr, who had sat through many such interviews and was in his own way a very hard man indeed.

"How did he do it to her?"

"P—, poison," O'Malley said. "Something new and quick. She didn't suffer a bit. Must have spiked her drink."

"But why?" Quirk asked.

"That's the reason we're here," said McGarr. "Perhaps if we can gather the facts quickly, we can get right on the trail of whoever it was. What can you tell me about your daughter? I understand she's been away for quite some time now." He stood, holding his empty glass.

"Oh," said Quirk suddenly. "Help yourself."

"It's a shame the cap's missing. All its strength will escape."

"Jim Cleary from next door gave it to me like that. Last night." Quirk turned to O'Malley. "Strangest thing. He just knocked on the door and when I opened it he thrust that thing at me. He looked like something or somebody had scared him witless. Do you suppose—?"

O'Malley shook his head. "Not Jim Cleary. He's just getting a little soft is all. Sure and you know him better than me. He's as gentle as a lamb and has always been. Even when he's on the drink."

But Quirk wasn't listening. Again he had turned to look at the picture of his daughter on the mantel. "She was a changed girl when she came back from America. Forgetful like, and distracted. She had something on her mind, that's for sure. First night, instead of staying home here with her ma and pa like she hadn't done in ten years, she went out to the pubs, like some day laborer or strumpet. I don't know what the world's coming to. When I was a lad, women stayed at home where they belonged. And they got married and had children. I don't know." The old man rocked his head from side to side. "I've always said the drink is the curse of Ireland, something gutter snipes and desperadoes use for blood." McGarr was just pouring himself another small glass. The old man added, "Begging your pardon, sir."

McGarr asked, "Did your daughter have a drinking problem?"

"Oh, God no. At least I would say that she didn't. I mean, I wouldn't rightly know. But every night she went out, Aggie and me waited up for her. Not once could I even tell she had had a drop. She wasn't tired or groggy. Several times we stayed up until dawn." Yet again he turned and looked at his daughter's picture on the mantel and then bit his lip. "I knew there was something in the wind. She wasn't acting like that because she wanted to. I don't care how many years she spent in New York. I know my May. It's the upbringing that counts." His hand jumped to his face. Not knowing what to do with it, he scratched his forehead.

McGarr took out his wallet and removed May Quirk's $27,000. He reached over and placed the crisp bills on the table beside Quirk. "That's your daughter's money, Mr. Quirk."

O'Malley glanced at McGarr. Officially, the money was evidence which should have been held until it was ascertained that May Quirk did indeed own it. But McGarr wasn't about to go by the rules with these people. He didn't think of the money as compensation, but it might help them over the months of sadness, when, he supposed, neither of them would feel much like working.

With quaking hands and fingers that seemed too numb or rough to separate them Quirk tried to fan the bills. "I don't understand. No amount of money will ever bring her back."

"And we don't want it, neither," said an old woman from a

doorway that led to a hall and bedrooms beyond. "That's dirty Fenian money it is, and what's responsible for my poor baby's death." Her hand groped for the jamb.

O'Malley stood to help her.

She fended him off and walked unsteadily toward the divan. Her legs were like thin sticks and red from sitting too close to an electric fire. She was wearing an old, flower-print dress—green holly sprigs with red berries—and a wool cardigan worn through at the elbows. Her hair was thin and very white. Her face had once been handsome, but, like her husband's, far too thin. Her cheekbones were prominent knobs and her false teeth seemed to be a bad fit. McGarr imagined that the Quirks, like many older people out here in the West, cooked only when they had company. Otherwise it was tea and cake, potatoes once in a while, and an odd rasher in the pot. Much of the produce in the garden out back had been left past prime.

When she had eased herself into the cushions of the divan, O'Malley asked, "What makes you say it's Fenian money, Aggie?"

There were red circles around both her eyes. Otherwise her face seemed bloodless. "Didn't she have a shooter in her hand-bag?"

Her husband was surprised.

"I saw it myself when she kept digging for them scented cigarettes of hers what smelled like a cabbage patch under the torch. Big as a gangster's it was. How else can you explain that?"

She didn't wait for a reply. "Oh, I know how it is. I've read about it in the papers. Our poor innocent kids get over there to New York and after a few years they think they know it all. And then they meet up with a cutie, some little good-for-nothing chancer from hunger who's got a nose for the fast buck and an easy mark. He gets ahold of a pretty young thing like May and asks her how Irish she is. And to prove it, over there where everybody's pretty much of everything and nothing much of what's good, she starts collecting money—handouts, mind you, just like plain begging it is—from other misguided country people. They think it's going to the patriots and rebels, you know, the ones what freed the country from the British. But it's not. It's going straight into the pockets of the dirty little dodgers like that one in New York, or them in Derry and the Bogside, the ones what would rather kill than work, the ones what are blowing people out of the seats in London restaurants. Or the one what did whatever he did to May." She made a fist with her right hand and pushed it into her forehead. "The craven coward, may he die a thousand hideous deaths!" She began sobbing.

McGarr waited until she had quieted. "What man in New York?"

"Sugrue, his name is." She stood and started out of the parlor toward the hall. "Wrote her just last week, he did. A little runt of a man. And without an occupation, either. She told me he was a fund raiser. Now then," she paused in the doorway, "wouldn't you call that tripe? A fund raiser! Isn't that what we all are in one way or another?"

When she returned from the bedroom she had a letter in one hand, a photograph in the other. "Look at him. A half-pint. Doesn't hardly come up to her shoulder."

McGarr didn't stand to take the photo from her. He didn't think he'd come up to the old woman's shoulder either. She was at least six feet tall.

And May Quirk was too. She and a man were pictured standing outside a bar named Mickey Finn's in what McGarr assumed was New York, since all the cars parked at the curb looked like ugly limousines. It seemed to be summer and she was wearing a tight lilac-colored pullover and short black skirt. Most tall women had legs that were in some way flawed, McGarr had noticed in the past, but in this picture May Quirk's seemed perfectly shaped. They were wrapped in dark hose, and she wore pumps with low heels. And she was in every other way a handsome woman.

The man, on the other hand, looked remarkably like McGarr but younger. He still had a full head of curly copper hair, and his smile seemed contagious and friendly, like that of somebody you'd enjoy knowing. He was small and thick and had placed his hand around May Quirk's waist in the casual way that people who have been intimate with each other adopt. He was wearing what McGarr speculated was an expensive light gray suit cut in the fashion of the moment, and shiny black shoes. He wore a green carnation in his buttonhole. A black silk tie on a gray shirt made him look like a successful entertainer or businessman.

"And just read the letter."

"Aggie," said Quirk. "You didn't."

She turned on him. "Of course I did, you poor old fool. I only wish I had earlier and showed it to Dan here, too. He might've placed her in his protection and she'd be alive this minute." The patent absurdity of her statement seemed to make her all the more aware of the situation. Her arm jerked toward the picture, which she grasped off the mantel and hugged. She then shuffled from the room, saying, "Ah, May. May."

McGarr read:

> Suite 70007
> World Trade Center
> N.Y., N.Y. 10048

May,
    In the past I might have told you I loved you. Forget all of that. 'Twas only said in the heat of the moment. Now that you've been gone for six weeks, I've had a chance—

free from your constant caresses and many charms—to think about us, you and me. And I have come to this conclusion.

We can't go on as before, meeting here and there—your place, my place, some rundown hotel up in Saratoga Springs. That's cheap. What's worse, my wife wouldn't like it. And with all the running around, I'm wasting away.

What? You didn't know about the wife? How about the thirteen kids? Do you think a handsome sporting gent like meself could long remain solitary and sexless? Give me credit for at least having had a little fun before I met you. (And I rue the day.)

Since, the certain matter about which you are aware has arisen, and I'm off to the Vatican for a special dispensation from my prior marriage vows, whence to the Holy Isle I'll fly, arriving at Shannon (14th August, 2:00 P.M., flight 509 Aer Lingus from London) and we shall tie the knot. Why knot? You know knot not, say not.

We've talked about it. You've never said no. You're home now among your people, and what better time and place for us to marry? What say? You can give me the answer at Shannon. If not (knot?), I'll just continue on back here and see if I can prise one of these thermopanes off the concrete blocks. I'll say a pray for you as I descend.

I love you and hope you'll meet the plane,

Paddy

It was the thirteenth of August.

"'A certain matter' indeed!" said the old woman, from the doorway. She still had the picture in her hands.

"Aren't you assuming an awful lot, Mrs. Quirk?" said McGarr.

"What? With that money and the gun? And him a 'fund raiser' as well as being a mouse and a gobshite? I know what 'a certain matter' means, if you don't, Mr. Policeman. Just like I know what he'd been up to with May. He was her lover. No two ways about it."

"But his intentions—" McGarr began to say.

"I couldn't give a tinker's damn for his intentions. It's the facts what matter. What sort of a constable are you, anyhow?" Her eyes cleared and she gave McGarr a close look. "You're nothing but half a man yourself."

Quirk got out of his chair and put his arm around his wife. He then led her back into the bedroom.

Superintendent O'Malley went into the kitchen, where McGarr heard him phone a doctor.

McGarr examined the postmark of the letter. It had been mailed in Boston five days earlier.

When Quirk returned, McGarr asked him, "Can you tell me something about what your daughter did while she was here? When did she return? What were her habits? Did she visit friends? Do you remember anything remarkable about something she might have said or done?"

Quirk reached over for the nearly full glass of whiskey. He wet his lips and winced. He was not a drinking man.

McGarr said, "Let's start with her friends."

"Male or female?"

McGarr cocked his head. "Female first." He wanted to get to know who May Quirk had been.

"Ach—the whole house was cluttered with them what are left hereabouts now. And who would have thought there were so many of them her age. I had thought they had all flown, like May herself, but they came from all over the county they did. Kids and husbands and all. May had always been popular, you see. She had a way about her. Had—"

It was plain the old man would give in to his grief if McGarr let him dote on her death. "And boys—I mean, men. Was she popular with the men?"

"You've got the snapshot in your hand, sir. You can tell by the look of her she'd be a favorite with any man, but there was

43

more, too. It was, like I said, the way of her that mattered. It was partly because of how winning she was that made her emigrate, I believe. That and her not wanting to be a farmer's wife, like she told us then."

McGarr kept staring at the old man, awaiting further explanation.

Again Quirk tried the whiskey but couldn't take more than a sip. "There wasn't a young man in the county who wouldn't have willingly made a marriage with her. First, there's the farm. Whoever married May got all of it, for we have no other children. Had—" He closed his eyes and continued speaking. "And then there was May, too. Nothing ever seemed to get her down. She was always May.

"The fellow next door approached me around the time she left."

"Jim Cleary?" McGarr asked.

"None other. His father had just died and left him over a hundred and fifty acres on both sides of the road. Some of his land was good then, and he had a tractor, a herd of milk cows, and even a truck, as well as an automobile. On the face of it, it seemed a proper match."

O'Malley said, "Why, he was nearly forty when May left for America. Right now he's just another old man in the local."

"Well, what eligible farmer isn't? Wasn't I thirty-eight myself before my father yielded me this place?"

O'Malley only took a sip from his glass.

"Anyhow, I asked May her opinion of Cleary. She said she didn't rightly have one. He was an old man. When I told her why I was asking she blushed and then laughed. I explained to her how it was a wise match, how in these parts Cleary was considered a rich farmer. He was a hard worker and, it seems, he

44

fancied her. She said she liked Jim Cleary very much as a neighbor and, you know, as an older friend. But Jim Cleary was not the sort of man she intended to marry.

" 'Well then, who is?,' I asked her. She said somebody strong and young and wild. Somebody with a dream. And courage, she added. I don't know—maybe she saw too many picture shows in Ennis, read too many books, or dreamed too many of her own dreams. One thing was for certain, she was never going to be a farmer's wife.

" 'And what's so wrong with being a farmer's wife?,' I asked her. 'Isn't your mother one?' And so she told me and it was the only thing she ever told me without so much as a smile or some playfulness about her. She said if she married Jim Cleary she wouldn't even own the dishes on the table or the farm that was her inheritance from me. Everything would go to Cleary and she'd be at his mercy. Then she'd have one child after another until she was spent, and she'd know nothing from nine months after marriage until the grave but steady hard work and service.

"I said it was the fate of a countrywoman in the West of Ireland.

"She said, 'That's just it, da. I don't plan to be a countrywoman in the West of Ireland.' And not long after that she left."

"Didn't she have any beaus among the young men?"

O'Malley answered that one. "As many young men as there were hereabouts."

"But anybody in particular?"

O'Malley and Quirk exchanged glances. "Rory O'Connor," said O'Malley, as though McGarr should know whom he meant. When after a few seconds of silence he realized that McGarr was waiting for an explanation, he added, "A big fellow. Wild as the west wind. Folks live out at the very tip of Nag's Head. That's not very far from the Cliffs—" O'Malley broke off. "You don't suppose—"

Quirk began to stand.

O'Malley waved his hand at him so that he eased himself back into the cushion. "Couldn't be. He left right before May did. Whole years ago."

"And she probably followed him, too, I bet," said her father.

"Do you have any proof of that?"

"Not a bit of it, but May wouldn't have mentioned a word of him to me."

O'Malley explained. "May had no favorites among the boys hereabouts but one—Rory O'Connor. And whereas he was big and handsome and likable in spite of all his foolishness, he was a wrecker if I ever met one. Raw as the place he hailed from—all emotion and strength and good looks and, some say, brains too, but not an ounce of discretion or concern for anybody but himself and—"

"May," said her father. "May too." He again touched his lips to the whiskey.

"But he wasn't anxious to marry her."

"Nor she him!" said Quirk in a rush. "They just wanted to rush off together, away from here to a place where they could live the way they wanted. When I asked them which way that was and where the place might be, they didn't have a clue. Just off they wanted to go together. And not married, mind you! Not so much as an engagement promise between them. May said that was the way she wanted it. That he wasn't the sort of man a girl actually married. 'Then what do you actually do with him,' I asked. When she didn't answer that, she didn't get what she wanted. I went out to Nag's Head and told O'Connor's father how it was—that this was my only daughter and I wouldn't suffer his son to ruin her, that if they would get married first I'd give them my blessing and eventually my farm too, but otherwise, his son Rory could go wherever it was he was heading alone.

"Well, Jack O'Connor was a fair man, I don't care what else has ever been said about him."

McGarr looked at O'Malley, who mouthed, "I.R.A."

"And he went into the barn, where Rory was stacking bales of hay. He was in there an hour. I heard them shouting and fighting and I didn't dare go in to see what was what, because there's no coming between a father and son, and as big as I was then, I was no match for either one of them alone.

"When Jack staggered out of the barn, he was a mess. He said, 'Rory's leaving tomorrow, alone. You have my promise.' And so he did. May never forgave me for that when she learned what had happened. And she too left the day after I admitted I had gone to see Rory's father."

McGarr asked, "Has O'Connor ever returned?"

"I don't think so. His father died a few years back. The oldest son was lost at sea, and the old woman is living there alone. Whenever I'm out that way, I stop in to see her." O'Malley got himself another drink.

"Has she ever talked about her son Rory?"

"Not a word. The way Jack dealt with him drove a wedge between husband and wife. Rory had been her favorite, you know. Her last son. She had spoiled him rotten, too. That's why he was the way he was. He didn't think there was anything he couldn't or shouldn't do. I wonder what happened to him and where he is now."

The phone began to ring.

All three men began to stand.

O'Malley said, "I'll get it," and went out to the kitchen.

47

McGarr asked Quirk, "What was May's occupation in New York?"

Quirk began rubbing his forehead with the heel of his palm. McGarr could tell the old man was getting tired. His wind-burned skin was beginning to look waxy, and his eyes were bloodshot. "Ah—she tried one thing and another for a couple of years. Then she became a journalist, first for the *United Irishmen,* a paper in the States for narrowbacks, don't you know. She became one of their editors in no time. May always had a way with words. And there was no denying her anything she wanted. If she insisted, she could get it out of you. She then joined the New York *Daily News.* Here." He stood and went to the sideboard. "May sent us a copy of every paper that carried one of her major pieces." He opened the doors of the sideboard, which was crammed full of newspapers. "I don't pretend to have read them all. It made me sick being reminded of how she'd probably never return." He took one of the top papers and handed it to McGarr. He was crying now. He walked out of the room, into the hall.

The newspaper had a tabloid format. The front page pictured a black young man sprawled on a sidewalk with a large white policeman standing over him. The officer carried a riot shotgun and was wearing a helmet with a clear face shield that made him look like a robot. The block capital letters read, "COPS IN BED.-STUY. CAUSE RIOTS," and the caption under the full-page picture read, "So Say Black Caucus Leaders. Story by May Quirk, page 2."

McGarr skimmed the article, written in the short, punchy writing style that some American newspapers favored. The article wasn't long, but the questions May Quirk had asked the black leaders revealed that they had little evidence to support their contention. One picture showed her interviewing a man on the steps of a brownstone. McGarr glanced at the date—June 22, 1969. May Quirk was about twenty-three then, and the editor had doubtless selected the picture not because the man being interviewed was important but because the people who read the paper liked to see pretty girls. She had her left hand on her hip, one foot on the ground, and the other on the first stair. The picture was shot from the side. It looked like she was taunting the big black man with the prospect of her upper body. He looked like a hairy, unkempt rabblerouser, she like a fine piece of work who was showing him up in every sense. But he was smiling at her too, a smile that seemed foolish.

O'Malley was standing in the door. "I'm wanted across the way. It's Cleary. He's having trouble."

McGarr put the paper aside. "Of what sort?"

"They say he's been raving around. He broke up all the furniture in the house last night and burned it and his old car out in the yard."

McGarr himself had seen a smoldering fire when they had passed by. The shell of the car had looked like a Triumph Herald.

"His cousin found him sitting against the kitchen wall in a stupor. He hasn't really been eating well, you know. Lives alone. Doesn't do much of anything anymore. Rented out his good land to some wheat farmers from Wexford. They poured on chemicals and used it up. Now it's going back to bush."

McGarr pulled himself out of the chair. "I'll go with you, if you think the Quirks will be all right."

"Your inspector wants to talk to you first."

It was Hughie Ward. He said, "Bernie got ahold of Scannell. You know, he's the one Hanly says cashed his foreign currency. Well, it's true, but not in big amounts. Five- and ten-dollar bills and never more than a couple hundred pounds' worth at a time.

49

"Then I've been around to the bars to check on the bottle of C. C. I got a warm welcome in the one you stopped in to."

"Tried to poison you, did they?" McGarr asked, keeping his voice very low indeed.

"Jasus," said Ward. "I've been drinking tea since I returned. But listen to this—not one publican in Lahinch has sold anybody a quart of C. C. in months. Hanly lied to us there, too."

McGarr also knew Hanly had lied to them two other times about how his car had come to be damaged, but he wanted to confront Hanly himself with that evidence. "Where's Hanly now?"

"In the next room. Liam has him. I don't know what he's got against that fellow, but he's leaning on him hard."

McGarr thought of May Quirk again and knew how O'Shaughnessy felt. If a low type like Hanly was responsible for May Quirk's death, McGarr would be put out himself. "Good enough. That gobshite is keeping something from us and I want to know what it is and why. Keep drinking that tea, boy, and spell Liam after a bit. I'll be there myself in a while."

"And McAnulty has been in touch with Phoenix Park." That was the site of Garda Soichana headquarters. "He wants funding permission to search the area below the Cliffs of Moher. Wants to hire some riggers and a mountain-climbing expert. He's also alerted the subaquatic unit. He said you've requested all that. The commissioner wants you to call him at his holiday house in Cork. Do you have his number?"

"Yes." McGarr hung up and called the commissioner.

"I've been waiting for your call." Fergus Farrell had hired McGarr. He was a gifted administrator in his late fifties. Rumor had it that he had stomach cancer. He was a tall man with large eyes that tortoiseshell glasses made look sad, but he never once mentioned his malady or missed a day of work. And his sense of humor was renowned. True, he drank a good deal so that his face, which some former skin condition had pitted, was red, but he never got out of the way or lost his sagacity. "What have you got out there?"

"A chance for some good publicity, I believe." Again McGarr kept his voice down.

"We need that." Because of the trouble in the North, the recent bombings in Dublin, and the seeming impunity with which gangs on either side of the political issue had been shooting each other along the border, it appeared as though the police were powerless to enforce the laws of the country. The thousands of crimes they had solved during the past year had of course not gotten the same attention in the press. Good news didn't sell newspapers.

McGarr thought of May Quirk. "I think I can promise you some results on this one."

"What do you know about the woman so far?"

"Tall, beautiful, a staff reporter for a big New York newspaper. Born and raised here in Lahinch. She may have been pregnant. She had twenty-seven thousand dollars on her person. Also, she was connected with an I.R.A. fund raiser in New York. The connection may have been romantic only, however."

"The papers will be making a big thing of this one," said Farrell. "They always do when it's one of their own. But then there's the expense of your request to consider. They could make a lot of that too, if—"

McGarr waited for Farrell to conclude the thought. He hadn't managed to rise to the top of three separate police organizations by being a skilled detective alone. When Farrell said nothing more, McGarr suggested, "Perhaps then we'd better make it look like we're breaking our backs on it. You know—as though we wouldn't want it to happen again to any other members of the glorious fourth estate." Also, McGarr wanted to bring Farrell in on the decision, just in case they spent large amounts of public money with no result. Many senior Garda Soichana officers resented the fact that McGarr hadn't passed his entire career with the Irish police. Because he had been with foreign police agencies, McGarr had not been involved in domestic cases that might have revealed his political leanings. And since his return to Ireland, McGarr had taken great pains never to reveal his political point of view. Thus, he had enjoyed an extraordinary press from nearly all Irish sources.

"If you think the operation is necessary." Farrell wasn't anybody's fool either. They were close, the two of them, but it was the affection that was built of mutual respect. If one of them had to go, there was no sense in the other being sacrificed too.

McGarr could have said, "McAnulty thinks so," but he didn't. He was sick of playing the organizational game, and he also really wanted to nab May Quirk's killer. "Yes—it's necessary. The dirty bastard who did this is going to the gallows, as far as I'm concerned." McGarr hung up.

McGarr was glad he had said that. When he turned around, he found John Quirk right behind him, lighting the top of the cooker for tea. The old man reached out his hand and shook McGarr's long and hard. "Thank you for everything, Inspector. You're the man for the job, all right. Would you care for a cup of tea?"

McGarr shook his head and left.

He was glad to get outside where the air was clear.

4

COUNTRY ILLS AND A COUNTRY DOCTOR

The color of the house across the road was not much different from the stones of the surrounding fields and hills—a drab, weathered gray. It was as though the great pitted rock that was Clare was reaching up to reclaim the materials from which the house had been made and eventually would subsume the mean, three-story dwelling. And it wouldn't be much of a shame, either, McGarr thought, since the building was an offense to both the eye and the persons who had the misfortune to live in it. McGarr knew its narrow windows made the interior dim and kept the rooms damp and mildewy, and that it was a cold, drear place in the winter but funky and hot in the summer. Several slates had been knocked off the roof and a quarter of the central chimney had fallen in a chunk onto the lawn.

Stepping out of the Cooper, McGarr and O'Malley had to walk carefully to avoid the cow pies that lay everywhere about the yard. Of the two towering cedar trees out front the nearer was dead, its needles gone and only the spiny skeleton remaining. The farther one was diseased and looking as though it was suffering from a special sort of arboreal mange. The grazing animals had not bothered with the grass against the side of the house. It clung to the foundation and mortar like a scraggly blonding beard on an old man's chin. There were two other autos in the yard—a Garda patrol car and an ambulance. The hulk of the Triumph Herald was still smoldering.

They stepped into the kitchen and McGarr had to catch his breath, step outside, and breathe again. The dank interior had the smell of a barn—ammoniac, pungent, the reek of animals and wet rotting straw. He ducked back in again.

Sitting in a battered rocking chair near an Aladdin paraffin fire, which a guard was trying to make burn evenly, was a man who looked crazed or ill or drunk. He had thrown his head of matted, greasy hair back on the rocker and was twisting his face from side to side. A patchy gray beard stubbled his face. McGarr guessed he was a very old fifty-five. A medical man was leaning over him, attempting to direct the beam of a small light into his eyes.

There was not one other item of furniture in the room besides the kitchen sink, which was filled with shards of broken dishes. Everywhere around the floor were newspapers so thick they felt spongy underfoot. The far window also had been covered by newspapers. McGarr poked his head into the adjoining sitting room. Newspapers covered those windows, too. In the dim yellow light he could see rusting food tins in a corner with some more broken dishes and pots. Heaps of newspapers were there too, but again not a stick of furniture. And that room was the source of most of the stench. Piss, McGarr thought. James Cleary hadn't been bothering to go outside.

Suddenly the man launched himself from the rocker, fell onto his hands and knees, and crawled in quick, spastic movements toward a corner of the kitchen, where he tried to vomit, with no result.

The doctor began preparing a hypodermic needle.

"His cousin says he's been like this since early morning," the guard explained. He had to speak over the man's agonized spasms. "At first the cousin thought it was just too much to drink, although Jim's a very moderate man usually. But the cousin returned later to find him burning more of the furniture, and that's when he called for us."

The doctor tapped the guard on the shoulder and they both approached Cleary. The guard, a big fellow, grabbed him under the arms and raised him to his feet. The doctor pushed up a sleeve of the greatcoat to expose an arm mottled with dirt and lice. The doctor had to rub a good while with a piece of moistened cotton before the spot for the needle's point was readied. The guard and an ambulance attendant carried the man out.

McGarr noted that most of the papers were issues of the New York *Daily News*, then went back outside into the fresh air. Shortly after, the doctor appeared. McGarr offered him a smoke and introduced himself. "Has he been like this before?"

"Twice." The doctor began walking slowly toward the van. He was young, no more than thirty. He had fine, pixyish features and a thin build. He was just a bit taller than McGarr and his accent placed him in Clare. When they had gotten beyond the ambulance and the other policemen, he said, "Nervous breakdown. I wouldn't tell anybody else that, of course."

"But I thought a nervous breakdown resulted from severe stress. You know, people who've got too much to do and no time and bills and . . ." McGarr's voice trailed off. "—city people." When it came to psychological classifications, McGarr was at sea. Once in Paris when he had investigated a series of murders involving mutilated corpses and aspects of gross indecency, he had immersed himself in books concerning deviant behavior. He had found them unavailing, since he had had to deal with an individual and not a type.

"Usually that's the case. But out here, things have changed almost as rapidly and perhaps more drastically than in the city. Take Mr. Cleary, for instance. He's got . . ." The doctor looked around the area in back of the house where the land was going back to scrub; in the distance a jackass was bawling, his gray head sticking over a wall. ". . . the mud and the weather, the house, maybe a neighbor forty years older than he, and not much else. He's got no wife, no kids, no family and no hope of getting one. His brothers and sisters have left and the last time he heard from one of them was in 1954 on his thirty-first birthday, when his brother sent him thirty-one pounds and advised him to have a bellyful of beer. He wound up in the Galway City jail.

"Cleary doesn't drink much anymore. He's afraid he'll go right off the handle again. So even the pubs are out for him. And anyhow, he's a quiet, withdrawn man. I don't think the pubs would help him even if he could drink regularly. And then the pubs in these parts aren't what they once were. Have you been in one recently?"

"This morning. Jolly place."

"It's the weather. And the tourists. You should try one in January and February. More like morgues. Nobody talks. Everybody seems almost stunned.

"And then Cleary isn't a religious man, either. There's nothing to support him here." The doctor squinted the cigarette smoke from his eyes and let his eyes scan the field and the hill beyond. "Emotionally, that is. All the young and the ambitious are off to Cork or Dublin or England or Canada. It's the city and the factory for them, and the sort of life they can see for themselves on TV."

McGarr had the distinct impression the doctor didn't care for the new way of life much. After all, he himself could have chosen to practice someplace else and been rewarded with all the things the younger people in Lahinch wanted, but instead he had chosen this drear backyard and his patient, James Cleary, who was now resting in the back of the ambulance.

56

"Could something else have brought on this attack?" McGarr asked.

"Like what?"

"Like May Quirk. She's home now. Wasn't Cleary interested in marrying her?"

"That was years ago."

McGarr had dealt with men like Cleary before, though—lonely, isolated men who had taken some small disappointment in their lives and built it into a tragedy, something to hang all their supposed failure on. "Has he ever talked to you about her, when, you know, you treated him in the past?"

The young doctor turned to McGarr. His eyes were small and dark and quick. "Certainly you don't think me that much of a bumpkin that I'd tell you if he had, Inspector."

"I don't think you're a bumpkin at all, Doctor. I'm only asking because May Quirk was murdered last night. I want to know if you think Cleary's behavior today is in any way extraordinary, given the problems you've treated him for in the past."

The doctor hadn't even blinked at the mention of May Quirk's name, although he must have been her near contemporary and probably had grown up with her. "No. He'd already burned the other furniture in the house. This was the last of it. The retching is usual too. I suspect he'll start tearing down the walls next. One room at a time. If he lasts much longer." He glanced back at the ambulance. "He hardly eats. He's somewhat suicidal, too. I can see that aspect of his personality growing stronger now."

"Couldn't you put him away where he could get some steady treatment?"

"What treatment—locked doors, a steady regimen of pacifiers, and an institution full of crazies? That would finish him off. At least here he can die among some people who know him."

McGarr looked at the diminutive doctor, whose shoulders

were no wider than the spread of McGarr's hands. He seemed strangely cynical for a man so young. Doctors, McGarr well knew, were like policemen in that they often had too much of people and had to protect themselves by becoming hard. It was just a veneer, however. A really hard man couldn't continue in either profession very long without the censure of his colleagues. But there was a half-note of bitterness in what the young man was saying, too. McGarr said, "What I've been meaning to ask is if you think Cleary is capable of murder. And specifically, of murdering May Quirk."

"I wouldn't know. I'm neither a psychiatrist nor a policeman."

"Did he mention where he had been last night?"

"I only got here a few minutes before you."

"Where would Cleary have gotten a bottle of Canadian Club whiskey?"

"I've already told you as much as I know of his drinking habits."

"Did you know May Quirk?"

"Yes. Of course. We went to school together."

McGarr flicked his cigarette onto the ground and stepped on it. He wondered why he smoked. He got such little pleasure from it. The whole process of lighting one up was automatic, a habit. "I've been having some trouble finding out who she was. Her parents, naturally, are distraught, and—"

"She left when I went to university. Only she never came back."

"Until now."

"That's right."

"Where did she go?"

The doctor glanced at McGarr. He realized McGarr knew the answer to that question. "Right into the center of the storm. New York City. She made a big hit. Everybody knew she would. Big-time reporter, they tell me. Tens of thousands of pounds per year. Powerful friends and a lot of power herself. Not an Irish-American in the 'New Land' who wouldn't invite her home for Christmas dinner."

"I.R.A. connections?"

"They say that too. It's the in thing, I suspect. Among all the protorevolutionaries in Manhattan."

"How would you know?"

"I went to medical school at Columbia."

"Then you *know* she was a staff reporter for a big New York daily?"

He nodded. "The biggest. The *Daily News*. Hard-hat newspaper. The sort of newspaper an I.R.A. gunman would read."

"And you read what when you were there?"

"The *Times*, of course."

"The university man's newspaper. The sort a bright young medical student, who wanted to help his people in a way different from that of a May Quirk, would read, eh?"

Again the doctor looked at McGarr. "Exactly."

"It doesn't seem to bother you very much that she's been murdered."

"No more than when any of my patients dies. No less."

"What did you treat her for, Dr. . . ." The young man had not given McGarr his name.

"Fleming. She had missed her period. She wanted to know if she was pregnant."

"And?"

"She was."

"Do you know who the father was?"

He shook his head. "Could be about anybody." He smiled slightly, then added, "Although that's not fair. I know nothing about May Quirk's sexual indiscretions. And don't want to know, either. Now that she's a historical figure, as it were, I'm sure the countryside will be crawling with types just like she was, all of them trying to dig up any squalid rumor about her past. I'm sure it'll all make interesting reading for some."

McGarr didn't care for this nasty young man. He doubted that Fleming was as disinterested in May Quirk's past and her untoward fate as he claimed. "Where were you last night, may I ask?"

"You may. I suppose it's the price I must pay for having been candid with you. I treated a local man for gout."

"Who is he, and what time was that?"

"Daniel Quirk." Fleming smiled wanly at McGarr. "He lives in the village. He was May's uncle."

"Yes; I know the man."

"Then I stopped in Griffin's, which is the pub on the corner across from the traffic standard."

McGarr raised an eyebrow. "So you drink?"

"I returned to Ireland, remember? It's my right, wouldn't you say? Anyhow, May was there with her following."

"Drinking?"

"Not really. She never ever really drank liquor. She'd buy one for herself as a prop, and she'd buy for anybody else who wanted one too."

"And her following?"

He shook his head. "As I just explained to you, Inspector. They're the kids who want to get out of Lahinch and Clare and maybe Ireland itself. They don't drink, on principle."

"Doesn't sound like much of a pub crowd."

"May made up for it. She made everybody merry with her banter and jokes. She had a tongue in her."

McGarr wondered if that was a wistful thought. His tone was unchanged, however. "Were you a part of May Quirk's 'following'?"

"Me?"

"For a different reason."

"And what would that be?"

"Love. Hate. Maybe you liked to look at a pretty girl."

Suddenly his delicate features froze. He looked McGarr right in the eye. "Let me tell you something, McGarr. If May Quirk was pretty, it was only skin deep. To me she had lost her looks. She wasn't very pretty. Not very pretty at all." He turned and walked back to the ambulance van. He jumped in and the driver backed them out onto the road, where they drove toward Lahinch.

"What do you make of him?" McGarr asked O'Malley, meaning Fleming.

"Just a daft farmer. A loner. Probably got himself a proper snootful last night. A couple of days in hospital, a bath, and a few good meals and he'll be on the mend. I'll get a social worker to look in on him from now on. Maybe the priest can organize a work crew to come out here and clean up the house a bit. The kids in town will do that now, you know. Sure, there's not much work for them lately." O'Malley looked at the house and shuddered, then walked over and shut the kitchen door.

When he returned, he realized McGarr had meant Dr. Fleming. "Oh—he's a fine doctor. Wonderful training. They say he's not just a G. P. but a surgeon, too. They offered him a fine post in Galway City and one in the States, too. Minneapolis, wherever the hell that is."

"As a man?" McGarr asked.

"A loner. His father wasn't much different, though, but hard workers, the both of them. The doctor was quite a scholar, too. A Gaelic language whiz, and mathematics and history and whatnot. They say some big foundation paid for all his years in New York."

"He struck me as a hard man. No sympathy for anybody who wants something different from him."

"Ach. We've all got to pick and choose. And everybody's glad he chose to come back. Sure, the sawbones we had before him knew the anatomy of a porter bottle and little else. And he's not as fussy as he'd let on, Fleming isn't. When the vet died he subbed at that too, and I'll tell you something—he was better at animals than the new boy. There's some farmers who refuse to go to anybody else when they've got big animal trouble. For operations, there's nobody like him. He's got small, fast hands and a good mind, too. Nerves of steel."

McGarr got into the Cooper and called the Lahinch barracks. Much to his surprise, his wife answered. "Everybody else is busy."

"They are, are they?" O'Malley was embarrassed. "We'll soon see just how busy, we will."

McGarr assumed O'Malley's notion of retiring had left him.

Noreen went on. "Hughie says you should meet him at Griffin's. It's across from—"

"I have Superintendent O'Malley with me now," said McGarr. "We'll find it." He wanted her to know of O'Malley's presence so she wouldn't make any observations about the barracks or the town.

"He says he's having a drink with a fella by the name of O'Connor, who was with May Quirk last night."

McGarr and O'Malley swapped glances. "Rory O'Connor?"

"He didn't say. But he added that the fellow either doesn't know or pretends not to know about the woman. He says rumors are flying thick and fast, but nobody's certain of anything. He imagined you'd want to talk to him immediately."

"I'm on my way. Meet me there too." McGarr threw the Cooper into first and pointed it toward Lahinch.

5

FLEETING THINGS

Griffin's Bar had leaded glass windows and snugs. In one sat Noreen, Hughie Ward, and a young man with a shock of thick black hair swept across his forehead. The snug door was open. The barman was bending to place a tray of drinks in front of them.

McGarr waited for the barman to complete his task. He then asked for a small Jameson. "The old stuff." He meant the twelve-year-old whiskey. He was tired of Canadian Club, as good as it was; somehow it just wasn't his drink. It was too light and didn't have enough taste for slow, steady drinking, which over the years had become McGarr's method of imbibing. He well knew the practice had become a habit for him, but he never allowed himself to get out of the way and he had the experience necessary to avoid hangovers. And for the connoisseur, which he undoubtedly was, alcohol in all its forms was such a pleasant habit. He stubbed his cigarette out before entering the snug, however. That habit bothered him, mostly because, he decided then, it spoiled the taste of anything with alcohol in it.

"Peter McGarr." He offered his hand to Rory O'Connor, sat, and gave his wife a peck on the cheek.

Noreen was a diminutive woman with delicate facial features

and a body the beauty of which relied upon proportion, not size. A tight nest of copper curls and a fresh complexion made her seem doll-like, perhaps the creation of a master craftsman who knew what would please the eye without being obvious. What was more, Noreen, like most Irish women, had a delicacy of manner. One glance at her and you knew she was polite, well meaning, and a person you could trust. Also, she was brighter than McGarr (which he admitted only to himself, of course), and she was twenty-one years younger than he. That fact he never forgot. Her passion was art history. His had long been women, especially those who had possessed one or another of Noreen's features and qualities. When he had met her, it had been as though some higher power had wanted to reward McGarr for having been dutiful. It had been in the Dawson Art Gallery, which her family owned. McGarr had gone there for some technical information on the theft of several prints from Lord Iveagh's mansion in Kildare. He had tried to kiss the young woman in the slide room to the rear of the shop. She had slapped his face and threatened to call the commissioner. That had been three years ago.

"This man," McGarr said, meaning Inspector Hughie Ward, "is a policeman. Has he told you that?"

O'Connor shook his head.

"I didn't think he was a braggart." McGarr was feeling good again, after having been somewhat depressed by the events of the day. Noreen always had that effect on him and what was more, she knew it, which galled him. That was a power over him, albeit a benign power, but nonetheless a threat of sorts. "And this hussy is my wife."

"*Your* wife? I thought—" O'Connor smiled. "Would you care for a drink, Mr. McGarr?"

"No thank you, Rory." McGarr then forced his own features

to become serious. "I've already ordered one, and I have some bad news for you."

"Is it about May?"

McGarr nodded, watching the young man's features closely. "People have been talking."

In spite of what McGarr had heard about Rory O'Connor's wildness, the big man seemed very gentle indeed. Like his contemporary, Dr. Fleming, he had the blackest of eyes, but his were large and soft. His skin was dark too, but clear. He was wearing a blue short-sleeved shirt with a black alligator on the pocket. The alligator's mouth was open and red, which made the teeth seem very white. Americans were a curious people, McGarr thought.

The barman set his whiskey in front of him.

"She's dead."

O'Connor blinked. He began shaking his head slightly. "What's that?" He placed his hands on his knees. His brow furrowed.

"Somebody murdered May Quirk last night. In a pasture near the Cliffs of Moher."

A large hand sprang from below the table and grabbed McGarr. Another hand swept across the table and struck the side of Hughie Ward's head, knocking him into the wall of the snug. "This had better be the sickest joke you've ever told, pal," a very American voice said.

McGarr was now raised off his seat.

Noreen rushed out of the snug.

"This won't help her, O'Connor," said McGarr.

McGarr saw the fist forming and the arm cock. It then lashed out at him. At the last moment he moved his head and the blow glanced off his jaw. The fist struck the padding of the snug cushions.

O'Connor dropped McGarr, picked up the table, and tossed it out the open snug door. The table was made of metal and cascaded across the stone floor, slamming into the brass rail of the bar. The glasses had crashed to the floor.

The barman had come running. O'Connor grabbed the man's face in his palm and shoved it into the wall of the snug. He then stood. He was one of the biggest men McGarr had ever seen.

The crowd that had formed outside the snug made an aisle for him. He walked up the aisle to the bar and grasped the edge of it until his fingers whitened. His body began to fold until one of his knees hit the brass rail. Then the other. His neck was bending too, until his forehead touched the bar. It was as though he was praying. But he sobbed. It sounded like the cough of a cow.

Slowly he got up.

There was not one sound in the bar.

He turned. His face was streaming with tears. With the back of his hand he wiped them off his jaw. He then started back toward the booth, where McGarr and Ward still sat.

He said, "Whiskey," in a big hoarse voice and closed the door very softly behind him.

Standing in front of the door, with his hands crossed over his chest, he said, "Everything. If you lie to me I'll kill you, so help me God. *Where* on the Cliffs of Moher?"

"The other side of the cut from O'Brien's Folly," McGarr said. He wasn't about to get into a fistfight with that man. His teeth were getting old, but most of them were his own and he valued them.

"How?"

"Pitchfork. Upper chest. One jab."

O'Connor's eyes closed. "No!" he shouted.

The people outside the door began mumbling.

McGarr heard somebody run out of the barroom.

O'Connor turned and drove his fist through the veneer of the snug wall. He pulled it out and struck a second time.

Hughie Ward sprang to his feet and punched O'Connor in the belly with everything he had. Ward, like McGarr, was a small man, but he had been a boxer and could hit.

O'Connor turned his head slowly and looked at Ward, who hit him again, this time lower.

O'Connor didn't move.

Ward hit him again.

Still nothing.

The snug door swung open and Noreen stepped in, holding a 9mm Walther in both hands.

O'Connor had begun to crumble now.

Even so, Noreen had to reach up to put the gun against the side of his head. "If you don't sit on the floor, I'll pull the trigger." Her voice was flat, businesslike.

McGarr imagined O'Connor had little choice. He melted onto the floor.

McGarr took the gun from Noreen. The safety was on. He stuck it under his belt and sat.

The bartender was standing in the door with a bottle of whiskey in one hand, a trayful of glasses in the other. He was an older man with silver temples and a pink pate. His eyes were wide with fright, his complexion blanched.

Noreen took the tray from him and shut the snug door. She held it while McGarr poured three glasses and then showed the bottle to O'Connor, who took it and drank long. He was gasping when he finished.

"One more time," said McGarr, who then took the bottle from him.

The three of them sat and stared down at O'Connor, who was still on the floor.

McGarr said, "You were with her last night."

O'Connor nodded. He reached out his hand.

McGarr handed him the bottle.

"She was pregnant."

O'Connor looked up at him.

"Yours?"

O'Connor turned the bottle over and poured the whiskey onto the floor.

"Buck up," said McGarr. "That's no way for a man to behave. You're acting like a child. Be strong."

O'Connor waited for the bottle to empty, then with a flick of the wrist tossed it at McGarr, who caught it. He said, "I've got something to do. I don't think you're going to shoot me." Then he looked at Ward. "Touch me again and I'll break you in half."

Slowly he stood. His legs were quaking. He opened the door and started through the crowd toward the street.

McGarr got out of his seat, reaching for his wallet at the same time. He began following O'Connor until he got to the bartender, whom he handed a ten-quid note. "You Griffin?" McGarr didn't take his eyes off O'Connor.

The old man nodded.

"On last night?"

Again he nodded.

"O'Connor in here?"

"Which one?"

"That one, of course," said Ward, at McGarr's elbow.

"Yes."

"Did he follow May Quirk when she left?"

"No." The old man paused. "Not that he didn't want to. She left with a German fellow in a big red Mercedes. Tall man like himself. Blond. A Viking if I ever saw one. Some of the boys thought he scared the lad."

McGarr doubted that. O'Connor wasn't the sort to be frightened by anybody. He heard a car starting outside.

"They talked it over for a while, him and her. And then she left with the kraut. He had another pint and left. What's this about May Quirk?"

On the way out the door, McGarr said, "She's dead. Murdered. Anybody who knows anything about her last night should tell Dan O'Malley about it."

Noreen was already behind the wheel of the Cooper with the engine running. O'Connor's car was just moving out of the square. McGarr could tell from the plates it was a Shannon rent-a-car. It was a red four-door Datsun and no match for the Cooper on any highway, much less the winding road toward the Cliffs of Moher.

It was twilight now, which in Ireland during summer meant a long gloaming when the sun seemed to catch on the very edge of the horizon and melt slowly toward darkness. And the road from Lahinch to the Cliffs of Moher put the Cooper's nose right into the banks of salmon clouds over the ocean to the west. It was as though they could sail off the precipice into the mauve medium between sea and sky and journey to the pink land in the distance, McGarr thought. There life would be different—no contention, murders, punches to the jaw, no need to hang back like this so that O'Connor wouldn't quite know if he was being followed. When they approached the scene of May Quirk's murder, McGarr had Noreen run closer to the Datsun, but O'Connor didn't even turn his head toward the collection of some half-dozen vans and the glare of blinding kleig lights that had been maneuvered to the edges of the cliff in three different spots and were now trained on the sea below.

McAnulty had spared nothing on this project, and he was getting what he wanted. McGarr saw a van from Radio Telefis

Eireann and the cars of reporters with the press passes on their visors lowered. McGarr only hoped that the Technical Bureau would come up with a pitchfork. It was important for the country to know that their police force was still capable of a thorough job, in spite of the chaos in the North, and that every murder was being investigated conscientiously.

Call signals now blatted out of the Cooper's police radio. It was Bernie McKeon in Dublin, the signal doubtless having been relayed through a transmitter here in the West. His voice was loud and clear. "Got a line on Hanly. Definite I.R.A. connections. Everybody knows him but nobody wants to talk about what he does for them. It's not the official I.R.A., neither. His brother Dick is a district Provo commander, Newry. It seems that Hanly's mother's people are from there. He grew up in Dublin until his father died. That was in 1950, which would have made him—let's see—fourteen or fifteen, you know, just young enough for him to get mixed up with all them muckers. At about age twenty, the family moved back to Dublin. That's when he first got into the dance hall racket, first as a bouncer out at the Royal in Bray. Eventually, he managed to weasel himself a cut of that pie, and from there on he set up his own spots in Dublin—Fifty-One King Court, then on the Howth Road, and then a spot in Baggot Street when the disco thing took over. The last one is the only one he keeps open now. They say that stuff is really the rage overseas, and the manager of the place claims they're currently operating at a loss, waiting to see if disco dancing will catch on here again.

"However, it seems our friend Hanly has the Midas touch. Along with dance halls, he began begging, borrowing, mortgaging, and cadging every spare quid he could, and around 1966 began buying pubs out in all the country resorts—Salthill, Killarney, Ballydehob, Kinsale, even here in Bray on the waterfront. If you consider the inflation and whatnot, he's loaded. But I can't find out, first where he managed to get his hands on all that money at a time when money was tighter than the belly button of a nun, and that's lintproof—." He waited for a reaction.

Hughie Ward moaned.

Noreen shook her head.

McGarr flinched and looked up the road. They were beyond the cliffs now, dropping down through a valley where the rock formation which is Clare eased its gray bulk into the sea. There the beach was heaped with boulders and faults that challenged the heavy swells of the Atlantic.

"And second, what he does with his enormous income."

"He lives well," said Ward. "Big car, good clothes, lots of liquid refreshment."

"If he tried to spend the money he makes in a year on such things he'd have to have a different car for every week and be changing his clothes on the hour."

"So?" McGarr asked.

"So I've been putting the thing together in my own mind. And I'm only guessing, remember. I think the I.R.A. financed him right from the start. He's their front. Back in '66 they had their contributions, even though it was a quiet time for them. They're not all gunmen, you know, and perhaps during that calm period they began to provide themselves with a mechanism that would insure a continuing flow of money and—what's more—a way to justify the cashing of foreign currency without arousing the suspicion of the government. Hanly's dance hall and pub schemes in holiday and resort areas was a natural. I don't have any facts to prove this, of course, and I'm not likely to get them, either."

"But where, then, do the Provos figure in all of this?" McGarr

71

asked. "Surely they didn't have the money or the organization to finance such a project in 1966."

"That's just it. I wouldn't know. Maybe they're trying to horn in on the thing now. They can be gangsters, you know. Hanly may have been connected with the Provos all along, through his brother. Maybe this Quirk woman was making some sort of payoff. And maybe I'm doing too much talking."

Nobody said anything. Whenever McKeon winged it without hard proof, he was always taken seriously, since he seemed to have a sixth sense for collusion and intrigue. He knew better than any of them how his countrymen thought and he had been keeping his ear to the ground for almost thirty years now. The transmitter popped and sputtered.

They were approaching Black Head, a bald outcropping of dark rock. Noreen had to slow the Cooper to steer a path through five donkeys. McGarr had once heard they were wild in these parts, having been abandoned by emigrating farmers. Certainly their hooves had never been clipped; they curled up like the tips of snow skis.

The lights of O'Connor's car were still in front of them.

McKeon continued. "About May Quirk. She was about six weeks pregnant. That probably places the happy event within this country, since she arrived back here about seven weeks ago, and—get this!—it wasn't a holiday at all. She was on assignment. Something about guess who?"

McGarr sighed. He didn't feel like playing guessing games, but he could understand McKeon's insouciance. The detective sergeant handled all the research and administrative details back at McGarr's office in Dublin Castle. He hardly ever got away.

"Rory O'Connor?" Ward asked.

"Who's he?"

"Ah—Bernie," said McGarr. "Spit it out."

"The I.R.A., of course. I just got through talking to the assignments editor of the New York *Daily News*. She was supposed to be buying a story about how the I.R.A. is financing the operations in the North and where all the American donations go. She had been working on the story first over there in the States, and then she got a lead and came over here. He said she was carrying a lot of the paper's money and wondered if we had found it." McKeon paused for a moment. He knew how McGarr operated. "I told him we hadn't as yet, but would look for it."

"And all along I thought the money was May Quirk's retirement benefit."

"I thought that's what might have happened to it," said McKeon.

McGarr wondered if Paddy, the I.R.A. fund raiser who had written the letter proposing to her, had known she was writing a story about him. One thing was certain: McGarr intended to meet his plane at Shannon tomorrow. "I want you to put a tracer on one Rory O'Connor. He's a Lahinch resident, living in America now."

Hughie Ward said, "New York also. He's a popular novelist. Evidently pretty successful. I gathered his books wouldn't get past the censor here."

McGarr then thought about how the three of them—Fleming, O'Connor, and May Quirk—had been drawn to the hub of New York and each in a different way had become successful and important because of the city. Only Fleming had chosen to return; at least until now. McGarr wondered if O'Connor wrote about New York or Ireland. Who knows—maybe he wrote about Afghanistan or Mars.

Suddenly the rear lights of O'Connor's car vanished.

"Where is he?" Noreen asked, slowing.

They were nearly at the end of Black Head now and had been

passing campers who had parked their cars off the road and pitched their tents wherever they could find shelter from the stiff breeze off the ocean. The horizon was layered with narrow bands of red light that glowed like ruby near the water.

Noreen stopped the car.

O'Connor could be anywhere among the rocks. McGarr opened the door and stepped out on the road. He counted seven campfires. Three of the cars were small, like O'Connor's Datsun. In the twilight everything metal looked red. The wind off the ocean was chilling but fresh. McGarr was hungry again. The surf made him think of oysters.

That was when he heard a car door slam. It was in back of them, down a sandy trail that led toward a small patch of beach between two massive boulders. In the shadow of one, McGarr saw O'Connor walking toward a blue tent that had a light on inside. Next to it was a large car. McGarr guessed it was a Mercedes. The license plate was oval, which made it foreign.

McGarr slid into the car. "In back of us and down the donkey path. Don't use your lights unless you have to." He pulled the Walther from under his belt and checked the clip. He slipped it into the nook below the dash.

"Do I need one of those?" Ward asked.

"Don't think so," said McGarr. "We'll let Noreen handle the Howitzer this evening. I'm just getting it out of my pants so it won't slow me down if that giant starts chasing me."

"If this is the German fellow I heard about, there's going to be trouble," said Hughie.

They were halfway down the path. The Cooper, which was light, was having trouble in the occasional patches of sand.

"Well, if you even see a gun, Noreen," said McGarr, "don't be afraid to use this one." He placed it in her lap. "The safety is on."

74

She glanced at him and tried to smile but only succeeded in looking slightly ill. Whenever in the past she had gotten into a dangerous situation while accompanying McGarr on his duties, she had exulted in having gotten through the scrape—but after the fact. During it, however, as in the pub that afternoon, she had performed well but seemed scared skinny every minute. McGarr had often thought about how she might one day be injured seriously, but there was no keeping her from the work. When McGarr had tried to keep her in the dark, she had threatened to sell the gallery on Dawson Street and become a Ban Garda, that is, a female Garda. She knew McGarr wouldn't have that.

They were close enough now to see figures silhouetted against the blue material of the tent. Two men of about the same height were standing nose to nose. The one closer to the flap had his fists clenched by his side.

McGarr supposed that was O'Connor. The other man had a large object in his right hand, pointed right into O'Connor's belly.

Before McGarr could snatch the Walther out of Noreen's lap, O'Connor grabbed the other man's wrist and struggled with him. They blundered to the back of the tent, then staggered toward the lamp, which they tumbled over. It went out, and then the tent collapsed.

McGarr popped open his door and began stepping out.

That was when a shot roared from under the heap of tent material and bucked through the radiator of the Cooper.

McGarr threw himself onto the ground and swore. From the report of the weapon, it was something powerful—a Mauser or Luger—and the bullet had probably shattered the block of the engine. Then McGarr smelled raw gasoline. "Get out of the car and run!" he shouted to Noreen and Hughie.

They did as he said, running off into the darkness. Noreen fell. Ward picked her up.

McGarr himself ran toward the men under the tent. If the Cooper exploded, it might set the tent on fire.

But again the gun exploded, sending a jet of orange flame from under the billows of tent material.

McGarr again dived onto his belly, but he saw the smoking protrusion that was the gun. He scrambled up and charged the tent. Using the very toe of his shoe, McGarr kicked at the gun for all he was worth and heard both men groan, but suddenly the protrusion was gone.

That was when the Cooper went up. The little car was blown right over onto its roof in a ball of white fire that turned yellow, then orange, then white again as a second explosion—the gas line—rocked it another time.

The tent in front of McGarr had small patches of flame the size of half crowns all over it, and something was burning McGarr's back. He tore off his shirt, pulled out his pocket knife, and made a rent in the tent material. Noreen and Hughie grabbed opposite sides and tore the tent open.

The two men staggered to their feet.

Hughie Ward fished around for the gun and came up with a Mauser just like the one May Quirk had been carrying.

O'Connor had only to realize that he was not going to burn to death before he gathered himself and lashed out at the other man. O'Connor had been in a crouch, and the punch came right up from the ground and caught the German under the chin. It raised him right off the ground and knocked him back several feet. He made an odd sound that seemed to come from inside his chest and did not move again.

Nevertheless, O'Connor started for him.

Hughie Ward jumped between them.

O'Connor wound up to punch him, but Ward was too quick. When the punch swept over his head, Ward pivoted back on one leg and kicked out at O'Connor. He caught the big man, who was now off-balance, in the kidneys. The force of the kick drove O'Connor's face into the sand. Ward followed him down, laying his knee on the inside of O'Connor's left bicep while he jacked the other arm up and snapped handcuffs on the wrist. By the time the big man had thrown Ward off his back, his hands were cuffed behind him.

McGarr waved the Mauser in front of his face and said, "Sit down."

Ward kicked one of O'Connor's feet out from under him and shoved him back. O'Connor fell back onto the sand.

McGarr went over to the blond man and rolled him over. He had a splotch of blood on the lower front of his green turtleneck sweater. His skin was waxen, like that of a man who had lost a lot of blood. His breathing was quick and shallow. McGarr lifted the sweater. There was a bloody gauze bandage covering his lower stomach. McGarr ripped the adhesive tape off that. The man had a bullet hole there with a drain in it. A professional medical person had worked on the wound. McGarr wished he hadn't wasted all the whiskey in his flask on Hanly.

Miraculously, however, another appeared in front of him. It was Noreen's. She always carried a spare for him. McGarr tried to lift the blond man to a sitting position. Noreen had to help him.

The man was young and very handsome in a Nordic way— broad forehead, long straight nose. He had a cleft in his chin. McGarr first wet his lips, then poured a drop or two on his tongue. The man jerked his head a bit but wanted more. He opened his eyes, which were blue beyond the glazing and seemed about a quarter-inch deep. He was in very bad shape.

Hughie Ward returned from the Mercedes, where he had been rummaging about. "Tax stamp says his name is Max Schwerr. He's not German at all. I mean, he lives in Blessington."

McGarr gave the young man another small dollop of whiskey. McGarr said the name over again. Two . . . no, three years ago he had investigated the theft of a race horse from the house of a family named Schwerr. They too had lived near Blessington, having bought a large tract of hilly, scrubby land after the Second World War. This they had successfully reforested. Now they were beginning to reap the harvest. McGarr could remember that he had been singularly impressed by the family. They had money, were foreigners of a sort, but were good citizens in every way—politically active and nationalistic, they had funded a chair at Trinity, built a wing for the new hospital in Wicklow, and generally taken an interest in the higher affairs (symphony, museums, opera) of the country.

He gave Schwerr a little more whiskey.

Ward added, "Here's an envelope. I found it in the glove compartment. It's full of money. Most of it's foreign. And—" he paused, "—there's a pitchfork in the trunk. May Quirk's missing shoe is under the back seat."

McGarr turned to O'Connor, who was still sitting where Ward had dropped him. "How did you know he was here?"

"Fleming told me."

"How did Fleming know he was here?"

"He worked on him. Some farmer called him out here. May shot him, I guess. Before he killed her. I only put it together when you told me about her. He came into Griffin's last night. She had been waiting to interview him."

"For what?"

"An article she was doing."

"On what?" McGarr turned his back to shield the man on the ground. The wind had changed briefly and pushed a gust of smoke from the turtled and still burning Cooper toward him. The smoke was black and pungent with the reek of plastic, rubber, oil, and petrol. It snaked in thick ribbons from the wreck. McGarr had really enjoyed owning that thing until he saw it like that and realized how silly it had been for him to have invested his feelings in something so unimportant and fragile. How precarious were all things tangible.

Ward was now trying to make the campers, who had gathered around the wreck, disperse.

"The finances of the I.R.A."

McGarr assumed Schwerr had something to do with that as well. He had been selected for this aspect of the illegal organization because he was German and his appearance probably kept him above suspicion, to say nothing of his wealthy background and patrician parents. If May Quirk had shot him before he killed her, McGarr wondered where he had gotten the pitchfork, why he had chosen to use such a weapon, and why he hadn't chucked it over the cliffs, as McGarr had suspected. That caused McGarr to think briefly about McAnulty and his crew and Commissioner·Farrell.

Schwerr stirred. McGarr gave him a bit more whiskey. He groaned and coughed. "Perhaps," McGarr had only to say and Hughie Ward started for the Mercedes. "And park it down the road, Hughie. Then insinuate yourself among the people who are with McAnulty and, when he's alone, tell him about the car. We'll let him decide how he'll say we found that pitchfork. Maybe he might want to work the car over right there in front of all those media types. That'll pacify him some. I hope."

Schwerr had his hand on the bottle. McGarr was choking him with the stuff.

McGarr lowered the bottle and asked, "She shot you, didn't she? That's why you jabbed her with the pitchfork."

Schwerr said nothing. He didn't even blink. Suddenly his eyes cleared and he looked at McGarr.

McGarr said again, "May Quirk is dead. You killed her with a pitchfork. After she shot you."

He turned his eyes back into the cloudless night sky overhead. He blinked once, very slowly, and reached for the flask. When he could, he said in a hoarse voice, "I don't believe you." He turned and looked at O'Connor, and then McGarr saw his eyes quaver. Schwerr realized what McGarr was saying about May Quirk was true. Why else would O'Connor have tried to kill him? He sobbed. He bit his lip. He tried to raise himself. The pain almost made him pass out again. "She shot me, that's true, but that's all. I'd never kill her. Never, never. I . . . she . . ." His voice broke.

". . . was carrying your child?" McGarr asked.

Schwerr nodded as much as he was able. His chin was resting on his chest.

O'Connor struggled to his feet and began walking toward the water, where the incoming tide was frothing through the rocks and up onto the small sandy beach.

"It was this business of an abortion," Schwerr said. "I mean—" He turned his face to McGarr. "My parents, they loved her. She spoke German. She was . . ." He looked away. "And then her talk of her career, and the questions again." He paused for a moment. "You're McGarr?" He was looking out to sea.

McGarr nodded.

"Then you know what about, the questions." His voice had just the merest foreign trace to it. Otherwise he sounded like a person who had gone to public school and university. "And

I put it together. She was only interested in me because I was involved with the people she was doing some work on. I struck her—I admit it—again and again. I had never dreamed she'd refuse me. If she hadn't shot me, I think I might have killed her myself. She said—" He glanced up at the moon again, "—she'd have it taken care of in New York. In passing. As if it were just some minor problem that . . ."

When he didn't go on, McGarr asked, "So you left the pasture? Was that where you were?"

He nodded. "Just across from O'Brien's Folly. I can remember seeing tourists with torches up there. But I fell down and maybe . . . I can't remember. When I got to my feet I shouted for her, but I knew I was getting weak. I managed to get the car started and I stopped at the first farmhouse. I asked the farmer if he had seen May. He hadn't, but saw I was bleeding. He brought me inside and called a doctor, who patched me up."

"What did you tell him? A doctor is supposed to report all bullet wounds to the police." McGarr then remembered Dan O'Malley's implying that Dr. Fleming was currently the area's only medical practitioner.

"He did. I heard him myself in the farmhouse. I told him I stumbled with it in my coat pocket. It looks like that, don't you think?" He tried to look down at the bullet hole in his side. "Anyhow, I'm licensed to carry that gun. When the gun licensee gets hurt with his own gun, the police don't seem to care much." He looked at McGarr.

"Depends on the circumstances." The explanation seemed too lengthy to McGarr. He wondered why Schwerr was trying to protect Fleming. Or, if Fleming had reported the incident, McGarr wondered why the report had gotten lost in the course of the day. O'Malley would certainly have told McGarr about it.

And then why hadn't Fleming himself noticed the incident, the murder and the gunshot wound having occurred within a half mile of each other? And why hadn't the doctor, if in fact it was Fleming, insisted on Schwerr's being taken to a hospital? "Didn't the doctor want you to go to a hospital?"

"Oh, yes. He argued. He told me I was a fool. But I had—" Schwerr tried to focus on his watch.

"To make a delivery? Where?"

Schwerr glanced at McGarr. It was obvious he was very tired. "In Galway. At the dance."

"Don't you mean Salthill? At Barry Hanly's dance?"

Schwerr tried to study McGarr's face, but his eyes were closing.

"How did the pitchfork that killed May Quirk get in your trunk?"

Schwerr closed his eyes. "I don't know. I can't believe she's dead."

"Did Hanly give you this manila folder with the money?"

Schwerr shook his head.

"Where'd you get it?"

"I can't say anything about that."

"And who was the doctor? Did you get his name?"

Schwerr said nothing.

"What did he look like?"

Still nothing.

McGarr stood. He turned to Noreen. "When was the last time I took you dancing?"

"Dublin Horse Show. August seventeenth, last year." She loved to dance.

"Well—we're going tonight."

"But it's so late, and—" She looked at the burning Cooper, then at Schwerr.

"A good dance in this neck of the woods might last all night."

McGarr turned to O'Connor, who was coming up the beach. "How would you feel about accompanying us to a dance, Mr. O'Connor? Maybe it will help you keep your mind off recent events. In any case, I ask mostly because I want to borrow your car." All the police vehicles at the Technical Bureau site on the Cliffs of Moher were official looking. McGarr wanted to keep a low profile. "You don't have to come with us, but I'd prefer it." In the car McGarr could question the young man in an offhand manner. He believed he knew far too little about the principals in the case, and O'Connor was very much a principal suspect.

O'Connor turned his back.

"We'll have to wait for the ambulance anyway. We can't leave Mr. Schwerr alone in this condition."

O'Connor looked down at Schwerr. It was plain he would have preferred to have left him, dead.

"Give me the keys to your car, please."

"They're in the switch."

Noreen turned and stepped through the sand. McGarr admired her narrow ankle and the line of her calf, the way the light green material of the summer dress crimped over her hips. Because of the heat she was wearing a tight, low-cut blouse. The skin of her upper chest was just delicately freckled and nearly the same color as her hair.

McGarr turned back to O'Connor. "Sit yourself down. It'll be a while."

McGarr himself sat near Schwerr. "Who's your contact at the dance?"

Schwerr was beyond answering.

Phil Dineen, McGarr thought. He was a Provo C/O who was presently operating out of Galway City. He had been a childhood friend of McGarr's. They had grown up in the Dublin slums together.

6

A THUNDERBIRD TRINITY

As the motor of the Datsun whined toward Galway City and Salthill beyond, McGarr asked himself what he knew about the murder of May Quirk.

She had been a New York reporter. She had been writing a story about the financial operations of the I.R.A. She had $27,000 to pay for information, but McGarr didn't believe she would have needed that with Schwerr. She had had another sort of power over him, yet the pitchfork that had killed her, and her shoe had been found in his car. Also, she had shot him. She certainly knew she was being attacked when she was jabbed, since her hand had been on the gun. How Hanly could have managed to have ended up in her lap was a matter beyond explication.

Also, she was pregnant. At least three men had been in love with her: Schwerr, O'Connor, and the I.R.A. fund raiser in the States; and young Dr. Fleming, her childhood companion, hadn't batted an eye when McGarr had told him she had been murdered. He hadn't told McGarr everything he knew, either, and an intelligent man such as he would have made the connection between the murder and the gunshot.

Everybody in Lahinch had been fond of May Quirk. She had been an extraordinary human being.

84

Where to start? McGarr usually began with the lies. Only Barry Hanly, the dance promoter, had actually told him falsehoods. Fleming had simply withheld information. McGarr had no reason to disbelieve what either Schwerr or O'Connor had told him thus far.

McGarr stopped in Kinvarra and put a phone call through to Bernie McKeon's home in Enniskerry, a suburb of Dublin. His wife said he was still at the office.

McGarr dialed that number. He wondered why Hanly had said that the man Scannell at the Provincial Bank cashed all his foreign currency when, it turned out, he had never handled a large sum. "Still at it?" he asked McKeon. "And all for a gold watch and a pat on the back. Some people are satisfied with little or nothing."

"At least I won't have to walk."

"So—you've heard about my car. Hughie has a big mouth."

"I was trying to raise you on the blower at the time. The noise almost knocked me into the Liffey."

"Would that the volume had been louder. Your head needs a good soaking." McGarr was in a hurry, though. "Look it, Bernie—what do we know about this fellow Scannell at the Provincial Bank?"

McKeon chuckled. "I'm way ahead of you, chief. I've got a man on him now, another is going to check the Provincial books to see if Hanly might have been telling the truth, and yet another is putting out feelers to see if he's I.R.A. or not. I just couldn't understand why Hanly would lie to you. He's too experienced for that. Unless he didn't lie and Scannell had been instructed to give that answer to any police inquiry. Why sacrifice the whole organization for just one man?"

"But he lied about buying a bottle of Canadian Club. And twice about how his car got banged up."

"Probably too jarred to know himself. You know how he is—all that money will eventually kill him. Like a Midas of another sort, he'll try to pass it down his pipe in a steady stream of rare aged rye. Which reminds me." He paused. "Holy God, it's almost ten o'clock." The pubs would close in an hour and a half. "I'm off."

The most salient oddity of the case, however, was how the pitchfork ended up in the trunk of Schwerr's Mercedes. Certainly Schwerr, injured or not, wouldn't have put it there and then forgotten it. He had had enough strength left to grapple with O'Connor, too.

When he got back to the Datsun, he said to O'Connor, "Tell me about your latest novel." He started the car and headed for the highway. "What's it called?"

O'Connor looked out the rear window of the speeding rented car at Galway Bay, which kept flashing a wavy image of the three-quarter moon. The surf was up. *"The Thunderbird of Madison Avenue."* He seemed disinterested in conversation. He had to sit with his legs across the back seat. The interior rear-view mirror was useless to McGarr, who was driving. O'Connor's torso obscured his view.

"What's it about?" Noreen asked.

After a while, O'Connor said, "I suppose you could say it's about the collapse of a city and a civilization."

"I meant," she qualified, "what happens in the novel. Tell us its plot."

They waited at least a minute. The traffic was fairly heavy and McGarr kept trying to nose the Datsun by the rear of a lorry so he might see to pass it, but he didn't quite trust the little car. It certainly didn't have the spunk of his Cooper. Also, the shirt Hughie Ward had brought him from the Technical Bureau van was too small, and it bound on his shoulders and arms. That was

86

bothering him. He just didn't feel right behind the wheel of the car.

In a bored monotone O'Connor told them the complex plot of his novel. To McGarr's mind there were too many characters, too many untoward or unbelievable occurrences. The people he described just didn't seem real to McGarr, who had to be convinced. But he didn't pretend to know much about the fiction or Manhattan, which was the setting of the novel.

"Then you're a Mannerist, I take it," said Noreen.

"What's that?"

"I suppose it's a term that's applied only to painting now but once was used to describe that sort of literature which is fantastical and—as I trust your writing is—polished, as opposed to literature that's based on experience. *Mannerismo* is art that is stylishly stylistic, like much of sixteenth century painting."

Said O'Connor, "I don't know anything about that. I just write the books."

McGarr asked, "How did May Quirk feel about New York?"

"She loved it."

"And your character in the novel—did he have a love relationship with his wife or girl friend or somebody?" McGarr watched O'Connor watch the southbound traffic flow by them.

"You mean to ask what my relationship to May Quirk was?"

McGarr said nothing.

"At one time you could say we loved each other." He paused for a long time. "But New York makes people different, especially two people with such different careers."

"But you were both writers," said Noreen.

"After a fashion. I'm a writer. She was a journalist."

McGarr said, "Which means you did your work in a room, at a desk or a typewriter, and she was out among people every day." McGarr could see O'Connor look at the back of his head.

87

"Yes."

"Were you jealous?"

O'Connor didn't answer.

"Of her career, her success?"

He laughed slightly. "There's more prestige, at least in New York, in what I do. And in an actual sense I was more successful than May."

"You were? But she was *very* successful," said Noreen.

O'Connor said nothing.

Finally McGarr asked, "Did you live together?"

"Yes. Right from the first. I mean, when she arrived in New York."

"About a week after you?"

"Three weeks. She took a boat from England."

"And, naturally, neither of you was successful then."

"No, but that was the best time."

Noreen asked, "How many years?"

"Three and a half."

"What did you do for livings?" asked McGarr.

"May tried this and that. I wrote copy for the public relations department of an insurance company and wrote my novels when I could, usually in the early hours of the morning before I went to the job."

"That must have been difficult, grueling," said Noreen.

"I only remember it as fun. The years just flew by."

"And then?" McGarr offered O'Connor one of his Woodbines.

"And then," O'Connor breathed out as though this were hard for him to say, "a publisher became interested in my work. More importantly, I made some contacts. My first novel got good reviews. They published the second right after, a third the next year. The fourth sold well.

"In the meantime, I began meeting many of the New York media people. May mentioned how she'd like to get into the newspaper business. She was a natural. She could make the pope confess to her and thank God he had."

McGarr said, "And that was the end of it?"

O'Connor said nothing.

McGarr continued, "You either stayed home every day or went to your office, but you had to work hard and all alone to meet that next deadline or the expectations of your publisher or your readers. She, on the other hand, was out in the world and meeting all types—big people, little people, white, black, criminals, professors, day laborers, cops, and derelicts. How could a novelist not be jealous of that?"

"What do you want, an admission?" O'Connor struck a match and lit his and McGarr's cigarettes. "Okay. At first I loved her all the more, and she me. How could we have helped that—both of us successful, young, big people." O'Connor paused for a moment. In present company that was something of a faux pas. "We were invited everyplace. Television people were trying to interview us. We couldn't go anywhere without somebody snapping a camera at us. And then—

"And then—I guess I realized—no, that's not right, I didn't *realize* anything." He paused again.

In the rearview mirror McGarr saw the head of the burning Woodbine glow bright as O'Connor drew on it.

"I began to feel cheated. First from a more active life. Every day she came home with stories of this and that, this one or that interesting person. I was getting all my information second hand. People *she* had met and written about started appearing in *my* books. At first I told myself what was the difference, as long as those characters were interesting and I was doing essentially what I wanted with my life and she with hers, but then it flagged—the workroom, the desk, the typewriter, the mail, the reviews, the business of being a recluse for pay."

"Big pay," said McGarr.

"*Any* pay," said O'Connor. "It was me, too, you know. I was the one who became bitchy. All was not right with me. I tried to pick a quarrel with her and she wouldn't have any of it. That made me madder. My sixth book wasn't the smash it was supposed to be. It 'got out,' by which I mean that nobody lost any money on it, but the people in the business began questioning my ability to write one hit after another. And I just couldn't handle that. I'd been too successful in the past, too long on my own."

"And so you took it out on her."

"Exactly. I told myself I was jealous. And then I became jealous. I followed her, made scenes in public. Eventually, she left me. I don't—didn't blame her. My seventh book came out then and went straight to the best-seller list and right to the top for thirty-two weeks. But it was too late. May was gone. I tried to get her back, but whenever we'd go out, she'd always go back to her place."

Noreen asked, "And that made you even more jealous of her affections?"

"Yes, initially. But I managed to tell myself that what we had become in New York was better than what would have become of us if we had gotten married and raised a tribe back home in Clare.

"And then, at the time, I began trying to write about us in an attempt to get it out of my system."

Noreen said, "It must be a different book from the one you described."

McGarr said, "I'd very much like to read that book."

"It didn't sell at all," said O'Connor. "My publisher did it just as a favor to me."

"And the reviews?" asked Noreen.

"Mixed. The papers out in the boondocks loved it. New York, Chicago, L. A. said it was old hat."

In spite of his temper, O'Connor didn't seem to McGarr like a man who could kill somebody with a pitchfork, especially May Quirk. She had shared too much of his life, and if he could be believed, O'Connor had been resigned to their drifting apart. On the other hand, however, this was a man who had proved himself very successful at telling all sorts of stories. "Did you have other girl friends?"

"Yes."

McGarr tried to see in the darkness. He imagined that a rich, successful young man with O'Connor's dark good looks would not want much in the way of female companionship. How many of these other women could have been persons on the order of May Quirk, however, McGarr could guess. Very few indeed. "And where was the good Dr. Fleming during all of this?"

"Around. He was in medical school at Columbia and later interning at Roosevelt Hospital."

"And you saw him?"

"Of course. Regularly."

"What was his attitude to May?"

"If you mean did he hate her, would he kill her? I think you've got him wrong." Suddenly O'Connor seemed on the defensive.

"You mean she and he didn't get along."

"I wouldn't say that. It's just that they both became different persons. At first, when we had just gotten to New York, it was like we had a conspiracy, the three of us. Us against the big merciless city."

"And then?" Noreen asked.

"I don't know. He chose to come back here, that's all."

McGarr said, "And for him you two had become the city."

O'Connor opened a rear window and chucked the cigarette stub out. "I can't see how you can say that. He was as good at what he did as we were at our careers. He got offers to stay on at

Roosevelt as a resident. Let me tell you—that happens to very few young doctors indeed. He got other offers, too. I just never could see why he chose to come back."

"And May?"

"No. She even tried to talk him into staying. They had a big argument over it too, in Mickey Finn's. It's the place we met every Sunday afternoon for a drink and some talk."

McGarr said, "Do you know a fellow name of Paddy? He's not half your size. He's got curly red hair and a thick body. A dapper fellow. Likes to smile."

"Paddy Sugrue," O'Connor said in a neutral voice.

"What do you know about him?"

"Fund raiser."

"I.R.A.?"

"Ah—"

"Don't worry. Nothing will come of this."

"I think so. Yes—why not admit it. He is. Provos, too."

"What about him and May?"

O'Connor laughed once. "Jesus—he's like a hound dog, that guy. He's got an eye for all the women and none more than May. While she and I were together, he just stood off in the wings and worshiped her from afar. I like him, mind you, but he's got all the vices—loves to drink, he'd gamble on a change in the weather, and he's always in some wrangle over a woman."

"Is he successful?"

O'Connor snorted. "I don't know how he has the energy left for the little work he does."

"Please don't misunderstand the intent of this question, but do you think he was successful with May?" McGarr, of course, had read a letter that implied as much.

"No," said O'Connor without hesitating. "May wasn't that sort of girl. She might have gone out with a lot of men, but she didn't sleep around. Especially not with Sugrue. He was too transparent. She told me so herself."

Probably, McGarr thought, to keep O'Connor passive. Perhaps May Quirk had not been a loose woman, but he couldn't believe that she had had only one affair. He said, "But the German. Schwerr. She was pregnant by him."

"Don't get me wrong," O'Connor clarified. "May probably slept with several men."

McGarr listened closely to O'Connor's tone. It seemed perfectly regular. Most good writers were good actors, too.

"The German included. It's just that I don't think Paddy Sugrue was her type. She used to like to banter with him in Finn's. They had the same approach to people, you know, as much as to say, 'I know that beneath your calm exterior you're really a desperado with a heart as big as a cabbage and you can't hide it from me,' and they both set about revealing it in the same wheedling, jesting way.

"It was marvelous to hear them squaring off against each other. I don't think May lost once, whether he was always letting her or not. Anyhow, it was plain he'd walk through coals for her.

"I once came into the bar and saw him mauling some big black fellow who had tried to pick her up. As small as he is, he made a mess of the man and chucked him into the street. The fellow later turned out to be a dope peddler and tried to rub Sugrue out. But Sugrue has his friends as well. Half the New York police force is Irish. Their relatives were either kicked out or forced to leave Ireland by the very people whom Sugrue purports to be fighting. The dope peddler tried to shoot Sugrue in a parking garage. Somebody called the police. An hour later there was one dead dope peddler down there and no sign of Sugrue.

The bullet that killed the man was not from a police gun. No-body—not even May—asked any questions."

McGarr glanced at Noreen. She was studying the road and probably thinking, as he was, of New York and all the terrible stories they had heard about the place. Doubtless, New Yorkers had heard the same about Ireland and had promised themselves they'd never go there.

He said to O'Connor, "What's your approach to the I.R.A.?"

Without hesitating, O'Connor said, "I support their cause, I deplore the violence. They're never going to bomb the British people into surrendering the Six Counties. Hitler tried bombs with a whole bloody air force, and he failed."

"Do you expect them to love the Unionists to death?"

"Not if death is the point they're trying to make. If they had just held pat in '69, maybe Britain—. But as it is, she can't. The bloodbath would be horrible."

"That sounds like hindsight, Rory."

"I suppose it is."

Suddenly McGarr was famished.

O'Connor said, "It strikes me that you don't think Schwerr murdered May."

"I've been trying to keep myself from thinking anything at all, until I learn the facts. And even if I had them, I couldn't draw a conclusion without some food in my belly." But yet another thought struck McGarr. "What brought you home after . . ."

"Thirteen years," said O'Connor. "I guess I wanted to take a look at the place again. And see my mother and cousins, of course."

"She lives alone, I understand."

"But I have seven brothers and sisters, Inspector. Half of them live in England. She has company much of the year. Twice since I went to the States she's come over to New York to stay with my sister Agnes."

"And your father."

"Dead. Five years now." O'Connor's face was impassive. McGarr couldn't read an emotion in it.

7

DUCKS, SOUR TEA, POTEEN, AND GELLY

They stopped at a large roadside restaurant. The parking lot was crammed with cars. Inside, they were lucky to find an unreserved table that had just been cleared.

Once the building had been a common roadside pub, and the new owner had taken every care to preserve the exposed ceiling beams, limed walls, tall hearth, and fireplace of gray stone while providing his guests with modern amenities such as indirect lighting, central heating for the winter, and comfortable chairs. The tables were covered with spanking white linen. The simple good taste of the restaurant cheered McGarr—so many new restaurants in Ireland tried too hard to be modern or Continental—until he saw the menu.

Here he was within sound of the sea along a coast so singularly well provided with fish that the Russians and Japanese sent whole navies to exploit the resource, and only fillet of sole was offered. More than any other fish McGarr had ever tasted, sole did not take kindly to having been frozen. The rest of the menu was standard Continental dishes that were now usually bad, even at their points of origin, where the youngest and as yet unjaded chefs early learned to shudder at their mention: Cassoulet Toulousain, Kasseler Ribchin, Sauerbraten und Kartoffelkloss, Pork Chops Robert, Chicken Kiev, Côte d'Agneau, and Vitello

Arrosto. McGarr asked the waiter if the sole had been frozen. He said no, but McGarr disbelieved him and thus ordered the soup de jour—onion—and found it undistinguished. It was thick. The gratinée was a rubbery Emmenthaler and not Gruyère.

While sipping this, McGarr watched the women who assisted the waiter in carrying appetizers to neighboring tables: the inevitable paté maison either canned or, McGarr guessed unfairly, a pork liver concoction with freeze-dried truffles; prawn cocktail swimming in some red sauce; clams casino, and a melon that hadn't seen anything but the inside of a refrigerator for the last month.

When McGarr asked the waiter if roast beef was offered, he received a peremptory reply that such fare was offered in the barroom.

O'Connor said, "That's for me. I've seen this menu maybe a thousand times before."

"You've eaten here?" Noreen asked.

"Never been here in my life." O'Connor was adjusting the belt of his pants. It was thick, with a silver buckle and a large turquoise stone in the center. The cowboy gesture of stuffing his shirt down his pants seemed out of place in that setting. People at other tables turned to look at the large young man. Eyebrows were being raised. He then pulled his fisherman's knit sweater over his belt. It was the sort only New Yorkers now wore. Otherwise he was wearing jeans and black cowboy boots with green cacti and bright red pears embossed on the sides. "Thousands of pretentious joints like this all over Manhattan," he said loud enough for the waiter and most of the guests to hear. He then ambled out to the bar. He soon returned with a slab of roast beef and two pints of lager. The waiter said not a word to O'Connor.

Noreen ordered veal.

McGarr sighed and said, "I had wanted fish," and waved the waiter off when he tried to point out the sole. McGarr nearly got his first wish, however. He ordered the Côte d'Agneau, which tasted like fish.

When the three of them climbed back in the car, he said to Noreen, "You know, good cooking has nothing to do with sauces and oils and expensive, complicated preparations. Good cooking should enhance the individual flavors of the materials the chef is working with. For instance, lamb has an exquisite and delicate flavor all its own, and anything applied to it that takes from that flavor is a mistake."

Noreen didn't say anything, though she knew he expected a reply. After a while she said, "Well, the atmosphere was pleasant."

"Ah. Even the waiter was a loss. He was trying to be snide, without knowing how." McGarr was feeling grumpy. He was still hungry, too. "How was your entree?"

"Tasted like duck."

"That's it! I thought my lamb tasted like fish. I was wrong. It tasted like duck."

"At least they could have served us a trencher of candied cherries."

McGarr laughed. "The sempiternal bing cherry! The necessary item in the creation of an unabashedly third-rate restaurant. How was the roast beef, Rory?"

O'Connor removed a fat cigar from his mouth. The back seat of the little car was a cloud of fine blue smoke. "Quack, quack."

McGarr chuckled. His mood had changed.

A half hour later they arrived in the vicinity of the dance hall in Salthill. They knew they were there because for at least a half mile both sides of the highway were solid with parked cars and both lanes were jammed. Young boys with pocket torches were directing cars into the driveways and onto the lawns of their families' bungalows for fifty pence. McGarr quickly tired of waiting in traffic and swung through a gate, around a garage, and under a clothesline.

"All the way from Shannon," said the boy's grandfather, who was sitting on the back stoop smoking a pipe filled with Yachtsman, a dark, pungent smoke that after O'Connor's expensive cigar smelled to McGarr like scorching donkey cack. "Yerra, I wish I was young and had me choice of all the women in Ireland of a Saturday night. Had I that," said he, "I'd look no farther. Evening, ma'am." He tipped his cloth cap to Noreen. He was toothless. A small portable radio next to him was playing a reel and he was tapping a heavy boot in the dirt. A glass by his side held an amber fluid. "Can ye dance?" He stood and nearly fell. He reached down and turned up the radio. He reached out for Noreen's hand. She took it and they danced a bit, moving only their legs and feet. It was like a tap dance, only less mechanical. The old man's brogans beat a tattoo in the dust, and a lit coal sputtered from his pipe and fell on his sleeve. He batted it off and stopped. "I'm tuckered. That was grand." He wrapped his arm around her and gave her a squeeze. "If I could wipe the slate clean of fifty—no, sixty—no, seventy years you could forget those two gombeen men and we could make a night of it, girl."

"Go on with you," she said. "Forty, thirty, or twenty is more like it."

He released her and stepped away from them. " 'Tisn't. James P. Creon is ninety and two if he's a day."

McGarr said the compulsory, "Sure and you don't look sixty-two."

"Hear that? Hear that, Midge?" he roared into the open back door of the house.

Somebody swore inside.

McGarr tried to place a fifty p. coin in his hand. "Cripes," said the old man. "How could I take that from you after you letting me dance with your pretty sister?" He gave Noreen a buss on the cheek. "If it was up to me I'd let the whole world park out here."

"You bring that money right in here, J. P.," a sharp old voice called out from the kitchen. McGarr could see a gray head bent over the sink.

"It's my daughter," he whispered. "A shrew. Can't dance a step." He put the coin in his pocket and sat.

Once a movie theater, the dance hall had a long stage at one end and a level wooden floor laid over its formerly sloping aisles. It was as hollow as a drum and roared under the dancers' feet.

Looking around at the meticulously coiffured hair styles, high shoes, tight pocketless pants, and open-neck shirts, McGarr believed he could well have been in London or Paris or Rome, but when the young people began to dance he knew he could be in only one place, for their step was little different from that of the old man where they'd parked the car. What was more, everybody seemed to be dancing together. The whole crowd moved up and down as one.

McGarr said, "I wonder if this building has been inspected recently."

Many of the young men standing near them were darting glances at Noreen. One girl nudged her friends and turned her head toward O'Connor. Another rolled her eyes.

"Do you dance?" Noreen asked O'Connor.

"I don't feel like it tonight, thanks."

"Oh, you'll not be able to refuse the girls here so easily." She took his hand and led him out onto the dance floor.

For a moment McGarr was a bit miffed that she hadn't asked

him, but he realized the situation was best for the business at hand. After inquiring at the bar for the manager of the dance hall, he was led up a circular iron staircase to the former projection room of the building. The bar girl pointed to a door at the end of a dark hall, then slipped back down the stairway.

McGarr could hear muffled voices behind the door. The hallway smelled sour, like cigarette smoke and old tea.

When he knocked on the door, the voices stopped short. He heard somebody push back a chair, approach the door, then hesitate before asking, "Yeah?"

"I'd like to speak to the manager."

"What about?"

"About Barry Hanly and Max Schwerr."

McGarr then heard several more chairs slide back and he wished he had brought more with him than the folder of money he had gotten from Schwerr. He took several steps back from the door and said, "I'm standing far back from the door, in the middle of the hall. I have my hands raised over my head."

He heard somebody within the room say, "I know that voice. Let me handle it."

A few seconds later, the light under the crack of the door went off and the door opened slightly, then farther, then a man stepped out. McGarr could barely see him in the darkness. He wasn't any taller than McGarr. He carried the tobacco and tea smell with him. Beyond that there was a sweet reek of porter and the bodies of many men. "Is that you, Peter?"

"Yes, it is. Who are you?"

"I was half expecting you, once we heard you'd lifted Hanly. What's this about Schwerr?"

"Who am I talking to?" The door was wide open now, and McGarr could hear the shuffling of feet in the dark room. He could also have sworn he heard the click of a hammer being eased back from the cocked position on a large-bore pistol. Or was that just his imagination? He knew his own figure was silhouetted on the yellow glimmer up the circular stairwell in back of him.

That was why, when the other man struck a match and held it to the end of his cigarette, McGarr said with somewhat more than usual enthusiasm at seeing his old friend, "Phil! Good to see you."

"And you, Peter. How's your missus?" Dineen had come to McGarr's wedding and they had been boyhood chums. Dineen had gone into the British army and risen through the ranks to become a major before he had a change of heart. He was a quiet man with thin features and the gentle demeanor of a pastor, which masked well his present activities. Dineen was the man who planned many of the Provo maneuvers in the North and elsewhere. In the past, McGarr and he had talked, argued, almost come to blows about the use of terrorist tactics. They were still good friends, however, in the way one feels very special about a person with whom he has passed the carefree days when the world was just revealing its sunny side. They had explored Dublin together, ducked under the fence at Croke Park, swiped apples on Moore St. and golf balls at the Royal course on North Bull Island. Once they had hopped on a C. I. E. coal barge together and taken it to Mullingar, where a Garda gave them, each in turn, the first lift back toward Dublin, on the toe of his boot.

"Fine. Noreen's downstairs dancing."

From inside the room McGarr heard a sharp report like a hand slapping the back of a head. Somebody whimpered, then a gruff voice said, "Get your arse down to that door or I'll pound the tripes out of you."

"But he'll see me." The voice was young.

"Let's hope his luck is better than that," said yet another voice.

"I know what it is," said the young voice. "You got me muney and now you chuck me out."

McGarr imagined they'd been playing cards.

"Pardon me a moment," said Dineen. He walked into the room and shut the door. McGarr heard a groan and the sound of somebody being driven up against the wall. Suddenly the door opened again and a form fell into the hall. That person scrambled past McGarr.

The glowing coal of Dineen's cigarette appeared in the hall again.

The whole building was rocking with the sound of the band and dancers below.

"Let's go in here and let the boys continue their game." He opened another door on the hall, stepped into a room, and switched on an overhead bulb that hung from the ceiling by its cord.

Although the light was dim, McGarr could see Dineen had lost a lot of hair since the wedding three years before. At that time McGarr had just taken the job with the Garda and necessarily he and Dineen could not continue to meet each other socially. What was more, Dineen had been implicated as an accessory in several I.R.A.–related crimes. In spite of their long-standing friendship, McGarr's approach to Dineen was little different from his approach to other I.R.A. members: many of the things Dineen and his cohorts did McGarr abhorred, but he looked upon their actions as mostly political. If no innocent party was hurt, he tended to turn a blind eye to them. McGarr disliked politics. It made things too simple, either black and white or good or bad. It ignored the fact that people are complex and various. In short, he wished his friend Dineen had had more sense than to involve himself in a cause that so often had been responsible for killing and injuring many innocent persons in Britain, the Six Counties, and in Ireland itself.

Dineen motioned to a chair around a large circular table the top of which was mottled with cigarette burns. He sat next to McGarr and produced a bottle and two paper cups. He half filled each. It was poteen, and very good at that.

"So," McGarr said, "how's the life."

"Any day now I'll grow a goatee and they'll start calling me the Ho Chi Minh of Connaught." Dineen smiled. Unlike many of his comrades, he had a pleasant sense of humor.

"Better than the British army, though?"

Dineen looked away. His eyes were hazel. McGarr noticed that his neck was getting scrawny. "Bridie wouldn't say so—no steady pay, no pension, no sick leave, no dispensary." He looked around. "Nothing but the back rooms of dance halls—if you're lucky; and a few pounds tax free to send home in a plain brown envelope. That's twice yearly. I haven't seen my family in a month of Sundays."

"Having second thoughts?"

"No man is without them." He glanced at the door, then said in a lower voice, "I can't say I agree with everything that's going on."

"You mean the infighting." Factionalism had long been the special curse of the I.R.A. In recent months it had led to open fighting. Over a dozen men had been assassinated, and they were the lucky ones. Several others had lost their kneecaps or other parts of their bodies. McGarr knew of a man who had been crippled from the neck down by a bullet that had been fired purposely into his backbone.

"That and the bombing."

"But you knew about the bombing plan when you joined."

Dineen's expression was more than pained; it was agonized. McGarr could tell he was in a quandary and wanted to talk. "I thought I was joining at the least a paramilitary organization. I was approached by a certain ex-officer who shall go nameless. He's quite a bit older and couldn't carry on anymore. He's got money and said he'd pay my rank and allotments and such and, in spite of my grousing, he's done it after a fashion. He said he was buying leadership, but here I sit, smack on my duff in some outback 'garrison,' trading in smoke and shadow. Every day I pick up the newspaper I'm embarrassed. Some nut has chucked a bomb into a crowd of civilians in the name of the cause. *My* cause. It makes me sick.

"Then the other news is the way we're chopping each other up, when all along I thought we were fighting for the same thing."

McGarr took a sip of the poteen. It was clear, colorless, and had a peaty flavor he enjoyed. "And what would that be, Phil?"

Dineen looked up at his friend. "Don't you know?"

McGarr returned his gaze. "I'd like you to tell me."

Dineen blinked once. "A united Ireland, of course. And a functioning egalitarian democracy."

"And you think fighting can bring that about?"

"Everything else has failed. The way the Stormont government had it, Ulster was the South Africa of Europe, only it was Paddies like you and me, Peter, who were the niggers. We could only work the most menial jobs, if we were lucky enough to get one. We had to carry passes, couldn't go into certain areas, either were kept from voting or had our electoral districts so devised that our votes wouldn't count. And at every turning we were insulted and vilified—had an army of bigots armed to the teeth marched through our neighborhoods on King Billy's birthday, and him the very one who first installed those mercenaries here three hundred years ago. And us native sons and daughters in our own country!" There was a flush in Dineen's cheeks now.

"But hasn't everything you've done only made the majority more sure that's the way they want it?" McGarr asked, referring to the clause in the Act of Union that committed Britain to maintain Ulster's firm relationship until a majority in the Six Counties should vote otherwise. The I.R.A. contended that Ulster was a part of Ireland and thus the majority of all the Irish people should determine its political destiny.

"Which just makes what we've done the more necessary, doesn't it? When England disallowed any other political solution, she must have wanted us to have no alternative but violence. The Act of Union is a political dead end. What other option have we?"

McGarr tilted the paper cup and looked down into the poteen. To him the I.R.A.'s policy was as blind a dead end. They were demanding nothing short of a united Ireland. The majority in Ulster would sooner see a civil war far hotter than the present hostilities there. The Dublin government hadn't gone out of its way to make itself attractive to the North, and some people in Ulster were more determinedly English than the English themselves. Some middle ground had to exist—another intermediary and independent Six Counties in which social, political, but also economic rights were guaranteed to all and time, the great healer, could bind the new wounds opened during the current spate of violence. Then perhaps years and years later some other political accommodation might be made.

McGarr said, "It seems to me you've got to identify the opposition. I don't think the I.R.A. has ever done that. The British people aren't your opposition, nor British politicians, nor even the British army. Most Englishmen wouldn't bat an eye if Ireland, all thirty-two counties of her, sank into the sea. And the R.U.C. and the U.V.F. and the B Specials aren't the opposition, either. The real opposition is the habit of mind that thinks of us," here McGarr meant Irish Catholics, "as the enemy, and vice versa. Then we've got to realize that the habit of mind is a form of ignorance, that there's no beating, bullying, or bombing it out of existence. If anything, that makes matters worse. What we've got to do is appeal to the better sides of the people who feel that way. And we've got to give them an alternative to our way of thinking, some middle ground. And if not to them, then to their children."

Dineen was smiling now.

And McGarr felt foolish. He knew the question Dineen was going to ask.

"And what middle ground is that, Peter?"

"An independent Ulster."

"Ah, yes—that old tuppenny upright, an Independent Ulster. Ulster itself wouldn't have her. Dublin wouldn't allow her out of the back alley."

"Oh, I don't know. I'm not a politician. We've talked about this before. I just hate seeing you all jammed up here." He glanced about the empty room. "Like this. Involved with a bunch of hooligans and psychotics."

"You mean you'd prefer to think of me as Major Dineen, your officer friend in the British army."

Now McGarr was feeling uncomfortable. "Yes, if you must know, that would be preferable."

"Well then, answer me this, Peter. Is it because you yourself feel guilty, being ensconced in your swell job in Dublin Castle, knowing what's going on in the North and knowing that people like me have thrown over similar cushy posts to do something about it?"

McGarr finished the drink of poteen. His job was neither swell nor cushy, but maybe Dineen had something there. To be very honest with himself, McGarr did feel guilty about what was happening in the North. But his guilt wasn't so much involved with not having joined in the I.R.A. fight as it was in not having done something about his idea for a middle ground. True, McGarr disliked politics, but he had not been a good citizen. He was perhaps as well informed as anybody in the country, he had an opinion about what should be done, but he had neither contacted his T.D. to let the man know his position nor had he tried to convince others of the rectitude of his plan. He had rationalized that by saying he could be a much more effective police officer if his political opinions were not known. That was true, but did he not have another obligation to his country as well? At least Dineen had come to a conclusion about how events should proceed in the North and was doing something about it. "Could be," he said sheepishly. "Could be."

Dineen pulled the bottle from his overcoat and added to the cups. "Does that mean you might be willing to help us in the future?"

McGarr said, "Consider my not having roused the Galway barracks tonight an act of assistance that contravenes the very spirit of my commission in the Garda Soichana."

"Touché," said Dineen.

"And my face is tired from winking at the antics of some of your hooligans." McGarr took another sip. A warm glow was making him forget his responsibilities. "And then, what other Garda officer would hand deliver all that cabbage," he said, pointing to the fat brown oak tag envelope.

"Anyone who was in need of a bit of information, I suspect. You mentioned Hanly and Schwerr. Hanly I know about. This is Schwerr's delivery. What happened to him?"

McGarr then told Dineen about May Quirk's murder. "As far as I'm concerned, it's a simple case of homicide *if*"—he tapped the folder—"I can keep these other complications out of it. That's why I'm here." McGarr met Dineen's gaze and held it.

Dineen said, "Hanly was acting under orders. *Not* to go and drink himself stupid, mind you, but to keep an eye on Schwerr. He's a new boy and, you know, something of an ideologue."

McGarr cocked his head.

"Wait—all of us are ideologues, I guess, but Schwerr had no real stake in the army."

Again McGarr seemed to object.

"I mean—he's wealthy, a kraut, been educated all over Europe. I wondered why he chose our cause. At first I had the idea his approach was romantic, so we gave him some pretty rough jobs."

McGarr didn't care to inquire what the jobs had been.

"He acquitted himself well. So we gave him the cash funds job with an eye to his replacing Hanly. Schwerr was just right—nobody would connect him with us—and Hanly is having big troubles with the devil in his throat. He's a good man, loyal and trustworthy when sober, but drunk he's different entirely."

"And what was his attitude to Schwerr?" McGarr asked. "No doubt he knew Schwerr was going to replace him. From what I can gather, it's a soft spot. Plenty of money, no way to account for it, lots of booze and companionship. I don't see Hanly doing anything more exacting for the cause."

Dineen shook his head. "He's been well provided for. And he's done more than his share in the past. At one time he had a Midas touch and earned plenty for us. Some of his investments were his own. He won't suffer for much."

"What were his orders in regard to Schwerr?"

"Just to follow him last night. The regular tail we put on Schwerr blew his cover, and we had nobody else available in that area over the weekend."

"But Schwerr must have known Hanly by sight?"

"As I said, Hanly's a pro. My bet is Schwerr never once saw him, drunk as he was."

True, McGarr thought, Schwerr had never once mentioned Hanly. Nor Hanly Schwerr for that matter, but that was understandable, given I.R.A. activities. Still, it struck McGarr that Hanly had been conspicuous. The men in the bar in Lahinch had described him right down to the odd brand of whiskey he drank. There was some discrepancy between what he was now being told and what had actually taken place. And the type and number of Hanly's lies reinforced that feeling for McGarr. "But *why* was Schwerr being followed?"

"Because of May Quirk." Dineen paused to light a cigarette.

The band had stopped now and McGarr could hear the crowd outside the windows of the room, taking a breather in the parking lot.

Dineen continued, "She was a journalist of the worst sort. A badmouther, I'd say. The idea was to make all the little people who read her reports feel good whenever she slew another giant."

That didn't seem far wrong. The *Daily News* was a little man's newspaper. McGarr himself had read an article written by May Quirk that had had such a slant.

"I had her checked out completely before I let her interview me, but we came to a decision about her I just couldn't support. We decided that too many of the Irish-American *Daily News* readers identified with the I.R.A., and her editors there just wouldn't let her do a job on us in the paper. I argued against it, but I was overruled. I told them I had gotten my facts from New York."

"Paddy Sugrue?" McGarr asked.

That knocked Dineen back. "No, somebody else; somebody closer to her."

McGarr wondered who could possibly have been closer to her than Sugrue. He then thought of Rory O'Connor, downstairs with Noreen.

"My thought was that she'd go for all the marbles with this story—you know, personal interview with I.R.A. finance chiefs—and try to set up syndication all over the States. If she did, her story could have hurt us bad. Above all else, May Quirk was a very ambitious young woman. *But*"—Dineen raised his palm—"we did not kill her. At least, I can tell you as an old friend I saw no order, heard no rumor, and wouldn't believe it if you told me now that we had anything to do with her death. And you know as well as I, neither Hanly nor Schwerr would have been called upon to do the job if we had decided otherwise. They are—*were*—too important to us. Cut off our money and—" Dineen let the silence carry his meaning. He pulled the stacks of money out of the envelope. A red rubber band bound each. These he removed and began sorting piles according to currency and value. "I guess I've been proven right, after all. Because of her, both of them are now useless to us, and we might have lost all this money as well."

McGarr said, "I don't see why you granted her an interview, feeling as you do."

"Orders. And if she was going to interview anybody, I wanted it to be me."

"And?"

"I got the distinct impression she was going to flay us in the article. Most of the questions were something like, 'Does it titillate your revolutionary ardor, Major, to know that your twenty-some-odd years of military expertise are being employed in the massacre of women and children?' 'Does your wife know she's

111

married to an archfiend?' 'What does she tell the kids when they ask if daddy's coming home for Christmas? He's over in London blowing Santa out of Harrod's basement?' "

McGarr smirked.

"Not exactly that, but you know what I mean. Sure, she asked a lot of important questions, too, but every once in a while she came through with one off the wall. I got the impression she was up to no good."

"Were you supposed to answer the important questions?"

Dineen's forehead glowered a bit. "I had my limits."

"About where the money was going and for what?" They both knew much of the cash donated in New York and other places was simply being stuffed in the pockets of either the intermediaries along the way or the Provo commanders who weren't as altruistic or well provided for as Dineen.

Dineen looked away. "She kept laying on that angle. She wasn't being straight with us. She had a hidden agenda. That O'Connor kid was different."

McGarr didn't say a word. He just stared at Dineen.

"Came along with her. Said he thought he'd write a book about us. I liked him. He asked questions that allowed us to put our best foot forward. He said we'd already gotten all the bad press we needed in the States. Also said the function of a critic was to try to understand a point of view thoroughly, to present it as completely as any of us would have it, and then step back to see how the reality of our efforts matched the ideal. You can't ask for any more than that.

"While he was saying that I watched her. She was just looking crafty, if you know what I mean. As though everything he was saying was just so much talk and she knew what she was going to do already."

"Maybe it *was* just talk. Did you investigate O'Connor too?"

"Of course. Thoroughly."

"And was he what he said?"

"More than she, who had only her New York *Daily News* ID and her word that she was going to write the piece. He had a contract with a New York publisher."

"What about the twenty-seven thousand dollars?"

Dineen tilted his head. He didn't know what McGarr was driving at.

"Her editor in New York sent her twenty-seven thousand dollars to pay for certain special information from a Provo source."

Now Dineen was very interested. "He did? From whom?"

"I'd like to know that myself."

Dineen thought for a moment.

"She had the money on her when she was killed, but whoever killed her either didn't know it or didn't or couldn't search her for it. Who else besides you and Hanly knew Schwerr was going to meet May Quirk in Griffin's?"

"Nobody else that I know of, but then again—" He let his voice trail off.

McGarr understood that the I.R.A., Provisional wing or otherwise, was not as tight-lipped an organization as some would have it.

Dineen said, "That's a lot of money."

"For one man," McGarr added. "The special information must have been pretty important stuff."

In a patently disingenuous manner Dineen said, "And I couldn't imagine what that would be, Inspector."

But McGarr could tell he was worried. "Where did you meet them?"

"In a pub in Lahinch."

"Does O'Connor know you use this place?"

"Don't think so. Of course, we won't be using it much longer."

"Does Schwerr have a temper?"

"Not that I know of, but I don't know much about him personally."

"Did you know May Quirk was pregnant?"

Dineen shook his head. "And, sad to relate, not by me."

"By Schwerr."

That interested Dineen. "She was a wily one, that one."

"Schwerr wanted to marry her. She mentioned abortion. He admits he blew his top. That was when she shot him."

Dineen thought for a moment. McGarr could tell the $27,000 and Schwerr's alliance with May Quirk were bothering him. "Even an I.R.A. man has a right to a little nonpolitical anger, you know, Peter." He looked away. "But Schwerr could have compromised us seriously with her. I wonder how much he told her. Have you found her notes yet?"

McGarr shook his head. "But I've posted an armed guard on her parents' house." That was a lie and Dineen knew it. He added, "If I find it, you can have it." He didn't have to add that he'd take a copy.

"I hope you find it, Peter. I really do." He paused. After a while he said, "You know, if I *had* known about her and Schwerr, I might have—"

McGarr scoffed. "She was a beautiful woman, you said so yourself. Don't tell me you've become a misogynist now that you've teamed up with these teddy boys."

But it wasn't a light moment for Dineen. "I could tell just by looking at her she'd have the hammer out on us the minute she got back to New York. There she was," he pointed to an empty chair, "all bright green eyes and chirpy like she hadn't spent a day of her life outside Clare and thought an I.R.A. CO was as lofty as a messenger from God, but I'd just read a sheaf of her articles on dope dealers, prostitutes, gangsters, corporate gougers, the vice-president who got the sack, and a labor union that was bilking its members. She had squashed them all as flat as ants on a pavement. And we were next, no two ways about it." He had the bottle out again. "Whoever did her in did us a favor. Have another drink, Pete."

McGarr didn't object. He was wondering about O'Connor and why he had lied to him about being here in Ireland. He was also wondering about May Quirk. Her image was beginning to tarnish a bit. She had been devious, ruthless, and inordinately ambitious. And McGarr knew Dineen to be a rare judge of character.

"Now what?" Dineen asked him.

"Don't know. Poke around a bit. Hanly lied to me about several things, not just the money."

"You'd think with how good we've been to him, he would have tried to play us straight."

"O'Connor lied to me as well. A certain doctor by the name of Fleming didn't tell me everything he knew, either." McGarr took a sip of poteen. Dineen had lowered his eyes at the mention of the name. "Do you know the man?"

"Which one?"

"Fleming."

"A doctor, you say he is?"

McGarr could tell Dineen was about to lie to him.

And Dineen knew McGarr knew. They had been friends too long. Dineen laughed. "Sure, I know him." He opened his suit coat and pulled his shirt from his pants. His ribs were wrapped. "Some bastard in Fermanagh tried to break me in half."

"Does Fleming work for you often?"

"That's a state secret. What state, you ask? Why, the state of being a doctor in the military sector that I control."

So that was the reason Fleming had not told McGarr about

Schwerr's gunshot wound. McGarr kept staring at Dineen until the latter added, "He's a good boy, Fleming. The best. Never asks for a farthing. Late at night, early in the morning. He's performed successful operations in barns by the light of a pocket torch on fellows that were half blown away. He's kept us in his office, his farmhouse. He gave us the loan of his car a couple of times. Fleming is a very special person to us. We wouldn't want a thing happening to him."

McGarr was a bit taken aback. "That's not a threat or a warning, I hope."

"Nope. Just a statement of fact. If Fleming got lifted, I don't know if I could restrain some of the crazies." The thought made Dineen's features glower.

McGarr stood. "Noreen's downstairs. Why don't you come down and have a snort on me."

Dineen shook his head. "Can't. Wouldn't be good for either of us."

"Ah—I don't care about that."

"But I do. May Quirk's death puts me in a bad light with the other CO's. They knew I didn't care for her. Then Hanly and Schwerr show up and get lifted at the scene. They're my men. At best they've only exposed themselves; at worst one of them gets charged with murder and the whole lot of us have got to run to ground. And then there'll be the charge of countermanding a council decision. No, Peter—somebody might misinterpret our drinking together in public. We wouldn't want that."

McGarr offered Dineen his hand. "You give me a ring if you need me, Phil. If you're in a jam, I promise I'll do everything I can. How are you fixed—"

Dineen stopped him. He tapped one of the piles of currency. "All I want."

That was when the bulb went out.

Then the door opened and McGarr heard something being slid over the floor.

The door was closed with a clap.

When McGarr heard Dineen fall to his knees and scramble toward the door, he knew what it was.

He jerked his head to the windows. His pupils had yet to dilate in the darkness, but through the yellow shade he could see the faint glow of the lights from the parking lot outside. At this he rushed and hurled his back into it.

Only when he felt the windows catch the weight of his body, buckle, then burst did he remember he was on the second floor of the building. McGarr tried to control his fall, to tuck in his appendages and shield his head, but the force of the bomb blast roaring hot from the shattered window drove him out across the parking lot in a wild tumble. He landed, back down, on the roof of a car and felt it collapse like a soft hat. The heels of his shoes smashed the windshield. He was then showered with debris from the explosion. Before the big stuff could fall on him, he had sense enough to roll off. He fell into the darkness between the parked cars and just lay there. Shards of wall and framing timber clattered over the sheet metal of the automobiles. The damp earth was cool on his cheek and temple.

There was no doubt about it now, he surmised—the I.R.A. had something to do with May Quirk's murder when they were willing to sacrifice one of their senior officers to sidetrack the investigation. Or could Dineen's disaffection for the cause have been deeper than he had let on to McGarr? Did certain of them see it as a chance to get rid of two thorns in their side? Or were they, as Dineen had said, just a bunch of crazies whom he couldn't control himself?

McGarr could hear the crackle of flames and the shrieks of the crowd, which was pushing from the lower levels of the dance hall in panic. He pulled himself to a stand. Fortunately, he was still numb. At first his legs wouldn't work and he had to use the sides of the cars like crutches.

He didn't stop at the dance hall entrance to assist the Salthill Garda. He knew he wasn't up to it. He caught a glimpse of O'Connor at the front of the crowd and, by standing on a bumper, he saw Noreen near him. McGarr managed to push his way, toward them, and they helped him to O'Connor's Datsun.

The front bucket seat wrapped McGarr's back like soothing hands. "Drive slow," he advised O'Connor. "Very, very slow. And avoid any rough spots, please."

"What happened?" Noreen had waited until then to ask.

"An attempted double assassination." McGarr thought about Dineen. The only way he might have escaped was through the door. McGarr imagined he hadn't had the time.

"Phil Dineen and you?"

McGarr nodded.

"When it happened, we were waiting for you near the ticket window in the front lobby," Noreen explained. "There was that terrible roar and then he came tumbling down the stairs, his face all covered with blood. He picked himself up, ripped off his jacket, which was on fire, and walked out the door as though nothing had happened. He collapsed when he got outside. Some men put him in the back seat of a car and drove off. Oh, Peter—that was a close call. I was so—" She couldn't complete the thought.

McGarr could see she was troubled. Her forehead was wrinkled, eyes wide with fright.

"Where do you hurt? Hadn't we better get you to a doctor?"

"I'm all right." He offered her his hand. "The hospitals and doctors will be busy treating all those people who got trampled. Did you see them?"

O'Connor was shaking his head. "Reminded me of a sheep dip."

"It was awful," said Noreen. "Are you sure? Where do you hurt?"

"I landed on my back. Tomorrow—" McGarr turned his face to the window. He knew how he'd feel tomorrow. His back would be a universe of pain and mottled with blue and green bruises. His neck and elbows were cut, too.

Noreen was holding a handkerchief to his neck. "Why you?" she asked. "What have you ever done to them? You've never gone out of your way to make trouble. You've even avoided arresting them, when you could."

"Why Dineen is the even more interesting question," O'Connor said. He was driving now. "Aside from the interest we have in your still being alive, of course."

McGarr turned to O'Connor. He was a cool one. "Why Dineen, why me, why a department store in Belfast or a restaurant in London? I don't understand why. These people are this island's deepest mystery. Madmen, capable of wreaking havoc for a cause that is votes and jobs one day, Holy Mother Ireland the next, and just bigotry and ignorance most of the time."

O'Connor was shaking his head. "No—this is different. As far as I know, Dineen is different. They need men like him, if they're going to drive the British out of the North. There's something else going on here."

McGarr let a few miles pass. Truly he was confused. Could it have been simple jealousy of Dineen—that he was a hard man in an organization not used to discipline and had provoked the attack? He looked over at O'Connor again. "What's in your literary future, Rory?"

The question caught O'Connor by surprise. "Another novel, I guess." The dancing with Noreen had seemed to cheer him.

"What about?"

"Maybe the I.R.A."

Noreen said, "That sounds like a change for you."

"I've always wanted to work in a realistic mode, but what with television and the movies, it's pretty hard to do it credibly. I've never really felt my talents were up to it. Maybe now—"

McGarr very much wanted to know what sort of story O'Connor had in mind, if he would write about May Quirk and what she had really meant to him. But he was tired.

"Have you ever thought about writing nonfiction?" Noreen asked.

O'Connor only nodded.

"It seems to me that a really good book has never been written about the I.R.A."

McGarr knew what she wanted to add: now that the I.R.A. might in some way be responsible for the murder of May Quirk, a woman O'Connor had loved, didn't he feel the need to come to terms with that organization?

But O'Connor said, "That's because the writer would have to define the organization, make some sense of the present fighting, the mayhem and the chaos, its goals, its needs." He looked out at the dark shop windows of Bealaclugga, which they were passing. "It's an impossible task, though May would have wanted me to try now, I'm sure."

A half hour later they were back in Lahinch.

Before going to bed, McGarr got Dan O'Malley, the Lahinch Garda superintendent, to put two of his best men at the Quirk farmhouse. He told O'Malley to make sure they were well armed.

"Pistols?" O'Malley asked.

"No. Whatever you've got that's heavier."

"Shotguns?"

"No. Automatic weapons, Dan." McGarr was exhausted.

"I don't think anybody knows how to use them. Sure I've never taken the bloody things out of the case."

"Pistols will be fine." McGarr rang off.

8

HISTRIONIC TOUCHES

The aroma of thick, black coffee awoke McGarr. At first he didn't know where he was. The smell reminded him of Naples and the Hotel Europa, where he and Noreen had lived for nearly a year in what had amounted to an extended honeymoon. That summer had been cool, the winter warm, and the staff of the hotel had served their Irish guests with the care that a despot might command, though not once had the small, red-haired couple asked for special attention. After the newspapers had pictured McGarr collaring an international dope smuggler in Herculaneum, the deference shown the soft-spoken man became embarrassing. The staff whispered to each other when McGarr and Noreen passed. In the reflection of the shiny pink marble that faced the sides of the elevator, McGarr had seen a bellboy imitating the way he walked. Noreen had heard the other employees talking about their manner of speaking Italian.

Here, however, McGarr was deep in the plush of a feather bed in a bed-and-breakfast three doors from the church in Lahinch. He had one pillow under and another over his head. On the nightstand was a pot of coffee and a bowl of sugar. The cup and saucer were reproductions of willowware, eighteenth century chinoiserie—pale blue patterns of rivers, trees, teahouses, a farmer in a field leading oxen at a plow—that reminded McGarr of his first cup of coffee, with his aunt on a little laneway off Baggot Street in Dublin. He had only one eye open. He could hear Noreen rustling around the room somewhere in back of him.

Suddenly, brilliant sunlight flooded the room and McGarr squeezed the pillow over his face. Just that little movement made him know why he didn't want to wake up: his back. It now began galling him. He lay as still as he could, and gradually the pain went away. He could hear a church bell clanking off in the distance. It was Sunday morning. When Noreen said, "Roll over onto your stomach," then placed several hot-water bottles on his back, McGarr was quite satisfied to be in an humble Irish bed-and-breakfast. To his thinking a good b & b, of which Ireland had thousands, was one of the most pleasant and relaxed modes of overnight accommodation one could find. He luxuriated in the warm numbness that then began to seep through his injured body. As far as he was concerned, May Quirk's murderer could go to hell, which was what the blackguard deserved.

He must have dropped off again, because several times he thought he heard a phone ringing someplace in the house, and finally Noreen said, "That's probably Commissioner Farrell for you, Peter. He's been ringing since eight thirty." She removed the water bottles from his back, fluffed the pillows near him, then helped him sit up and lean back into them. "How's that?"

"Not so bad. Now. Thanks."

She poured the coffee, which was obviously a fresh pot. It steamed up into the cool air of the bedroom. She added two lumps and handed the cup to him. "I'll go speak to him." She started toward the door.

"Missus McGarr. Missus McGarr," a voice was saying in a whisper behind it. "It's him again. The commissioner."

"What time is it?" McGarr croaked.

"That's last Mass ringing now, sir," said the proprietress in through the door. "Would you care for breakfast, or"—she paused—"'brunch." The word was odd in her mouth; she was trying it out.

McGarr tried to say "breakfast," but only managed a cracked, throaty sound.

"Right away, right away." The woman rushed off.

McGarr began looking around the room for his clothes, but more for the flask he kept in his pocket.

"It's gone," said Noreen.

He then glanced at her handbag.

"Mine too." She closed the door.

McGarr shut his eyes and wondered why he had chosen at age forty-five to get married to a woman twenty years younger than he. He was no match for her. Right then he was acting like an octogenarian. True, he needed the coffee that was burning the palms of his hands, but much more he needed further sleep or at least several stiff eye-openers.

After a while the door creaked again.

McGarr didn't bother opening his eyes until he heard and felt something being poured into his cup. He then smelled peat smoke and, lifting the cup to his face, inhaled the lovely essence of vaporizing malt whiskey. Using both hands, he drank long from the cup. When he lowered it to his lap again, he had begun to think somewhat differently of the advantages of having a young wife. "Was that Farrell?" He opened his eyes.

Noreen was standing beside the bed with a large, full bottle of Powers in her right hand. She was wearing a white blouse that seemed almost transparent in the sunlight and blue slacks paler than the china. Her skin was golden. She gestured at the bottle.

McGarr nodded. "What's he want?"

"From his tone, maybe your head."

McGarr pulled the covers off his legs, which he swung out of bed. "Tell him he can have my back."

"I've been telling him about your back all morning."

"Then tell him to buzz off. It's Sunday. I'm tired." McGarr didn't think he had enough energy to stand. He took another sip from the cup.

"Liam says Hanly's so soft he's mush now. And you've got that plane to meet at Shannon later this afternoon. Schwerr's father and mother are waiting for you at the barracks. The Garda you posted at the Quirks' has called twice, too. McAnulty reports there's not a print on that pitchfork. For that matter, there's not a fleck of paint or anything to make it the murder weapon. He says he'd like to talk to you before you speak to the commissioner."

McGarr gently got to his feet. The pain wasn't so bad. He knew what McAnulty wanted.

"And then there are the reporters. Two of them are in the dining room. They've taken picture after picture after picture of McAnulty's operation on the cliffs, and now they want the story from you."

McGarr took a step toward the sink. He was dressed in a pair of tan boxer shorts. He looked in the mirror and winced. He looked ancient—fifty-five, at least. He had tufted bags under his eyes, which were red. The light shadowed the red stubble on his chin, making it look like dirt. Thin wisps of red hair along the sides of his bald head bristled.

Noreen wrapped a bathrobe around his shoulders and opened the door. McGarr followed her down the hall to the phone.

"McGarr here." Through French doors he could see the two reporters in the dining room. They were smoking and talking, tea cups before them.

"Just back from Mass?" asked Fergus Farrell.

"I said a prayer for you."

"That's only fair, since I've been invoking the Spirit that Negates All to intercede for me in whatever dark affairs you've been pursuing the morning long, Chief Inspector."

"And there all the time I was having a nightmare. I dreamed I'd become commissioner and was trying to get in touch with my chief inspector of detectives. I wanted to know if the big search he initiated and I had okayed and the media people were watching was fruitful. I waited forever, it seemed, through one whole night and a good part of the next morning, and when I finally reached him by phone, what should I get from him but lots of lip and the knowledge that the Technical Bureau had managed after all to come up with a pitchfork."

"They did?"

"So I've been told. McAnulty is very thorough."

"Where did he find it? Below the cliffs? What luck that must have been!" Farrell's tone had changed.

"As I said, McAnulty is good. If he can't do it, nobody can."

"Well, what's next?"

One thing about Farrell, he was nosy. What was more, he had a right to be involved in the planning of any investigation, but it had long been McGarr's policy to tell his superior as little as possible about the manner in which he pursued a criminal. McGarr's methods were never the same and not really known to him until he actually decided upon the course of action. Even more to the point, however, was the fact that Farrell was an administrator, pure and simple. He had always been an office man, like McKeon back in Dublin, and had gone to too many criminology conferences and university lectures about police procedures, and thus he had many impracticable ideas about investigative methodology. McGarr had never once questioned the value of somebody like McAnulty, but Fergus Farrell's contributions to an investigation were always slightly suspect. McGarr knew this was a sort of cabin fever, however. Farrell was bound to his desk. But McGarr saw no reason to allow the commissioner's insouciance to get in his way. And so McGarr answered, "Don't know."

"You *don't know?*"

"No, sir. And I'm not going to try to think about it until I'm fully awake."

"And when, pray tell, will that be?"

"This after', perhaps; or maybe tomorrow. Even the Bible doesn't exclude policemen from the proscription, you know."

"Are you putting me on?"

"I wouldn't dream of it, but if it's going to ruin your weekend otherwise, I'll check back at half-hour intervals."

"McGarr!" Farrell hung up.

McGarr opened the French doors and stepped into the dining room.

The two reporters stood. One fumbled to close the newspaper he'd been pretending to read as both of them had strained to overhear McGarr's conversation with Farrell. The other offered McGarr his hand.

McGarr sat down. "What gives?"

The young man smiled. His name was Quinlan, from the *Press*.

Fogarty, from the *Times*, was older. He had been their police reporter for ages. He said, "The May Quirk murder, of course. Remember, Inspector, they have to pay us to speak to you. It's not my idea of fun to be gassing with you of a Sunday morning." Fogarty had a large hairy mole on the left side of his bald head, but otherwise his face was hawklike and tough. He wore a dark suit.

Quinlan said, "They're coming from America in droves, so it's said. You know, guys like Jimmy Breslin and such. Newspaper people and writers. She had a lot of friends." Quinlan was young and a better reporter than Fogarty by far. He had a large handlebar mustache and long brown hair. He wore a green knit shirt.

McGarr shook his head. "Never happen. They'll turn rabble like that back at Shannon."

The woman of the house was leaning in front of him, setting a place there, though she'd already arranged McGarr a table in front of a window. Seeing his cup empty, she rushed to fill it.

"Don't want 'em," McGarr continued, "don't need 'em. Probably not a line between 'em that'd get by the censor." He waited while the woman added some Powers to the coffee. If he wasn't tough with Fogarty, the old man would badger him into a bad mood. "Parasites. Trading in tragedy and sorrow." Fogarty was the only member of the Irish press corps who had it in for McGarr. McGarr didn't know why.

Fogarty looked away. He'd been watching the whiskey spill into the hot coffee. The woman had even stirred the cup for McGarr.

Quinlan said, "They say it's an I.R.A. thing. Now, how do you suppose somebody like her from the New York *Daily News* and all ever got mixed up with the I.R.A.?"

"Why ask me?" said McGarr. "The procedures of your craft" —he waited until Fogarty looked at him, then smiled—"are a mystery to me." He took a sip from his cup. There was almost enough whiskey in it to make him gag.

"Eye-opener?" Fogarty asked.

"Enough to pop the pennies off the eyes of a dead man." McGarr fluttered his eyelids. "Or woman."

The woman set a hot plate in front of him. On it were two fried eggs, rashers, pork sausage, a tier of broiled cherry tomatoes, and hash browns. Another dish was heaped with white and brown breads, especially the whole-wheat soda loaf McGarr favored. There were also scones and sweet biscuits. The pot of coffee was enough for the three of them. The spread wasn't specially for McGarr, though. The newspapermen had probably been served a breakfast that was no less grand. There was nothing fancy about an Irish bed-and-breakfast, but a guest certainly got value for his money—plain, honest, wholesome fare and a good bed.

McGarr said, "I make it a point to do as little supposing as possible. But between both of us, the I.R.A. bit is a red herring. A man who might have I.R.A. connections through his family happened to discover the body. Right now he's assisting in our investigation. No charges have been placed against him, and probably none will."

"What about Schwerr?" Fogarty almost snarled. When McGarr had been appointed to his present post, Fogarty had written a feature article asking the Garda why it had to break with tradition and appoint an outsider when so many senior officers were also qualified. It had seemed a fair criticism to McGarr at the time, but the fact was that McGarr had the job and Fogarty, who would have to work with McGarr, had been stupid to release the column in his own name. If he had thought he could intimidate McGarr, he had been mistaken.

"Gunshot," said McGarr. "In the side."

"We know that." Fogarty's face was impassive, but his eyes were watching every bite McGarr took. And he wasn't liking what he saw.

McGarr added, "Nice boy. Good family. Good *Irish* family." He knew how Fogarty would receive that.

The old man turned his body from the table and looked out the window. His bottom lip was working.

Quinlan asked, "Who shot him?"

"Can't say until I hear from Ballistics."

Fogarty muttered something. He couldn't bring himself to look at McGarr anymore.

"Did May Quirk shoot him?"

"Could be."

"Why would she want to shoot him?"

McGarr hunched his shoulders. His mouth was full.

"What was she doing with him, anyhow. She's a New Yorker. He's—" Quinlan let his voice drop off, "—a country boy. In trees, I think."

Fogarty liked that least of all.

"Maybe romance," said McGarr. "But don't quote me." He was playing Fogarty like an organ now. Everything he said made the old man twitch.

"What about Rory O'Connor, the novelist?"

"Pleasant fellow. Big, bright, good looking. Credit to his country."

Even Quinlan was smiling now. Fogarty was fuming.

"Wasn't he in love with May Quirk?"

"Couldn't help but be," said McGarr. "She was the very best of what's meant by the expression 'a fine piece of work.'" McGarr took another sip of coffee. "But don't quote me. I don't think her parents would appreciate that, coming from me, an outsider."

Fogarty stood, grabbed his hat and camera bag, and, never once looking at either of them, left the dining room. He didn't bother to close the French doors.

Quinlan looked at McGarr, who said, "Did I say one word against the man?"

"No."

"Did I answer the one question he asked me?"

"Yes."

"Then I find his behavior here today inexplicable and insulting. To have waited here how many hours?"

"Three."

"Only to get the chance to walk out on my press conference is a cut that only a man as big as I can forgive." McGarr smiled.

Quinlan chuckled.

"We wouldn't want him to lodge a complaint against me with the commissioner, so I hope you'll cut him in on what I'm about to tell you." McGarr knew that would happen anyway.

McGarr then told Quinlan the details of the murder and how he had checked with the I.R.A. and learned how they had never marked her for execution and how the manner in which she had been murdered, coupled with Schwerr's gunshot, indicated it was a crime of passion. "Right now Schwerr is the most obvious suspect, though I've not placed him under arrest yet."

"Why not?"

"Because I just don't think he'd kill her. Temper or no. He would and did knock her around some, but the last thing he'd do is jab her with a pitchfork."

"Isn't that supposing too much?" Although mild, Quinlan was as aggressive a newsman as Fogarty.

"Yes and no. I interviewed Schwerr at a time when he had little opportunity to construct credible lies. He spoke openly to me. And remember, I've had some experience at this business of question and answer."

Quinlan smiled.

McGarr added, "Let's say as of now the investigation is progressing, and an arrest seems imminent. Two men are assisting the police."

"Are you trying to write my story for me?"

"No, but if you'd like me to repeat that, I'll speak more slowly."

They both laughed.

McGarr could see Fogarty outside the bed-and-breakfast, pacing the sidewalk, smoking a cigarette in a savage manner.

At the Garda barracks a half hour later, Hughie Ward said to McGarr, "The Schwerrs are in O'Malley's office waiting for you. No fingerprints on the pitchfork, and Superintendent McA—"

An interior door opened and McAnulty shuffled in. "Ah, there you are, Peter. Before you talk to his nibs—"

McGarr raised a palm. "It's all taken care of. I told him you found the pitchfork, only I didn't know where. I told the papers that too. It's another coup for the Technical Bureau if, as planned, you go on holiday to some distant outpost beyond the reach of the commissioner of police."

"You're a wonder," said McAnulty. "A savior, a saint, and a horrible liar who told that whopper on your own recognizance and without my knowledge." McAnulty cast his small, black eyes around the office at the Garda constables. "I wonder if I could catch a lift out to—"

Walking toward O'Malley's office, McGarr said, "I'm going to Shannon in about an hour, if you wouldn't mind waiting, Tom."

"Don't know if I should be seen in his company," McAnulty said to Ward. "A man who can circumlocute the truth without any coconspiracy with his fellow senior officer whatsoever." But he sat on a bench and dug out his smokes. He and McGarr seldom got the chance to talk, and the automobile ride would be a perfect occasion.

McGarr had remembered the Schwerrs as being older. Perhaps it was the summer clothes—she in a natural linen dress and a wide-brimmed hat with a black velvet band, he in a light khaki suit and mauve shirt open at the neck—that made the difference, since several years before he had interviewed them in their chilly drawing room in the middle of the winter.

She was tall, Nordic, and not really blond anymore, yet her face was still handsome, her skin unwrinkled. Her son resembled her closely.

Herr Schwerr was perhaps seventy, and though as tall as his wife, his body had begun to shrink. Somehow the shoulders of his suit seemed large. His hair was cut short and was very white. His eyes were blue. He suspirated his consonants just a little too much to be mistaken for an Oxbridgian Englishman. "I'd like to say I'm glad to see you, but the occasion doesn't warrant that, I believe."

"Why not? I'm certainly glad to see you. Please have a seat." McGarr sat behind the desk. He looked at them.

They were worried. Her face was drawn, her cheekbones obtruding, her jaw set. "I spoiled him. That much is true, Inspector. But Max is a good boy. Maybe he's got too many—" She paused and glanced out the window into the sunny courtyard of the barracks, "—romantic notions. That's my fault too. He was our youngest, please understand, and I doted on him. His father always tried to be firm with him, but I—"

Herr Schwerr broke in. "Does Max need a solicitor, Mr. McGarr?"

McGarr cocked his head. "That's always best. Although he hasn't been charged."

"Will he be charged?"

"I really don't know."

She said, "I realize you deal with affairs like this every day, but I hope you can appreciate—"

McGarr cut her off. "Have you seen him?"

They nodded.

"How is he?"

"The doctor says the wound is going to heal, but he also has a concussion. It seems," she looked down, "he hit his head in an altercation."

"I hope he has a good doctor."

Herr Schwerr said, "Dr. Fleming."

"Ah, yes, he's tip-top," said McGarr. "What made you select him?"

"He's a long-time friend of Max's."

"And of the family," she added. "They went to school together."

"U.C.D.?"

They nodded.

"Was your son involved in," McGarr gestured his hand, "romantic causes there?"

Schwerr said, "Like most undergraduates, he was against war and the bomb and the United States and," he added somewhat sheepishly, "capitalism."

"What did he tell you about Friday night?"

They looked at each other.

McGarr added, "If you believe he told you the truth and he's not guilty of murdering May Quirk, then there's no reason for you not to discuss it with me, is there? Obviously, part of the reason you came all the way out here was to put your minds at ease. I'm willing to tell you what I know."

Schwerr said, "Well, I don't think we should tell you certain—"

"He's involved with the I.R.A.," she blurted out.

"I know that. It doesn't interest me. If I began arresting every I.R.A. contact in this country, I'd fill the jails in a week."

Schwerr said, "Well, it bothers me. It's not legal."

"And it's dangerous!" she added.

"And stupid." He uncrossed his legs and crossed them the other way. "To think a man so well educated would involve himself with those thugs."

She said, "He told us he was coming out here to ask May Quirk to marry him. Did he tell you that?"

134

McGarr nodded.

"But he didn't tell us what else he was doing. About the I.R.A. money. You know about that?"

McGarr nodded again.

"He said he asked her to marry him and she refused. But she told him she was pregnant." Her lower lip shuddered. Her eyes were watery now. She began digging into her handbag. "She said she preferred to terminate the pregnancy artificially. Over in America. And that she didn't think she and Max could make a match, that she had her career. Do you know the rest?"

"I'd prefer to have you tell me, if it's not too trying."

Schwerr spoke. "They were in the field where she was found. Another car pulled up alongside Max's. She began walking toward it as though she was going to leave in it. Max thought it was the O'Connor fellow. He was a rival for her affections. He tried to stop her and she shot him. Eventually, he staggered to his car and left."

McGarr had to force himself to pause before asking, "Did he get a look at the second car?"

Schwerr said, "He told me he can't remember its being there when he got into his own car. I asked him if he didn't imagine the second car, or if it might not have been just some lost car wandering up the laneway between the pastures. He said no. They both turned when the lights went on them, and she started for them right away. Maybe shock prevented him from noticing the car as he left."

McGarr was thinking of the bruise on the left side of Hanly's face. "Did he say anything about the driver of the car?"

They looked at each other.

"Did he mention a man named Hanly?"

Schwerr said, "No."

McGarr said, "I'm going to be honest with you, too. Your son never told me about this second car. It could be he didn't remember at the time, or that he didn't want to incriminate Hanly, who also has I.R.A. connections. It could be, however, that this isn't the only bit of information he's withholding from me. Perhaps you'd be well advised to get him a solicitor or else tell him that when I talk to him next he'd better have the whole story for me. That's if he's innocent of killing May Quirk."

What he had said seemed to make the Schwerrs feel ashamed.

McGarr waited a bit before he asked, "What was your opinion of May Quirk?"

The Schwerrs exchanged glances again. He stood. "Perhaps we had better take your advice, Inspector, before we say anything else."

"Suit yourself." McGarr stood. He then opened the door for them. They thanked him and left.

McGarr waited by the window, watching the Schwerrs leave the barracks. When they had first begun to talk to him, McGarr was almost positive their son had not murdered May Quirk. Now he wasn't so sure. If May Quirk had shot him just as Hanly had arrived, then perhaps he might not have had an altercation with Hanly that resulted in Hanly's bruised face. But then, when he came to, why hadn't he been able to find her? She had been jabbed or at least had finally come to rest against the wall quite close to the stile that Schwerr in his injured condition would have had to use to get over the wall. The sky had been clear that night, the moon in the third quarter. That must have made the meadow very bright, since the sky in Ireland, cleared by winds off the Gulf Stream, is as limpid as any.

McGarr craned back his head and hollered, "Hanly! Where the hell is Hanly!"

The door to O'Malley's office burst open. "Sir?" asked a young guard dressed in a tight blue uniform with silver buttons.

"Hanly!" McGarr roared, and pushed by the guard into the

136

outer office. "Where the hell is Hanly, that miserable, sniveling meld of some bloody bastard's spawn! Hanly! Hanly!" He began opening all the doors in the office, the closets, the cloakroom, the firearms room, kicking each one, fumbling with the handles, wrenching them open, then banging them shut, shouting "Hanly!" over and over again until his face grew red. Twice he passed right by the dayroom door without stopping.

The young constable kept touching McGarr's sleeve, trying to tell him Hanly was there.

Superintendent McAnulty, sitting in the corner, was smiling broadly: for once he was going to be treated to a performance from McGarr. McAnulty waited until McGarr had made himself red from shouting, then walked over to the dayroom door, opened it, and stood aside.

"Is he in there?" McGarr demanded. "Is that little lying bastard, that drunken lump of Liffey shit, that sniveling, measly, sonofabitch of a liar in there? Nothing browns me off like a liar!" McGarr started for the open dayroom door. His face was crimson now, his eyes bulging. He was sweating. He had his fists curled into tight yellow balls.

Hanly was sitting on the edge of a chair in the middle of the room, trying to see around Superintendent O'Shaughnessy, who was standing in front of him.

His face was haggard. He hadn't shaved, and his heavy beard shadowed the furrows between his chins. The sacks beneath his eyes seemed to have collapsed and were dark, almost blue. His forehead was greasy with old sweat. Accordion folds creased the sleeves of his blue blazer, and a tail of his shirt stuck from the waist of his gray slacks. His expensive loafers lay askew nearby, where he had kicked them off during the night. The room stank of cigarettes, tea, and Hanly's feet.

"There he is!" McGarr roared.

McAnulty followed him into the room, then stepped out of the way.

McGarr reached behind him and slammed the door shut.

"Don't," said O'Shaughnessy. "Don't do it, Peter. The likes of him isn't worth it. He'll get himself a lawyer who'll plaster it all over the papers."

"Hanly!" McGarr roared, and tried to rush around O'Shaughnessy, who was six feet eight inches tall and solid. "You lied to me. Not once—oh no, not once!—but six! Count 'em! Six goddamn times, which is six goddamn times too much, you dirty little bastard!" He tried the other side of O'Shaughnessy.

Again the Galwayman restrained McGarr.

"Nobody lies to me! Not Phil Dineen, not anybody!"

Hanly blinked several times at McGarr's mention of Dineen's name. Hanly was breathing through his mouth now. He wiped the sweat from his right eyebrow.

"Calm yourself, Peter." O'Shaughnessy had his arm around McGarr's chest now. "Calm yourself."

"Why? Has he been lying to you too?"

"All night. All night long. But don't let it bother you." O'Shaughnessy's voice was soft, soothing, so low Hanly had to strain to hear him. "You don't want what happened to Bates to happen to him too, now do you? We could cover that up back in Dublin, but here? Never. We'll clap him in the cooler sooner or later. What did Dineen say?"

McGarr took his eyes off Hanly and looked up at O'Shaughnessy. McGarr blinked and relaxed his muscles. He stepped back and tucked in his shirt. "Hanly's on his own. He'll get no help from that quarter. He had a thing about Schwerr, thought the kraut was going to take over his job. And he was right. They were easing him out, so he knocked off Schwerr's girl and tried to frame Schwerr for it, after—get this: *after!*—" McGarr shouted again, "he extorted twenty-seven thousand dollars from her."

Hanly was shaking his head. His forehead was furrowed.

"What?" McGarr asked in a voice that was tight with anger. "What did you say?"

"Nuttin'. I didn't say nuttin', I just shook me head."

McGarr went to step around O'Shaughnessy. This time he let McGarr pass. "That's good," said McGarr. "That's very good. I don't want to hear you open your lying mouth to me, jocko. Get me? You don't speak until you're spoken to. Try it! I'll pound that piece of flab you call your face into pudding. Understand?" he roared.

Hanly nodded. The fear in his small yellow eyes was unmistakable.

"Now then." McGarr fixed him with his gaze. "We'll take it lie by lie. I want you to tell them to me again, loud and clear.

"First, the bit about your car. How'd the left rear bumper get crushed?"

O'Shaughnessy had his note pad out now, pencil in hand.

Hanly wrenched his eyes from McGarr's. "Aw—I don't rightly know, I guess."

McGarr didn't say a word. He waited until Hanly got tired of looking at his shoes, the floor, the sides of the walls he could see with his head down like that. When Hanly finally chanced a peek at McGarr's face, McGarr again fixed him. "Where did it happen?"

"Didn't I tell ya? I dunno." When McGarr's eyes didn't move, Hanly added, "And that's the truth. Honest to Jesus, Super, it is. But," he looked down again, "I guess it didn't happen out there." When McGarr still didn't say anything, Hanly continued. "It happened a few hours before, I guess. Back in Ennis."

"How?"

"Backed into an alley. It was dark. I hit the wall."

"Trying to keep Schwerr from seeing you?"

Hanly's head jerked at the sound of the German's name, but he kept it lowered. He nodded.

"Why did you lie to me about that?"

"Cripes, I had to." He held his fat palms out. His eyes were bulging; he looked hurt. "If I started blabbering every time I got lifted, I wouldn't be much of a man, would I?"

McGarr let the silence prevail until Hanly lowered his hands. Then he said, "Not blabbering is one thing, lying quite another. You lied to us about that dent, you lied to us about the bottle of Canadian Club, you lied to us about the bank in Dublin, you lied to us about knowing May Quirk, and, Mr. Hanly, you lied to us about not seeing another car when you got up to that murder scene on the cliffs, and finally, you lied about how those scratches got on your car. They were made with a pitchfork, the very same one that you used to kill May Quirk and the one you then stuffed in the trunk of Max Schwerr's Mercedes. That's what you really wanted, wasn't it? To get rid of Schwerr, your rival, the fellow who was going to take over your job. You saw her shoot him, you saw your opportunity to hang a murder charge on him. That's the long and short of it, and I've got enough on you right now to put your neck in the noose. Not a jury in this country would deliver any other verdict."

Hanly looked from McGarr to O'Shaughnessy to McAnulty, who was standing in the shadows of a corner, and back to McGarr. "What do you mean I lied about the bank in Dublin? Didn't you get ahold of Scannell? It's the Royal Provincial Bank headquarters right there on Pearse Street, across from the college. They call it the United Bank now." When McGarr still didn't say anything, he again glanced around the room. He was

140

panicky now. It was one thing for the police to accuse him of a capital crime, quite another for the I.R.A. to cut him off. Knowing as much about I.R.A. operators as did Hanly, he knew they couldn't allow him, a man with a weakness for liquor, to stay on the loose for long. He had worked for them for over twenty years. He knew too much.

Hanly looked down at his hands. He then touched the bandage on the side of his face. He shook his head and said, "Now that you reminded me of it, Super—I did see another car up there on the bluff. And two people, him and her. They turned when my lights flashed on them. I'd lost Schwerr in Lahinch. His car was faster or the booze was getting the better of me or something. Anyhow, he got the jump, and that area is all raths and glens. I knew I'd blown it when they saw the lights. They both knew my car. She'd interviewed me already once. Schwerr and I—" He looked up at O'Shaughnessy, who was noting everything in shorthand, then hunched his shoulders and continued. "We'd never gotten along. I knew from day one he was the bloke who'd put me out. I even tried to stop drinking, ordered lemon soda every time I went into a bar. I'm only telling you all this because I really didn't kill her, honest I didn't. I'm only telling the truth because I'm innocent. Jesus, Super, give me a break. I'm on my own here, you know so yourself."

McGarr said, "I'll be the judge of both your honesty and your innocence. Where'd you park the car?"

"In front of his."

"Why in front?"

"I know what you're thinking, but you're wrong. I was jarred, like I told you. I thought maybe I'd just buzz right by them, let them see it was me, that the guys like Dineen had me—Hanly, who Schwerr thought was washed up—following them. But the laneway was blind. Once I got my car beyond his, I saw that.

And I knew I'd never get it back onto the access road without scraping up one or the other of them. Not in my condition. That was when I heard the shot.

"I couldn't see what had happened, and, to tell you the truth, I didn't really care."

"You mean to tell me the twenty-seven thousand dollars didn't interest you?" McGarr asked.

Hanly looked down into his fat hands again. "That was just a little sweetener. I thought somebody should squeeze her a bit for all the information she was getting. After all, if she did a job on us in the press in the States, then that would hurt us bad. The money wouldn't begin to make up, but at least it would be something."

"In your pocket."

"No, honest. Everybody knew about it."

"Not Dineen."

"You've got him?"

McGarr nodded. "And we've got you. For murder. You were saying you heard a shot."

Hanly looked bleak now. If the Garda had Dineen that meant that Hanly would be held responsible for exposing the whole district I.R.A. contingent. That meant Hanly was a marked man. They'd get him sooner or later; they always did. "Whichever of them it was, it meant trouble for Schwerr, which was all right by me. But I knew I had to get out of there too.

"I switched off the ignition and the lights. I got out and started over the wall, trying to be careful, just in case it was Schwerr who'd fired the shot. I couldn't see a thing. It was thick there and wet and I must have slipped. What else I told you, including the bank, that's the God's honest truth; I swear it, so help me, Super. I woke up in her lap, and I'll tell you this—it's Schwerr. It's got to be. He's big and strong enough to be carrying her and me around. Why wasn't his car there in the morning? There was nobody else there either. It's got to be him. Dineen and the others are only protecting him because—"

"He's got a future," said McGarr. "And you're headed straight for the gallows. Tell me about the bottle of Canadian Club you spoke of before. You lied to me about that, too. You didn't get that in Lahinch. We've checked."

"Oh, that's right," Hanly said, much too quickly. His brow was just slightly too furrowed in mock insouciance. "Ennis. I think—*yes*, Ennis. I must have bought it in Ennis."

"Where in Ennis?"

"Don't know. Couldn't remember. Some joint or other."

"Ennis was where you got the call from Dineen, wasn't it?"

Hanly nodded.

"You didn't stop there to buy yourself any bottle of Canadian Club before getting out after Schwerr. That thought never passed your mind. You were too totally consumed with getting something on Schwerr. You just hopped in your car and took off." McGarr was winging it, but he felt sure he had hit on what had happened.

O'Shaughnessy stepped toward McGarr. "You probably haven't had a chance to see this yet, Peter." He took an investigation report from the back of the notebook and handed it to McGarr. It was blank.

Before McGarr could finish pretending to read it, Hanly began speaking. "Jesus—what a jam I'm in. I'll be hung if I don't tell and shot if I do. Has Dineen told you about Fleming?"

McGarr didn't look up from the blank report.

O'Shaughnessy was writing again.

McAnulty was still sitting in the corner, watching everything closely.

"He's a doctor fellow here in Lahinch. He's helped us out a

lot. Schwerr stopped in to see him before reaching the town. I knew he would. It was all part of the schedule. I knew Schwerr's next two stops in Lahinch. And I knew he'd finally wind up in Griffin's. I had some time, so I popped into Fleming's, like I was just passing through. He's a good man, the doc. He's always got the warm welcome out and a jug and whatnot."

"And that night he just happened to have a big bottle of Canadian Club?" McGarr asked.

"Why not? I paid him a thousand fecking pounds for services rendered. He said he'd gotten the bottle from May Quirk, if you really want to know. She'd gotten it going through the duty-free shop at Shannon when she flew over."

That seemed reasonable to McGarr, who remembered the bottle on the sideboard in Quirks' house. If O'Connor could be believed, there was no enmity between Fleming and the murdered woman. Fleming was just a dour young man. "How long did you stay there?"

"Enough for a bit of a drink."

"And talk?"

"We're neither of us deaf mutes, you know." Hanly seemed to be feeling somewhat cocky again.

"You told him what you were doing there right after Schwerr?"

"I did not. I know my job."

"You talked about Schwerr?"

"Had to. The doctor mentioned his just having been there."

"And you?"

"I acted surprised, of course. Said I was sorry to have missed him."

"And then what happened?"

"The doc asked me for a lift into town. Said he had left his car there. Turns out he'd left it right there at Griffin's, so I had to

144

beg off going in with him for a drink. Instead, I drove on up to the last bar and parked my machine down the alley, out of sight."

"How many drinks did you have in there?"

"One too many. I'd just ordered the last when I saw the lights of Schwerr's Mercedes whip by. I had to belt it back. It finished me. Then I was having some trouble with the barman. Hicks, you know. They don't like nobody who might know more than them."

"And they could tell you did?" McGarr asked.

Hanly didn't say anything.

So McGarr added, "As I can. I found the bottle top from a quart of Canadian Club in a pasture a couple of hundred yards from the murder scene and right on the edge of the cliffs. I bet you know how that got there."

Hanly looked up and blinked. "I don't; honest, Super. I've told you everything I know. I just said that about them bunch of shit-heels in the bar because it was plain they was prejudiced against city people like me. Not a donkey and a hundred quid between them."

"Nor a Jaguar XJ12L," said McGarr.

"No, nor that, neither. Which I worked for and hard."

McGarr turned and started for the door. "No, nor a Jaguar XJ12L, neither," he said, mocking Hanly's thick Dublin accent, "with scratch marks down the side that were made with the pitchfork that murdered May Quirk and not caused by backing into any rock wall." McGarr stopped at the door. "Let me tell you this, Mr. Hanly. You've got yourself in a pickle. I want you to keep thinking about all the little details you've misremembered, mistaken, or misconceived. As far as I'm concerned, we can hold you now on the Offenses Against the State Act. Indefinitely."

"How?" Hanly shouted. "I wasn't packing a shooter, like Schwerr. I wasn't carrying explosives or ammunition, nor did I have any plans for anything like that."

"No. But you were carrying the money that was going to be used for all of those things."

"I never said that. That money was from me dances and such. You won't be able to prove it. I'll sue you for false arrest and"—he looked up at O'Shaughnessy—"harassment and torture."

"By your own admission."

"What admission?"

"That you paid Fleming for services rendered. What services? When was the last time you needed a thousand pounds' worth of medical attention?"

Hanly's eyes darted wildly around the room. "That was a mistake. I just said it because it was what you wanted to hear, and after your man here kept badgering me all day and all night and all day again. You won't be able to make it stick."

McGarr was in the doorway now.

Hanly shouted at him, "And you'll have to arrest Fleming, too. People around here won't stand for that. They'll let us both off."

When McGarr turned his back, Hanly added, "And I've told you everything I know, anyways. What in Christ's name haven't I told you? I want to know. McGarr? Superintendent?"

"Enough," said McGarr. "You haven't told me enough." He was in the main room now.

"Like what?" Hanly shouted.

"I'll leave that up to you to decide. Names of your contacts would be a good beginning, and then a full description of your finance activities for the I.R.A. Like the stuff you gave May Quirk and Rory O'Connor. Only in greater detail again."

Hanly roared, "Well, let me tell you this then, McGarr. You can't push me around. I've got friends. *Political* friends. And I've got money. I want a solicitor!" He was standing now.

O'Shaughnessy put his hand on Hanly's chest and shoved him back into the chair. "You *had* friends, and all the money in the world won't help you now."

McAnulty left the room.

McGarr had his hand on the doorknob. "What's your solicitor's name? I'll call him for you. Maybe he can explain why it's best for you to tell me everything." McGarr knew that none of the solicitors who sympathized with the I.R.A. would care to represent him now, and Hanly probably didn't know any other lawyers.

"Could you call one for me, please?" Hanly asked McGarr in a meek tone of voice. "You know—somebody you've worked with before and trust. Somebody good. I don't care what it costs."

McGarr said, "I don't run a legal assistance bureau," and closed the door. He could hear O'Shaughnessy saying, "What time of day was it when you arrived at Dr. Fleming's house? Where is that, anyhow? I've got a map here and you can point it out to me."

Noreen had just arrived at the barracks, saying they'd better hurry if they were to meet Paddy Sugrue's plane at Shannon later that afternoon and still manage to drop McAnulty off at Kilbaha. For this they got the loan of O'Malley's personal automobile, a new Triumph Toledo that didn't have a speck of dust on it, inside or out.

9

JUST LIKE THAT

Noreen drove. The fair weather was holding, and they clipped down the Clare Peninsula with the ease that a Sunday noon in a country as devoutly Catholic as Ireland allowed. Only at churches in Milltown, Malbay, Quilty, Kilkee, Carrigaholt, and, finally, Kilbaha did she have to slip the Triumph into lower gears. Otherwise, she let the new car hum, and they made the thirty-five or so miles in nearly as few minutes.

The Atlantic was on their right and, whenever the car climbed a promontory, McGarr caught a glimpse of the ocean swells rolling gray and bluish like the belly of a salmon in the full sunlight. In the valleys where the land eased gently into the sea myriads of bright tents had been pitched. Almost all the cars near them were foreign. With Ireland's entrance into the Common Market, Europe's middle and lower classes had discovered the pure water and clean air of her beaches and rivers, and the West country was fast becoming a playground.

None of this bothered McGarr at all, as long as his countrymen were not swept into the pursuit of the tourist trade to the exclusion of all other considerations and made of the stark, treeless scarp of shale a Brighton or Bray or Coney Island or La Spezia. The outlanders were flocking here now just because most of the land remained as it had always been—barren, windy, and wild, long undulating ridges rising from plateaus to occasional flat-topped hills and dropping down toward the sea again. Atlantic Ireland: even the hawthorn hedges seemed to have given up their unequal struggle against the blasts off the water, to be replaced by gorse and then, like hands raised and imploring the elements to be gentle, walls built of single flagstones set on edge. In the lee of these McGarr could see a few lean sheep huddling, even on this, one of the finest days of the year. It was their only protection from the salt spray of high tide.

Glancing in the side mirror, McGarr noticed a black Mini with Northern plates. The car had been following them from Lahinch, hanging back whenever Noreen had to slow down. There were two men in it.

After a while, McAnulty said, "It's Hanly. It's got to be. I know I shouldn't be jumping to conclusions with our investigation only a couple of days old, but there's something sneaky about him. Something devious." McAnulty was bunched into a corner of the back seat of the Triumph, looking out at the passing landscape, smoking a cigarette with great concentration. His black, bushy eyebrows were knitted together. His small, dark eyes were squinting, but focusing on nothing. "How many times have we lifted him before, Peter?"

"Only a couple, a long time ago."

"Really? I could have sworn he was acting. Just like playing a part, he was. Like he knew you were going to try to scare him, so he decided to go along with you and act scared. And that bit about you getting him a solicitor. I didn't buy that at all. And he's got the motive, all right. He's the sort of man who'd be lost without his job."

Noreen glanced at McGarr and smiled slightly. McAnulty was also a man who would be lost without his job. It was obvious he was reading his own personality into Hanly's motive.

Said McGarr, "You're right about jumping to conclusions so early in the investigation, Tom. This is one case where we're not lacking for suspects. But I credit your intuition—I don't think we've gotten the total story from Hanly yet."

"Who's this Dr. Fleming?"

"A young doctor in Lahinch," said McGarr.

"He bears watching," said McAnulty. "Or a little warning, as well. It's one thing to sympathize with the I.R.A., quite another to be in the thick of the comings and goings." He paused for a while. "Where was he when May Quirk got jabbed?"

"Don't rightly know," said McGarr. "As far as I've been able to learn so far, his night looks like this: he saw Schwerr, then Hanly, and got a sizable payment from him for past services to the I.R.A. Hanly then drove him into Lahinch and he either had a drink first, then treated May Quirk's uncle Daniel for gout, or vice versa. Then he got called to a farmhouse near the murder scene and treated Schwerr for the bullet wound. We can't pinpoint exactly what time she was stabbed, but if it's shortly before or after Schwerr got shot, then he'd have to have had a jet to have done it himself."

"If she got stabbed before Schwerr got shot, then Schwerr must be the prime suspect himself, somebody else having shot him," Noreen concluded.

McAnulty was shaking his head. "It's very hard to pinpoint that time, since she may have taken a long time to die. Also, Schwerr himself has said he passed out before Fleming tended to him, so—" Again McAnulty began taking short draws on his cigarette. He was filling the interior of the car with smoke. "What about Fleming? What could be his motive?"

"He disliked May Quirk."

"He did? That seems odd for a man his age. I didn't think she knew a soul who didn't love her in one way or another. The whole town seemed to worship who she was and what she'd become. I've done some asking myself along these lines, you see."

McGarr looked out the side window, then rolled it down to clear the smoke from the compartment of the auto. They were nearing the western edge of Loop Head.

Here beyond Kilkee the landscape was utterly barren. The thatched roofs of the cottages they were passing had to be secured by ropes that then were tied to pegs set in stone walls that surrounded the houses.

"Well, first off, he said she sympathized with the I.R.A., and that bothered him. But he was just trying to throw me off his own involvement with them, I guess. Yet he made no bones about his feelings toward her: she had opted for New York and modern ways, he had chosen to return and work with his people here. Her choice was easy, his hard. Her salary, position, notoriety supported her decision, whereas Fleming had no societal support for his except his own opinion that he was performing a service for his own people here and the occasional accolade from a grateful family or a local newspaper.

"But that doesn't strike me as enough to cause such a man to murder, and surely not in that manner."

McAnulty said, "But he knew Hanly was following Schwerr, probably learned from Hanly that Schwerr was going to meet May Quirk at the bar. He was there near the murder scene to work on Schwerr. He had a car. And he was not without the sort of motive that to a man of his intellect may be very important. Also, have you read my report yet?"

McGarr shook his head. He had the report in his lap.

"There was a third set of fresh tire tracks at the murder scene. One tire, the right front, was worn so smooth the cord was showing. That'll make the auto very easy to identify. I gave the

151

information to your man Ward. I think he's got some Gardai running it down now."

McGarr also had Ward checking over May Quirk's files and personal effects at the farmhouse. He was looking for her notes on the finances of the I.R.A. McGarr doubted he would find them, since he was beginning to suspect that in part she had been killed for that information. He believed that somewhere along the line she had gotten purchase on facts that would have proved extremely compromising to whoever had killed her. "Big car?"

"No. Something small. From the axle width, I'd say it was a Renault or a Japanese car."

"A Datsun?"

"Or a Toyota or Mazda. Honda or Mini would be too small." McAnulty thought for another minute. "Of course, many of the older English cars would match too. Is the doctor married?"

"No."

"Does he have a girl?"

"I don't know."

"I bet he doesn't," McAnulty said quickly.

Noreen laughed. "What makes you say that?"

"A solitary, lonely, young, handsome-in-his-own-way, and brilliant doctor who's returned from great opportunity in America to minister to his people is confronted by the woman who would have made an ideal match for him had she chosen to stay. But instead she's not only chosen the bigger world but has also reappeared to taunt him with her dark good looks and city ways, her money, her success, her worldliness. And by that I mean Schwerr and O'Connor. And then there's the I.R.A., an organization that he's befriended at times. Her purpose in coming back isn't totally selfless. She's here to do an exposé of the most vital aspect of that cabal."

Now McGarr was laughing too. "First it was Hanly, now it's Fleming, next it'll be O'Connor."

They were close to Kilbaha now. Across the slate blue expanse of the mouth of the Shannon, McGarr could see the rugged coastline of Kerry Head and Brandon Mountain in the far distance. But closer lay the sheer sea stack of Dermot and Grania's Rocks that the rolling waves clapped against and sent up spumes of foamy brine, which the stiff breeze held for whole seconds before spewing back into the sea. And then, off to the right, he saw the Bridge of Ross, two arches of—he remembered from a short course in geology he had taken in Christian Brothers' school and barely passed—Namurian rock through which the sea was boiling.

"O'Connor," McAnulty was saying, "O'Connor. I bet him and her were close at one time."

"Close?" Noreen asked. "How do you mean? Is that a euphemism?" She was carefully steering the car down a narrow, rutted laneway with low rock walls on either side that led to McAnulty's holiday house. It was a thatched-roof cottage, recently limed so that it was nearly too bright to look at directly in the full sun. His children, having seen the car, had run into the house to get their mammy, and now she appeared in the doorway, hands on her hips. She was wearing a house dress, an apron, and red knitted socks. A black and white dog with a thick coat barked at the car and nipped at the tires.

McGarr said a little prayer that it wouldn't jump up and scratch the finish of O'Malley's new Triumph.

"Have they checked O'Connor's mother's house for a pitchfork? That one in the trunk of Schwerr's car couldn't have been the only one up there, you know. It didn't have the paint particles from the Jaguar on it. And the rake lines down the side of that car happened in the pasture. And there wasn't any blood on it, either, so far as we can tell out here. And the O'Connors would have one, you know." McAnulty was loath to get out of the car. His wife's eyes were blazing.

"They had several," said McGarr, "as does every house, barn, and hayrick in Clare. You know, Tom," he added, "you can't sit here forever. Eventually you're going to have to pluck up the courage and go in there."

McAnulty's small eyes fixed on the house and the woman standing in the dooryard. It was as though he had put family matters so far out of his mind that only now did he realize where he was. Suddenly, he looked bleak. "Noreen," he said in a conspiratorial way, "why don't you go talk to my missus like a good girl. There's something desperate important I've got to discuss with your husband. Alone, if you don't mind."

Noreen turned right around and looked at him full. "You mean you want me to break the ice."

"Ice is just the word," he said, without moving his lips. "Just look at her. She'd freeze a volcano."

But it was too late. She'd already started toward the car.

"Unfortunately," said Noreen, hopping out, "I know of none in these parts."

Said McAnulty, "Jesus—aren't they all the same? Ungrateful and thankless, when all we've been doing is a bit of work to support them in style." He waited awhile before getting out of the car, however.

McGarr stayed where he was.

The black Mini picked them up again on the main road.

Shannon was crowded with tourists and returning Irishmen whose families, with children and dogs, were clustered around the debarking gates of the vast airport buildings. McGarr marveled that these monumental expanses of green Connemara marble could ever seem filled.

He consulted his watch: 2:10 P.M. He then tried to see the arrivals board in the distance, but the summer sun glared through the western windows, making it impossible.

And the crowd had snatched them up, at least that part of the crowd who with bags in hand or on dollies were pushing toward the foreign-exchange counter of the Bank of Ireland, just opposite from where McGarr had wanted to go.

That was when a pleasant female voice with just the trace of an Irish lilt began saying over the public-address system, "Miss May Quirk, Miss May Quirk—would you please come to the information booth beneath the clock."

McGarr checked his watch: 2:17. Paddy Sugrue could not possibly have gotten through customs and immigration with such speed unless the airplane had made time, yet only somebody who had spent the better part of the day in the air would not know of May Quirk's fate. The murder was front-page news in every Irish paper, and Reuters and all the New York dailies were covering it as well.

Fortunately, the crowd was driving McGarr and Noreen toward the clock, but at the last moment a rush pushed them right past.

McGarr stopped, planted his feet, turned, and using his shoulders like paddles, dipping first one and then the other into the crowd to usher a few people past, managed to make a bit of headway toward the information booth. Noreen followed in his wake.

But the belly of a large man stopped him. It was bound in a print shirt of some chemical weave that pictured buffaloes grazing on a limitless range with nary a cloud in the sky. The belly was very soft. "And where the hell do you think you're going, sonny?" The man was staring down at McGarr's head. McGarr placed the accent as decidedly west—once West of Ireland, now the Midwest of America, probably Chicago.

Noreen, who was staring at the buffaloes, said, "I believe we're about to hear a discouraging word."

McGarr said, "My wife—she's going to have a baby."

"She is?" The man stepped back and pushed a number of people around him.

They objected, shoving and grumbling.

The big man began observing Noreen closely as McGarr led her through the space he had made. "When is she going to have this baby, bud?"

"Come nine-month. Count on it." Now McGarr was well past him. "We'll send you an announcement."

The man wizened up his big puss, made pink, McGarr supposed, from a day-long bash aboard some transoceanic jet. "Nothing I hate worse than a wise guy. You wanna step outside with me?"

"Cripes," said McGarr. "I wouldn't care to step on any side of you, what with all those bisons grazing on that nifty sarong of yours."

The man howled in outrage and tried to reach for McGarr.

People around him began giggling.

One woman said, "Move it!"

"Get the lead out!" said another.

McGarr turned to Noreen. "Americans—I love 'em. Remorseless. They'd pig-pile a pope for his first peccadillo."

"But they're Irish-Americans," said Noreen.

"And none more savage," said McGarr. He could see the big man in the distance. He was turning around to stare in their direction. His face was scarlet, his jaw set.

At the information desk, McGarr said to a young woman with a round face and sloe eyes, "Who's wanting May Quirk?"

"I'm afraid I must reserve that information for May Quirk." It was the same dulcet voice. With fair skin and hair parted in the middle, the young girl wore a light green suit and a white blouse open at the neck. In all, she appeared to be innocent and inexperienced, like somebody who might easily be cowed. But McGarr noticed the fire blazing in those dark eyes and decided he wouldn't try to pass off Noreen as May Quirk.

Instead he showed her his identity card. "May Quirk was murdered yesterday. Perhaps you've seen the papers."

The young girl nodded and wrote McGarr's name on a pad in front of her. "What can I do for you?"

"You can tell me why you're paging May Quirk."

"I have an envelope for her. May I ask your name?"

Noreen told her. She noted that on the paper too.

Said McGarr, "I'd like to see it, please."

Without blinking, the girl said, "I'm afraid I can't do that without permission from an officer of Aer Lingus." She smiled at McGarr. The smile wasn't fresh, just disarming.

"Well, would you do that, please." McGarr checked his wristwatch. As he had understood Paddy Sugrue's letter to May Quirk, Sugrue was just stopping off at Shannon. Flight 509 was merely refueling here. McGarr wanted all that time to talk to Sugrue. But he wanted to know what was in the envelope first.

"As you can see, I'm all alone here." Still the smile. She was like something nice and soft and fragile. McGarr could imagine himself crushing her.

"Look," he said. "I don't believe you understand the gravity of this situation. This is a murder investigation. You have my name. You've seen my identification. I'll take all the responsibility. Time is of the essence."

Yet she didn't alter her smile or those damnably soft dark eyes for the longest time, until they quavered once slightly. She said, "All right." She reached below the counter and picked up an envelope. "If you'll give me one of the cards I saw in your wallet."

McGarr complied.

Not only did she countercheck the card with the name she had on the pad, she also picked up a telephone and called the Shannon Airport barracks of the Garda. The officer there asked to speak to McGarr. He wondered if McGarr might need some assistance.

McGarr said, "There's a black Mini with Northern plates parked someplace in the airport compound, probably in lot E," which was where Noreen had parked O'Malley's Triumph. McGarr turned and scanned the crowd around the information booth. Cupping his hand to the speaker, he asked Noreen, "Do you see the men?"

"Behind you, near the bank counter. They're pretending to look at the exchange rates."

McGarr asked into the phone, "Do you have Gardai in the area?"

"Seven, sir. All have radios. I can reach them immediately."

"Good. But I'd advise you to send armed personnel and make sure there's nobody about. Perhaps if you could wait for them at their car."

"When do you think they'll return to it?"

"How long do you think it'll take you to get your men in there, find the car, and clear the area?"

"No more than five minutes."

"That's fine." McGarr gave their descriptions and rang off.

He wondered why the I.R.A. had put a tail on him. It could only be that they believed his investigation of the May Quirk murder might expose them even more than it had already. That being the case, McGarr wondered what he had missed. There had to be something else. First they had tried to kill him, not caring if they got Dineen as well. Now they were watching his every move.

The young woman handed McGarr back his card. "I hope you can understand my reticence." She still carried that little smile, which intrigued McGarr so much he almost wished his wife hadn't accompanied him. "We've been fooled before by persons misrepresenting themselves." Her hands were folded in front of her. She seemed so calm that McGarr wondered if she was breathing.

McGarr opened the envelope. In it was an Aer Lingus ticket to New York. The booking was for flight 603, which would depart in less than an hour. The stub had been endorsed for a return flight at an open date. On a small sheet of paper a Telex message read: "Very busy flew direct N.Y. Please follow love Paddy."

McGarr sighed. "Where was this sent from?"

The girl reached for the letter and McGarr handed it to her.

"London. Earlier today. Eleven forty-nine, Heathrow."

McGarr checked his watch: 2:22. That made it mid-morning in New York.

McGarr sorely wanted to speak to Paddy Sugrue. He wondered if Sugrue had visited Ireland while in England. Also, he wanted to visit May Quirk's haunts, to examine her apartment, her files, and just generally circulate in her milieu. True, it was a whim, but as in so many other cases when he'd been presented with a plethora of suspects, he had learned more about each only by examining the victim's background more closely. And in this case, where as many as five men had some motive for murdering May Quirk, none had an overriding reason. Maybe McGarr might discover that in New York.

He turned to Noreen. "What say we subject Rory O'Connor's opinion of New York restaurants to an empirical test."

Noreen was surprised. "How do you mean?"

McGarr waved the ticket. "The I.R.A. is paying your way, the Garda Soichana and Aer Lingus mine." Officials of McGarr's rank rode free on all Irish commercial flights.

"Are you serious?"

Even the girl in the information booth seemed shocked.

"But we haven't anything to wear."

"We'll buy something there."

"But our passports? We'll need money. What about Commissioner Farrell?"

McGarr tapped his wallet. "I never go out of the house without my passport. You don't need yours." McGarr had had his amended to include Noreen. "We won't really need any money, although I've got some. And Farrell is just a born worrier. We'll give him something to chew on for the next couple of days."

"Just like that?" the girl asked McGarr.

"No good in being an irresponsible Irishman unless it's just like that, is there?"

Noreen was still stunned. "I've always wanted to go to New York, but not exactly on the spur of the moment like this."

"It's the only way to go to New York and not be disappointed. This way you'll see all the good things and ignore its monumental ugliness." McGarr reached for the phone again. He imagined that the Gardai were now in place and the area around the Mini cleared of people. He dialed the barracks number, then turned toward the two I.R.A. men still standing near the bank exchange-rate chart.

When one of them glanced over at McGarr, he waved to the man, then pointed to the phone.

The first man nudged the second. They both looked over at McGarr.

Again McGarr pointed to the phone.

The two men swapped glances and bolted. They couldn't get very far very fast, however, since the terminal was still clogged with tourists. McGarr imagined it would take them at least ten minutes to get back to their car.

"Where's the Telex?" he asked the young woman.

"There's one at the Aer Lingus office over there." The girl's smile had changed somewhat. Now there was interest in it. She wouldn't have minded going off to New York with McGarr, just like that.

And McGarr wouldn't have minded taking her along with both of them, just like that. During other times in the old pre–British Ireland, monogamy was unknown. But Noreen's hand on his arm brought McGarr back into the twentieth century. Nevertheless, McGarr found this imaginary womanizing most enjoyable, especially when the dilemma posed necessitated a choice between two particularly fine beauties. And then again, McGarr passed through Shannon many times each year.

10

FINNLANDIA—ORCHESTRATED DEALS

The flight was pleasantly uneventful. McGarr never felt comfortable on an airplane. There was no margin for error. One fault and the whole ship and its passengers were dashed to bits or, worse, immolated. McGarr enjoyed gambling in all its forms, but the odds against surviving an air disaster were just too unequal.

But after the first meal had been served, he felt drowsy. Noreen rested her head on his shoulder, the curtains were drawn for the movie, and they both nodded off.

McGarr's sleep was fitful. Occasionally he awoke and glanced at the screen, which offered the saga of a South African gold-mine venture, or out the window at the clouds or the ocean far below. Flying due west, they were chasing the sun. New-foundland and Nova Scotia seemed like barren islands, as tree-less as Clare. The Maine coast was rugged, but low cloud cover quickly obscured the rest of New England.

McGarr began to feel queasy and knew it would get worse. He could skimp on either sleep or food, but never on both. Thus, he forced himself to eat some of the two undistinguished meals that were served aboard the jet and also later a fine dinner at the Irish consulate in New York.

That began with a Caesar salad of crisp romaine lettuce, progressed to roast chicken rosemary served with Franconia potatoes and fresh asparagus tips hollandaise, and ended with a lovely Black Forest cake from which McGarr's sempiternal bing cherries were gushing. "But they belong in the cake," McGarr observed, and Noreen nodded. The wine was a hearty California red with lots of body and just the hint of muskiness that McGarr enjoyed, especially with the aroma of the rosemary in the chicken. Cuban cigars and cognac completed the repast, and, if the venture to New York proved no more useful than to have assuaged McGarr's yen for a good meal, he believed he would think it well worth the cost, for he was a belly bourgeois.

From Shannon, McGarr had Telexed for a consulate car to meet them at JFK Airport. McGarr dreaded driving in New York as much as driving in New York with a New York cabbie, and thus he had trusted in his own. The choice had been correct. An ancient Hibernian with a face as creased and folded as that of a lizard had guided the long Cadillac into the city. In a deep green hush it whispered through the dark canyons of the metropolis. It was Sunday here too, and, although the streets in the center of Manhattan near Central Park were crowded with strollers, there was little vehicular traffic.

Now the Cadillac pulled to the curb outside Mickey Finn's on East Sixty-third Street. McGarr had an official from the New York Police Department with him. Noreen was back at the consulate resting up. Tomorrow the consul's eldest daughter was going to take her to a Pierre Lesage retrospective at the Museum of Modern Art. Later Noreen wanted to tour the art galleries in Soho. Of course, there was the question of clothes to be bought. And the consul had invited them to dinner at what he claimed was one of New York's finest restaurants.

The N.Y.P.D. official was a tall man who had arrived at the

consulate after dinner. He was wearing a shiny gray suit, like a weave of some special alloy, and walked like a duck. His nose was flat, his face sagging, and his lips seemed very wet from the long green cigar that stuck between two fingers of his left hand. All in all, however, the impression he created was that of a still handsome and jaunty man.

His arms had swung slightly with each odd step he took through the long room toward the consul and his guests. He hadn't waited for the consular official to introduce him. "Simonds here. I'm from the commissioner's office. Don't worry about my name. I've worked with so many Irishmen in my time I'm greener than the guano on the bells of Saint Patrick's Cathedral.

"Just look at this." He had reached into the jacket pocket of the gray suit coat. Somehow the material didn't bend in any recognizable way and was more like armor than cloth. Simonds had extracted a long pocket secretary, which he opened. From this he took cards, as he said, "Gaelic Hurling and Football Club, Hibernians Unlimited, Friends of the Knights of Columbus, the Dingle Club, the Irish Society for the Prevention of Cruelty to Non-Irish Cops—that's a joke—and, of course, the St. Columcille's Boys Club. I'm not going to bore you with the names of the several dozen Irish barrooms I subsidize whenever my boss wants to talk in private.

"There, that's my identification. Where's yours?"

After McGarr had explained the May Quirk case to Simonds, the latter had said, "I know Paddy Sugrue well, and," he had checked his watch, "I know where we can find him right away, if he's in town."

Simonds had continued, "He's cute. He keeps a low profile and he's got the gift of gab. There's not an important Irish cop in the city he doesn't know on a first-name basis, including me."

"What do you know about May Quirk?" McGarr had asked.

164

Simonds had shrugged. "Sometimes read what she wrote. I remember once I took a long look at her long legs and got myself a long thirst. I went home and picked a fight with my old lady."

Now McGarr was surprised to find Mickey Finn's packed. It was just like a summer Sunday night in a resort town back home. But here most of the people seemed to be wanting to forget they had to go to work in the morning. Most were young men and women wearing expensive but designedly casual clothes. The men had on dark glasses, like those aircraft pilots used, even though the interior of the pub was dim. Some of the women wore glasses too, but they preferred the Italian kind that May Quirk had worn, each lens the size of McGarr's palm, the frames outsized and ludicrous. As well, they used lots of makeup, a big patch of rouge on each cheek, their eyes heavily shadowed. Shag haircuts, tight-waisted jackets, and bell-bottom trousers made the men, young and old, look alike and, to McGarr, somewhat androgynous.

Mixed drinks with fruit were flowing freely. Waitresses in short red dresses and black net hose were jockeying trays from the bar through the men standing near it to the tables in other sections of the tavern. Nobody could keep his eyes from the crevice of flesh that spilled from the tight bodices of the waitresses' dresses. And McGarr had the impression he could touch the smoke that filled Mickey Finn's. But it was the contrast between the empty, quiet street outside and the din of the barroom that interested McGarr most. It was as though the tavern was not simply a social center but rather a world apart, a better microcosm in which to pass one's time.

And Simonds was right.

Sugrue sat at the far corner of the bar where it met the wall. The area was enclosed in deep shadow and separated from the other stools by the barman's walkway, which a chain covered with red velvet blocked. In front of Sugrue were a telephone, an ashtray heaped with spent butts, and a cocktail tumbler. He was tapping a fountain pen on a note pad, making dots all around the border. The pad had phone numbers on it.

McGarr, glancing over Sugrue's shoulder, saw they were Irish numbers—the Lahinch Garda barracks, McGarr's Dublin Castle number, and three others he didn't recognize. Near the wall was a copy of the New York *Daily News*. Before Simonds could introduce him to Sugrue, McGarr stopped him. McGarr stared down at the pad and memorized the three phone numbers he hadn't recognized.

McGarr would have preferred to have taken another barstool close by and to have observed the man for a time, but when the barman neared, Simonds said, "A drink for Paddy, me, and— what are you drinking, Peter?"

"Bourbon," said McGarr, trying to make his accent sound neutral.

"Jack Daniels," Simonds clarified.

Sugrue was now looking at McGarr, who turned to him.

Sugrue was a short, thick man with curly red hair. He was wearing a tan suit and his shirt, which was open at the neck, was blue. He had been drinking, but McGarr could tell he was in a mood that alcohol couldn't touch. To expedite matters, McGarr reached over and picked up Sugrue's pen. He drew a line through his office number and laid the pen on the paper.

"What are you doing here?" Sugrue asked.

"Looking for you."

"Why me?"

"I read your letter, got your note at Shannon. I figured you knew her as well as anybody."

Sugrue drank off his old drink, put the glass down, and reached for the fresh glass. "Obviously not. If I had, I could have prevented this."

A man was passing down the bar, shaking hands and slapping

people on the back. He knew everybody by his first name. When he approached Sugrue, the barman caught his eye and with a shake of the head warned him off.

Another person then whispered in the man's ear. The man grew suddenly grave.

McGarr tasted the whiskey and made a mental note to take some back with him. It was sweet without being cloying, had the bite that every good whiskey requires, yet there was a smoky, hickory dryness about it, too. Over crushed ice like this it was a special sort of American ambrosia.

"Who killed her?" Sugrue asked. "That's all I want right now." The tightness in his voice was anger. "I figure you should know, McGarr."

"Not yet. Tell me about Rory O'Connor."

"Did *he* do it?" Sugrue started to rise off the stool.

Simonds put a hand on his shoulder and eased him back.

"What do you think?"

Sugrue shook his head. "No. I can't see that at all. At one time, maybe. When they were—together. Perhaps then, but now, I mean—they were like old friends. There was feeling there, but it was warm, not hot."

"Then Schwerr."

"Don't know him. He's new to the organization."

"She was pregnant by him."

Sugrue stopped drinking from the tumbler and slowly lowered it to the bar. He turned to McGarr. "This is a hell of a time to be saying something like that."

McGarr just stared at him. After a while he said, "Tell me about your relationship with her. How did it start?" McGarr signaled for another round.

"This going to be all on one tab, Sid?" the barman asked Simonds.

"Yes, mine," said McGarr. He took off his Panama hat and

167

placed it on the bar. In the past he'd found younger people more willing to confide in him when he looked like an old man, a father figure perhaps. "And do you think she might have developed you and Schwerr and Hanly," McGarr studied Sugrue's face closely, "only because she wanted to write the article on the financing operations of the I.R.A.?"

Sugrue turned to Simonds. "This guy must think he's back at Dublin Castle with a couple battalions of blue boys out in the yard—talking like this here and now." He then whipped around on McGarr. "Hanly? *Barry* Hanly? You think May went and seduced Barry Hanly to get information out of him? Let me tell you something, copper. I was the one who first proposed that she do the article."

"Why?"

"Because I figured if the average Irish-American wage earner could see how the cash got to those who need it the most, he'd be more willing to give. The way it is now, most of them think it's just going into my pocket or some pack of gangsters back home."

McGarr didn't care to pursue that line, although Sugrue seemed to be living well off the donations to the I.R.A. "The autopsy said she was six weeks pregnant. Could she have been pregnant by you?"

Sugrue shook his head. He was irked that McGarr had continued to belabor the point. "No."

"You were in England."

"Yes—but not in Ireland. Don't you check on this stuff first?" He pulled out his wallet and a small green book with a gold harp embossed on the cover. "I've just been declared an enemy of the state." He scaled the book at McGarr.

It hit him in the chest and dropped onto the bar. McGarr opened the book—Sugrue's Irish passport. Stamped across the first page was, "Revoked 9th August, 1975."

"That's why I couldn't meet her at the airport."

"Then why didn't you tell her that in the letter?"

"It's not the sort of thing you just bawl out. And then—"

McGarr waited.

"—and then she had a dream, you know, of returning home one day for good."

That surprised McGarr, though he didn't let on.

"I didn't want her thinking I'd never be allowed back. I didn't want to hurt any chance I might have had with her."

McGarr said, "She slept with O'Connor and Schwerr. Did she sleep with Fleming too? How did you feel about that? You know, her being the girl you wanted to marry and all. She told Schwerr she wanted an abortion."

Sugrue cocked his body and launched a punch across the corner of the bar.

McGarr only had time to pull back. The blow glanced off his chest. He grabbed Sugrue's wrist and pinned it to the bar. With his other hand he tossed his drink into Sugrue's face. "Simmer down. Did she sleep with Fleming or didn't she?"

"I don't know. Ask Fleming. I think maybe she did. So what? What of it? Things are different over here."

McGarr released his hand. The barman tossed Sugrue a bar towel. "Try to control yourself, Paddy. I've got my business to think of."

Most of the conversation at the bar had stopped and people had turned to them.

McGarr said, "It's just that I want you to put yourself in my shoes, Paddy. I've got plenty of suspects with all sorts of motives. I'm just looking for the handle now. You loved her; help me out. Who or why. Think, give me an impression. She was writing an article on your bunch. You know all of them. You know O'Connor, Fleming, Hanly. You know something about Schwerr. If you want to do something for May, tell

169

me something. Anything. Even if you think it's unimportant."

Sugrue blotted his face. It wasn't just the liquor he was drying. McGarr could see tears in his eyes.

Sugrue said, "Well, I've been thinking about that. Ever since—" He reached for his drink. "And—" He shook his head with a snap that tousled his red curls. "I can't. Believe me, McGarr. I can't. It's not just May we're talking about. It's—well, it's me and the army. Do you understand me now?"

It was McGarr's turn to shake his head. "It's May and nobody else. I broke the news to her parents—two big, honest, and worthy country people who had lost their only child. And I made a promise to John Quirk. I told him I'd see the bastard who did it in the dock, and I aim to keep my promise. Help me."

Again Sugrue shook his head.

McGarr reached over and handed him his drink.

"Jesus, McGarr," Sugrue said in a rush. "You're putting me in a terrible spot. I want to help you, sure I do. But—" he brought the glass to his mouth and the liquor spilled over his chin, "—the most I can say is that you should look at Fleming's place closely."

"His house?"

"That's all I'm going to say, so don't ask me any more. And that's got to be between the two of us." He looked behind him.

Simonds pretended he was looking at a waitress who was passing.

McGarr said, "I didn't get the impression Fleming was much of a friend of hers."

"That was the case only after the article she wrote about him, the one that said he was throwing away great opportunity here to go back home and treat a bunch of farmers and fishermen.

170

She as much as said he was an oddity and there was some flaw in his personality that made him want to escape."

A thought struck McGarr. "And did she write about O'Connor too?"

Sugrue nodded. He sipped his drink.

The barman placed another bourbon in front of McGarr.

"What was the tone of that piece?"

"That he was wasting his talents, too. His last novel—"

"*The Thunderbird of Madison Avenue?*"

"—that's it. She said it was unnecessary, that Rory was a man who had quit on his talent and was now just satisfying his avarice. And then, when the game he invented came out right after, she really let him have it."

"Game?" McGarr questioned.

Simonds cut in. "It's called Potlatch. After them Injuns out on the Coast. My kids are nuts about it. O'Connor must have made three fortunes on it. It's a craze."

Sugrue was talking now, and sounding a bit drunk, too. "She did a comparison of him with another writer, some guy nobody but book reviewers and professors had ever heard of. She showed how both of their first books were about equal in talent, and from there each took a separate way."

Simonds said, "O'Connor opted for the bucks, the other guy for immortality. Personally, I never ate me no immortality, so I wouldn't know. Hey, Sandy," he shouted at the barman, "you got any immortality on that menu? Give me a big slab of it, rare."

Everybody else in the bar was talking about as loud as Simonds. McGarr judged it was the loudest single room he had ever been in in his life, but nobody seemed to mind.

"The article didn't do O'Connor much good," Sugrue went on. "He started trying to write artsy-fartsy short stories for the

New Yorker. Then he just stopped writing altogether. He can retire, you know, with just what he's got from the game. But I don't think that's what he wants."

McGarr waited at least several minutes, watching Sugrue and the others drinking and the barman making them refills. Everybody in the bar looked prosperous and slightly overfed. And nobody seemed hesitant about drinking, either. People were bashing them back without pause. At tables in the dining area he could see men and women talking animatedly over food they could barely see. Their eyes were bright and flashing, and McGarr could tell booze wasn't the only cause—deals were being made this Sunday evening. He could hear as much from the snatches of conversation that came to him through the din. These Americans were a busy people, self-confident, talented, and not a little bit crass. They seemed to like it that way, so much so that they were changing the world to their point of view.

McGarr could imagine May Quirk getting caught between the two worlds in a way that was similar to the choices Rory O'Connor and Dr. John Fleming had made but was poignant as well, for May Quirk had been called upon to judge the dilemmas of the other two and their decisions. She labeled Fleming's choice escape, when he returned to Ireland, and O'Connor's crass commercialism, when he chose to please American readers. Another thought struck McGarr. One of the poet's functions in Gaelic Ireland had been satire—that of ridiculing the words and deeds of those who had strayed from accepted standards, in order to reassert the traditions of the society. People had feared the tongue of a poet perhaps even more than the wrath of the priest. McGarr remembered the description of May Quirk in Griffin's Bar. Nobody dared match wits with her; her tongue could singe. "Could it be that she was a badmouth and—"

"—had the hammer out on everybody?" Sugrue cocked his head as though listening to some special voice. "I've thought of that. It sometimes seemed so. Why even she and me—well, that's how I met her. Being so short, I'm a bit sensitive about my height and—"

"But can you ever remember her backing anybody whole-heartedly?"

Both Simonds and Sugrue tried to think of somebody but couldn't.

McGarr asked Sugrue, "Did she work at home?"

"If you mean did she do the writing at home, yes."

"Do you have a key to her place?"

"No—May was a great one for privacy."

"What's the address?"

Sugrue wrote it on his note pad, then handed the sheet to McGarr. "Are you going there?"

McGarr nodded.

"Can I tag along? My staying here won't do May much good."

McGarr paid the tab and they left.

11

IN THE SHADOWS
OF MANY GUNPERSONS

At the door to May Quirk's apartment Simonds asked, "Can you pick it?"

There were few locks McGarr couldn't. "Think so."

"Good. I'm going to walk up the hall and around the corner so when I return I'll find the door open. Paddy, you're my witness." McGarr watched Simonds saunter up the hall. The way he put his feet down, he probably never wore out a shoe.

The apartment wasn't empty.

An old woman, her gray hair braided and piled on top of her head, stood in front of them. A Mauser automatic no different from those McGarr had recently dealt with in Ireland was pointed at his chest. "Come in and shut the door."

McGarr didn't move.

She was wearing a gray dress, an apron, and heavy black shoes. "Get a move on. Quick. Quick." She jerked the gun. "I can hit a pig's eye at thirty paces, and the two of you are closer than that. They'll not put an old woman like me in jail for shooting a couple of gunmen."

"Nora Cleary," Sugrue began to say, "it's me, Paddy—"

But she cut him off. "Muscha, it's you all right. A gunman like the ones who stuck my May. Put up your hands and face the wall."

When McGarr and Sugrue had complied, she said, "Now lean your hands against it and step back three paces."

She walked over to a table, took the receiver from its yoke, and began dialing a number.

But a knock came on the door.

"Who is it?" she yelled.

"Police." The voice was Simonds's.

She cautiously moved to the door, keeping the Mauser trained on them. "Prove it."

Simonds slipped his identification through the mail slot.

She opened the catch box, took the card out, and studied it. She then went to the phone and dialed the number on the card. She listened for a bit, hung up the phone, and went to the door. She opened it.

Simonds stepped in.

"Raise 'em," she said. She had backed into a corner where she could cover the three of them.

Simonds put up his hands.

"What's your assistant's name?"

"Arnucci."

"What's his rank?"

"Detective sergeant."

"All right. Frisk them two fellers and if they're packing shooters I want you to chuck them on the couch. Then lift that feller's wallet. Toss that on the couch too." She waited until Simonds had done that before she said, "Now, take off your jacket and sit on the floor."

Simonds shook his head. "Geez," he began, "I been made a monkey of in my time, but—"

"No yap. Just do it," she said in a manner that cut him short. He did it.

After a while she said, "You, McGarr—come over here."

McGarr kept his hands in the air as he turned and walked toward her. He judged her to be a woman of her word who wouldn't hesitate to shoot any of them, Simonds included.

"Where were ye born?"

"The Royal Hospital, Kilmainham."

"When."

"July twenty-second, 1927."

"Father's name?"

"Hugh Frances."

"Mother's."

"Cecilia Agnes Ford."

"Says here your eyes are blue. Look gray to me."

"It's fear," McGarr said. "I'm not used to you New Yorkers."

She snorted. "I'm not a New Yorker. What are you doing here?"

"Trying to find out who murdered May Quirk."

"Here?"

"I want to read her files."

The old woman thought about it. She had a red, bulbous nose and a square jaw. Her forehead was low. She wore glasses. Her own eyes were gray, too, and quick. "What do you need them for?" She meant Sugrue and Simonds.

"One to hold the files, the other to turn the pages."

"You're from Dublin, all right." She turned to the other men. "You two. Get out."

"But I'm—" Simonds began saying.

"I couldn't care if you were the man in the moon. Beat it."

"Aw, Nora—" Sugrue pleaded.

"Don't 'Aw, Nora' me, you worthless little shite. Now that May's gone you're not welcome here, and if I had had my way you'd never have shown your tinker's fishy head in this house and she'd be alive today.

"Now scram, before I give you what you deserve."

When the door closed, she threw the night latch and turned to McGarr. "Tea?"

"Love some."

"You'll find what you're after in the bedroom, over there." She pointed to a door. It led to a room two walls of which were glass.

McGarr was presented with a magnificent vista of lower Manhattan at twilight from this the thirty-seventh floor of a new high-rise. He walked right by the desk and filing cabinets, opened a sliding glass door, and stepped out onto the balcony. The hot, sulfurous stench of a city that had been baking under the summer sun rose to him.

In the distance McGarr could see the curve of the island packed tight with buildings, bristling with piers and jetties. The twin towers of the World Trade Center, two outsized boxes taller even than the Empire State Building, were straight ahead. In comparison, the older big buildings (perhaps only twenty years less recent) seemed like relics of a more refined age. Whatever little gilding or grace each possessed welcomed the eye: the gentle ripples on the Chrysler Building's dome, the treed tiers of older hotels on the East Side, even the neon sprawl of Broadway, Seventh Avenue, and Forty-second Street. At least the scale of those areas was somewhat human.

Nevertheless, the view that May Quirk had had from this balcony was spectacular. Above the Palisades, across the Hudson River in New Jersey to McGarr's right, a flame red sun was sinking into a bank of purple clouds. The lights of the city were just going on and the brilliant specks rivaled the majesty of the heavens. McGarr felt suspended in an interstellar void with stars above and below him.

Even now, on Sunday night, the city was noisy. The sounds of jackhammers and rivet guns, the droning of tugs in the harbor, and more than one jet overhead assaulted the ledge.

McGarr stepped back inside and closed the door. The noise died quickly and all he could hear was the hush of the air-conditioning system.

In addition to the bed, which was a huge, canopied affair at least a hop off the floor, the room contained an oak roll-top desk with banks of metal file cabinets on either side. One group contained May Quirk's research, the other, old articles, correspondence, and personal affairs. Everything seemed to be in order, the files neat and arranged according to chronology. The desk also was uncluttered. The drawers held office equipment, paper, pens, pencils, a box of typewriter ribbons, carbon paper, supplies for a copy machine that sat in the corner.

"She did all her work in that bed, with the curtains drawn. The poor, darling girl!" said the old woman, placing a tea tray on the desk. "She ate here. Breakfast and, when she needed it, tea."

McGarr had opened the folder marked I.R.A. It was thick—loaded with newspaper clippings, notes from a work diary, and other trivia. McGarr set this near his teacup.

"I see you went right to the source," Nora Cleary went on. "Them being the low-lifes who are responsible for her demise."

"How can you be so sure?" McGarr asked, although he continued to leaf through the folder.

The tea was black, some Oriental variety with a delicate jasmine scent. Hot scones, the aroma of which McGarr had been smelling since he had entered the apartment but only then placed, were also on the tray, alongside a boat of unsalted butter.

"Wasn't she working on them when it happened? Didn't it happen back there in some bog? I tried to warn her off that

178

tinker Sugrue and his ilk, but no, she was strong headed. I've tried to call her folks, with no luck. And what's to happen to all her stuff and this apartment and the car in the garage and all her bank accounts and things? She owns this place, you know, McGarr. It's a con-dome-inium." She paused. "And another thing, what's to happen to me?"

"Have you no savings, no relations? Couldn't you find another job like this one?" McGarr asked, if only to make conversation. He was still leafing through the files, munching on one of the scones. The taste was light, buttery, with just the hint of soda beyond. "The way you handle a gun, I could probably put you to work back home."

"I suppose a job like yours makes a person hard. Death doesn't touch you."

"To tell you the truth, it usually doesn't, but her death did. That's why I'm here."

"Can you tell me about it?" she asked, her voice suddenly old. "I hope you can understand me wanting to know. I'm not a ghoul nor nothing like that. It's just that she was from my village. I've been with her lo these ten long years and she was like me own daughter."

McGarr looked up from the file. It was only then that her name struck him. "Are you related to James Cleary?"

She looked up from a bit of knitting she'd been doing while McGarr talked. Through her octagonal glasses McGarr could see she had been crying, but silently. She blinked several times. "Indeed, he's my youngest brother. The baby of the family." Her voice was thick. "Why do you ask?"

"He had an attack the day after May was murdered."

She cocked her head. "An attack? What do you mean? Jamie was always as strong as a bull, never had so much as an extra hour in bed." She thought for a moment. Then her eyes seemed

179

to clear and she stood. "Certainly you don't think he—" She then caught her breath. "Oh, my God!" She took a step toward the file cabinets, but stopped. She turned her head to McGarr again. "What do you mean by an attack?"

"He had a fit of despondency. The doctor said it was a nervous breakdown. Spasms of nausea. And he tried to damage himself, too."

She caught her breath, bit her lower lip. Standing in the middle of the modern room like that she seemed massive and out of place, a huge, matronly West Irish woman dressed as she would have been in any Clare kitchen. "Then maybe you should see this. As much as I love him, his being my baby brother and all, May was worth a thousand Jamies, and murder is murder. God help me!"

Her step was more a waddle. She opened a drawer of the cabinet marked C, and took out a thin folder. In it were three letters, all written in the labored script that McGarr recognized as the sort taught in the Irish national schools. His own hand was little different, though fluid.

The first, which was now over eight years old, was a simple statement of intent: James Cleary was asking May Quirk to marry him. He straightaway set out the advantages of such a match—the propinquity of their farms and families, his desire to have children, and most particularly his admiration and affection for her. It closed on a note that was almost fawning:

> I know a big-city person such as yourself would probably feel a little strange at first back here with me and the cows on the farm, but when you think how fast time flies and why the good Lord put us here and how he intended us to live, I'm praying you'll see life here is best with your own kind doing what He intended. May, I dream of the day you will return and accept this lonely farmer's plea, for I know

in my heart of hearts it is what Jesus Himself wants for the both of us and our children. You will make me the happiest of men saying yes and I will work my fingers to the bone to serve you. I beg Jesus, Mary, and Joseph to bless this petition. So far I have led a good life and will ask Them for nothing else will They but send you to me. With all the love of my heart I am your idolator.

James Frederick Joseph Cleary

Sitting as he was in the desk chair of a former staff reporter for one of the world's most powerful newspapers, McGarr was filled with profound pity for Jamie Cleary. Here was a simple peasant's plea for perhaps the only woman in his life who might have made him an acceptable match, and she had been so worldly and contemporary that she could only have thought of his proposal as ludicrous or pitiable too. There had never really been a chance that she might have consented to marry him when she was still back home, but the prospect for the aging bachelor once she had established herself here in New York was hopeless. Although separated from each other by a short, affordable plane ride alone, they were whole worlds and centuries apart in their expectations.

The next letter had been mailed a year before, in the spring. The tone was strident. It even contained a veiled threat.

I don't know what I might do if you don't return to me. Twice now I have driven to Shannon Airport to watch the aeroplanes fly off to America. If you don't answer this letter I plan to take out the papers I need to visit you there. I know it is not you, May, who wrote me that letter six years ago but some other person who the big city has changed. Tell me there's hope, May. Just one little ray or maybe will be enough. I'm desperate lonely and I love you more dearly with every passing day.

Said his sister, looking over McGarr's shoulder, "She wrote him a long, kind letter telling him she had indeed changed and had no intention of marrying, ever. Here," she said, placing a photocopy of a typed letter in front of McGarr. "Jamie is—" she paused, "—a country man. He—" She was on the verge of tears again.

"You don't have to explain. I've met Jamie," said McGarr. He turned to the final letter, dated two months before. It read:

> Your father told me this morning that you are coming home soon but you are not coming home to me. When he left I got down on my knees and asked Blessed Mary Mother of God to intercede for me to give me guidance to help me understand why you have been so heartless over the years, so deaf to my pleas. I must hear your denials from your own lips, May. I pray that She will protect you on your air flight over the far ocean.
> Your loving and still hopeful petitioner,
> James Frederick Joseph Cleary

"And to think," his sister said, "that he then would have killed her. Ah, God—life is strange."

McGarr stood. "I see no reason to assume your brother murdered her."

"You don't know him like me, McGarr. He was the youngest and as spoiled as any old cow's calf."

McGarr remembered then having heard just about the same remark about Rory O'Connor.

She continued, "My mother doted on him. He had everything he ever wanted, which gave the poor man a temper. I once saw him break down a door to get a new pair of shoes that were locked in the bedroom when my father was away.

"And the pitchfork you mentioned." She was rubbing her

upper chest. "That would be his way, it would. He wouldn't have the knowledge of a gun."

McGarr opened a drawer of the filing cabinet and replaced the thick I.R.A. folder. Most of the information in it was general, cuttings from her own and other newspapers, notes taken from her reading and research in the United States.

McGarr then moved to the files on the other side of the desk. Here he found the classification People. He discovered a file marked "O'Connor, Rory," and another, "Fleming, Dr. John." He removed these. He was unable to find listings for Max Schwerr or Paddy Sugrue.

In O'Connor's file were the two *Daily News* articles Sugrue had mentioned earlier. With them were photographs that hadn't been used in the paper and the notes and rough drafts she had made in working up the stories, which were in no way flattering.

O'Connor, she intimated, had been prodigal of his talents. He had squandered his time on literary dreck, catering to the current tastes of New York critics. He had created a sort of pop novel filled with fantastical scenes and cardboard people when, in fact, he had shown in his earlier books that he was capable of creating real people and placing them in situations relevant to the lives of present-day Americans.

The second article was a virulent attack upon O'Connor. It had been issued only six months before, either on or about the date of the release of O'Connor's game, Potlatch. She called it "The Game an Artist Would Never Play." The photograph showed O'Connor reclining in the deep plush of a fur-covered couch, his hand to his brow as if he were slightly ill, the game board and pieces on a coffee table in front of him.

The piece ended with a cutting remark, "The big game O'Connor has always had in him is the charade he's currently playing with both the moguls of the trade book industry and critics and, most lamentably, the gullible reading public—that of 'being an artist.'

"Have you played Potlatch?" the article asked. "The game is well named. O'Connor calls it a fun game. His giggle comes when you throw your money away on it."

The file also contained reviews of O'Connor's books, letters he had written her over the years, photos, and other memorabilia like a rose pressed in a thin volume of Lorca's poems, a snake skin he'd sent her from Arizona, a menu from their first big celebration in New York, the one they had following the acceptance of his first novel.

"Rory," said Nora Cleary fondly. Again she was looking over McGarr's shoulder. "The apple of me eye. A fine big man and so successful." She began tsking. "But, alas—it wasn't to be."

"Why not?"

She sighed. "I suppose it's all right to tell about it, now that she's dead. The truth of it is he broke her heart. Big and successful and handsome, there wasn't a woman in the world who wasn't after thinking him a great catch. And when he got to drinking, he'd grow wild. It was during one of his toots that May returned suddenly to town here and found him down in his studio in bed with some mutual friend's wife. It was only a fling, don't you know. But May was just a country type at heart, like my poor brother Jamie, and never forgave him.

"Then she went a bit off the deep end with men. For a few months she hardly spent a night home here in this bed. And—" She stopped speaking.

McGarr said, "She had to have an abortion."

"How did you know?"

"Just guessing."

"An abortion," the old woman said with awe. "Just think of that. May Quirk having to abort some bastard's spawn. The shame of it! She never recovered from that, I don't think. I mean, in her mind. And she blamed Rory O'Connor as the source of her miseries. If she had had any real city savvy, she would have turned a blind eye to the transgression. He's the sort of fellow who needs a whore now and then."

"What about his game, Potlatch?"

"Sure it's not as bad as she paints it. A gambling game it is. Sporting people think it's a gas. They say he dreamed it up on one of his escapades. In spite of what she said, some people think he's a genius—for business and writing and games."

"And women, it would seem," said McGarr.

"Maybe the truth is he was too—much for her, or for any woman. Maybe she was spared the travail and heartache of being a wife to a man who can't help being a bounder.

"Who knows, maybe she's better off dead. Some of us, like May, do big things and die young, while others like me and my brother Jamie do nothing and live long."

"How do you know Jamie does nothing?" She had told McGarr she hadn't been home in forty years.

Her eyes didn't waver. "I could tell as much from the way he wrote and what you said."

McGarr doubted that and reached for the teacup.

"Could you use something a bit stronger?"

McGarr nodded. "Please. That'd be lovely." He closed O'Connor's file and turned to Fleming's.

Nora Cleary shuffled out of the room.

The article on Fleming had been sold for national syndication in the color magazine sections of American Sunday newspapers. The first paragraph read:

> While the trend among young doctors is to specialize and pursue private practice in big cities, Dr. John Xavier

Fleming, whom his colleagues call "brilliant, gifted . . . a doctor in a million," has decided to abandon his budding career in New York for the rocks of County Clare, Ireland.

The article went on to explain the details of Fleming's career—First Honors, chemistry, U.C.D., Columbia Medical School, Roosevelt Hospital, his area of specialization, which was internal medicine and surgery—and then described an interview with him in which he was portrayed as a taciturn, dour young man. The implication was that some character flaw or innate morbidity was driving him away from an international reputation to a sort of purgatory in a dying country society. She kept asking him why. He kept mentioning how he felt a duty to his people.

Nowhere in the Hippocratic Oath is a doctor enjoined from accepting any case but one which will advance his skills and enhance his reputation. That's what I find myself doing over here. In fact, right from the start of my practice, my advisors have counseled me to husband my energies, to concentrate on the new, difficult operations, to research new methods. The idea is that I might develop techniques which will aid hundreds of other doctors and thousands of patients. Indirectly.

Well, I've searched my soul. What they say may be true. But that approach is not for me. For too many years now I've been studying and learning and putting off my involvement with those whom my training should be helping. I'll leave the research and new methods to other minds and hands.

Quirk: But I'm told nobody's mind or hands are quite like yours.

Fleming: That's flattery, but far from the truth. This country has dozens of doctors who can replace me. Right here at Columbia and Roosevelt Hospital I know three. One is a woman.

Quirk: But why Clare? Couldn't you satisfy this other desire to have a general practice by taking on a small number of patients from a private office here in New York?

186

Fleming: No. First, I couldn't do justice to both posts. Each is a full-time commitment. Too many doctors have large practices. That's unfair to the patients.

Second, New York is a dead end. The economic system it represents is at its last gasp. All over the world people are realizing this—in Portugal, Spain, Italy, England. It's dying. One reason has to be because it's wasteful. On one hand you have unlimited personal expectations, which are expressed in material goods, and on the other hand rapidly diminishing resources. Future generations will judge the twentieth century as a potlatch of the earth's irreplaceable natural wealth.

There was that word again, thought McGarr. He wondered how close Fleming and O'Connor really were. After all, it had been Fleming who had told O'Connor where Schwerr was camping on Black Head.

Fleming had continued.

How many people who own electric pencil sharpeners, plug-in waffle irons, or power toothbrushes really need them? This isn't just another depression we're in. We have inflation *and* unemployment, rising prices along with economic stagnation. I don't doubt for a moment that this country won't stage an economic recovery, but the handwriting is on the wall. The capitalist way of doing things, which I define as having each person out to get absolutely as much of everything that he can, is no longer practicable, if indeed it ever might have been. There simply has to be a new order. I think the seeds of a new order are not to be found here in this moribund giant of a metropolis but in a place like County Clare. Each of us should make an adjustment to accommodate himself to a more human, familiar, cooperative way of doing things. My adjustment is to return to Clare.

Quirk: But *why* Clare? The emigration statistics for that barren land are still shocking. The young no longer even return for Christmas or the summer to get the hay in. The place has fewer people than it did in the fifteenth century when Europe's population was less than 10 percent what it is today, and most of them are old men and women.

Fleming: It's curious that you should mention the fifteenth century. It's precisely because the Renaissance never touched Ireland that piques my interest right now. Up until—let's see—say, the middle of this century it was possible to talk to old men and women who had had few dealings with a money economy in their lives. My belief is that the kind of sharing and mutual support that obtained in those old Celtic communities might still be there in a residual way. Perhaps some of us can revive those ideals.

Quirk: You sound like a dreamer, not a doctor. And one who wishes to return to the land of the saints and scholars, which never really existed. It would seem to me that you're trying to deny the actuality of having been born a twentieth century man and having found your place in this city.

Fleming: You could be right. But the actuality of 125,000 heroin addicts, more persons than that treated yearly for serious mental illness, the deathly grinding pace of this town and society in which few if any human needs are cherished—that's a twentieth century actuality that can't be denied either.

You ask if I am a doctor. Yes indeed, I am a doctor, but I am also a human being who cares enough about the continuance of the human race in a form which is bearable that I'm choosing to try to make an area that might hold some hope for us habitable again. County Clare needs a doctor with my training. I don't wish to stay here and become one of the wealthy who will preside over the demise of a civilization and the deaths-in-life of tens of millions of people. The way I see it, I'm opting *for* life.

Quirk: You mean you think New York is already dead.

Fleming: Dying. From a terminal condition. Greed.

Quirk: And you're fleeing the ship.

Fleming: Rats are survivors. There's another sail in sight.

Thus the article ended.

But McGarr got a surprise. There was a second article on Dr. John Fleming. This one had been filed only two weeks before and was a follow-up to the first.

188

In it, May Quirk asked Fleming if he had found the seeds of his new economic order in Clare. He said she had mistaken him. His intent in coming back was to contribute his skills as a doctor and thereby make the place more desirable. He wasn't a social architect or historian. His tone was sharp.

"But perhaps you're a politician," she said. "You're involved with the Provisional wing of the I.R.A., are you not?"

"Only insofar as every Irishman should identify with the cause of a United Ireland. If Attila the Hun showed up on my doorstep with a hole in his belly, I'd help him out."

May then asked Fleming if he had expected to have to pinch-hit for the local veterinarian. "They tell me you delivered a litter of piglets last week. The farmer claims you're miles more talented than your competitor. He says he wouldn't have anybody else for man or beast."

"I'm flattered. Out here that's a compliment. I only hope your reporting this won't drive the vet from the country. Who knows, he may have to stand in for me."

"What's the most common malady that you treat in Clare?" she asked.

"Depression."

"Of what sort?"

"Mental depression."

"What causes it?"

"Most of it comes from the breakdown of the nuclear family. When nearly all of the children get to be about eighteen or twenty, they leave. They don't want a family life for themselves. There's little cash in it and still less glamor."

"Then capitalism is alive and well in Clare?"

"If you define capitalism as the pursuit of cash and glamor. That'll change."

"When? When the gunmen whom you support take over?"

Fleming sidestepped that slash. "When the real truth is known about city life. When the glamor fades and other values are chosen."

"For instance."

"Cooperation, self-sufficiency. Perhaps the implementation of some of the tenets of living put forth by your countryman Henry Thoreau. Had he come to this country before *Walden*, he would never have needed to write the book."

"But Thoreau was a nineteenth century philosopher espousing ideals which were current in the twelfth century. My countrymen, as you call them, considered him an interesting crank."

"Look around you here or in New York. Surely twentieth century ideals aren't achieving very much in human terms, are they?"

The article closed with a description of Fleming standing on a barren rock overlooking a leaden sea. May Quirk assumed that he was looking off over the Atlantic and perhaps thinking about his former possibilities and the choice he had made.

McGarr skimmed the other material in the Fleming file. It seemed that Fleming's hobby was literature and that he was a Joyce aficionado, having contributed several scholarly articles on facets of *Finnegans Wake*. He also had a private collection of Joyce memorabilia: a signed copy of *The Mime of Mick, Nick and the Maggies*, and many of Joyce's daughter's prints and paintings.

In all, McGarr decided, a rather complex young man.

A loud knock came to the front door just as Nora Cleary was setting a tray with a decanter of amber whiskey and two glasses on the desk in front of McGarr.

She rushed to answer it.

McGarr poured himself a drink, wondering what the folders on O'Connor and Fleming had really told him: that, as he had supposed, the relationship of the three Clare emigrees had become complicated once they had arrived here in this Babylon; that both men had had a sort of falling out with May Quirk; that she had then pursued each of them while ostensibly practicing her journalistic profession but had failed in her obvious purpose of portraying them as in some way inadequate to the challenges that the city had offered them; that there was an essential contradiction in her wanting O'Connor to reject the lure of the metropolis for art and wanting Fleming to accept the challenge in the name of science and fame.

McGarr heard Nora Cleary shout, "Villain! Blackguard! You dirty, shameless heathen!"

McGarr rushed into the living room.

Simonds, the New York detective, had one of Nora Cleary's arms pinned behind her. His other hand was on her wrist. She was holding the Mauser. Simonds shook the wrist. The gun fell onto the carpet. In back of Simonds were two other men. At one glance McGarr could tell they were cops. Paddy Sugrue was standing farther down the hall.

Simonds said, "You're not licensed to carry this gun. You pointed it at a policeman. That's a felony. Consider yourself under arrest. You have the right to consult a lawyer, the right to remain silent. Anything you say may be taken down and held against you."

"Low-life!" she shouted. "Scum!"

He clapped the handcuffs over each of her wrists.

"You broke and entered here earlier. Take that down if you dare. They'll have you in a blue coat and arch-support shoes before I'm done with you."

The other policemen took her away.

Simonds explained to McGarr, "We can't have people running around with toys like this in their hands." He was hefting the

Mauser. "But she's got a point. She wasn't exactly running around with it, was she."

Said McGarr, "No, but it was unlicensed. And it was a question of pride, was it not?"

Simonds reddened a bit. "You're damn right it was. Being in, you know," he waved the gun, "public relations, I don't get much chance to—"

"Muscle up old ladies," said Sugrue.

"—to *serve* the public in my usual capacity." He was chewing his cigar butt now, trying to justify the arrest. "And you get soft, out of shape. You tend to think making arrests is somebody else's job. You begin to wink at crimes, let criminals go. But—"

"What are you going to do with that thing?" McGarr meant the Mauser. He imagined that Simonds was well suited to his public relations job.

"Evidence. We've got to impound it."

"Could you run a ballistics test on the thing and send me a copy of the report?"

"Sure." Simonds looked down at the gun. "Why? You don't think that old babe—"

"And I wonder if we could learn if she's left this country recently."

Simonds thought for a moment. "We can check the status of her passport with the federal government. Maybe she'd surrender it voluntarily. If not, we could—" Simonds cast his flat black eyes around the apartment, "—subpoena it, if we believed she had committed a felony and could convince a judge of her probable guilt. And then Paddy and me could take another of our celebrated long walks down a short hall. I'll be in the stairwell, having a confab with the cockroaches." He sauntered out the door, which McGarr closed.

After a long search McGarr found Nora Cleary's passport in a battered black handbag at the back of a closet in the bedroom the old lady used.

She was an American citizen now. The slim blue booklet had a Shannon entry date inscribed "12th August" and a Kennedy Airport return stamped "8/13."

McGarr then went into the kitchen, where at a small desk he had seen a collection of bills and correspondence in a hand different from that of May Quirk. He sat and leafed through the pile until he got the copy of the past month's telephone bill. It listed calls to three numbers in Ireland, all of them outside the Dublin area. Alongside these McGarr wrote the numbers he'd seen over Paddy Sugrue's shoulder. Two matched.

On the pad of his pocket secretary, McGarr made note of all the numbers. He then picked up the phone, dialed customer service, and claimed that he was about to leave the country and wanted to pay his bill beforehand. If she could go through his current bill telling him his long-distance calls, the dates and amounts, he would pay them. But the woman told him all charges for the current month were in the computer and he'd just have to wait. She thanked McGarr for his concern but allowed as how the New York Telephone Company would doubtless survive the interval without his payment.

McGarr put down the phone, wondering why everybody in New York had to have a smart last word.

That was when Simonds appeared in the kitchen door. He said, "I've got nine fifteen, shamus. That's a howling hour of a Sunday night." The brogue he was putting on was thick but accurate. "I've told a bunch of the lads up in Queens about you, and they're dying to get the message from the olde sod. Big beery police types and not a one of them that don't get misty when hearing Dennis Day do 'Danny Boy.' Kate Smith works them over pretty good, too. I've told them you're a real Irish cop, not the inflated pink hippo variety from Jamaica Plain."

The situation was even worse than Simonds had intimated. The beer joint had no windows. From the outside it looked like a squat fortress of yellow brick with a heavy cast-iron grate over the door.

Inside, only a dim lamp by the cash register, some bulbs under the bar, and the blue glow from the jukebox and television set, which were battling each other for auditory dominance, lit the interior. The place stank of cigarettes, the sweet reek of cheap blended whiskey, lager beer, and a chemical cleanser that came from the open door to the latrine.

Simonds was welcomed volubly, and before they could reach the clusters of men who were squeezed into the bar the proprietor had poured them shots of Jameson and glasses of stout from small amber bottles.

All eyes were on McGarr, the smallest man there. The bar conversation had died. McGarr judged he was expected to knock back his drink. He removed his Panama hat and placed it on the bar, then raised the shot glass. Most of the men, he had noted, were uniformed New York policemen. They wore blue trousers and white short-sleeved shirts. Some had on windbreakers to cover their badges and name tags, but from the hips of most bristled the walnut and cold blue butts of Smith & Wesson service revolvers. McGarr had the feeling of having stepped onto the set of a special sort of American western movie, one staged in the East at a saloon filled with pistol-packing good guys who could not afford to be as lenient with desperadoes as had the heroes of the old horse operas. McGarr also realized why they had insisted that Simonds bring him there: they needed reinforcement, needed to see the genuine version of what they purported to be—the Irish cop who was at once tough on criminals but gentle with friends, capable of utter ruthlessness in situations requiring action, yet supportive and helpful at other times, interpreting the law on terms that were somehow fairer than the cold print on the pages of the law books.

McGarr imagined it must be extremely difficult to be anything but a hardened professional here in this megalopolis. For instance, most of the buildings McGarr had seen in the neighborhood outside the bar looked as though they'd been ravaged. Many had been razed and were now just piles of brick or gullied lots with pools of fetid water, trash, and—McGarr had assumed from the stench that a torrid wind had wafted to him as he had stepped from the large police car—garbage. The structures that remained were dilapidated, the wooden porches of the apartment blocks faded and sagging, the bricks city-worn, the small houses shabby behind chain-link fences and plastic overhangs on the front doors. It seemed as though the denizens of the area, few of whom were on the street, had abandoned the idea of community for a perverse sort of isolation. It wasn't only behind the gates of a plumbing wholesaler that McGarr had seen a large Alsatian guard dog but in the backyards of several houses as well. Bright red alarm bells and warnings to would-be thieves were numerous.

Thus McGarr told them what they wanted to hear. "To Irish cops," he said in a loud voice. "The world over. And especially to Irish cops who started with two shoes, two fists, a hard head, and a big heart. The shoes may have been worn to a frazzle, the fists to scars, even the head taken on a shine," he touched his own bald pate. "But the heart, gentlemen—in spite of all the bastards we've had to run in—that's where we're special. We've got heart." McGarr drank off the shot.

The others followed suit, and before any of them could speak, McGarr added in a rush, "I say this with authority, having consulted my cardiologist before coming over here. He said no fatty foods, no smoking, and most of all, no booze. Bartender," McGarr tossed a blue ten-pound Irish bank note on the bar, "pour a round of drinks on the Garda Soichana."

A huge policeman almost wrenched McGarr's arm stuffing the note back in his hand. The others pushed their own separate piles of American money toward the barman.

McGarr guessed he was, in for a wet night. He could hear somebody asking Simonds, who was standing as close as he could to McGarr, "What's his job back in the old country?"

Simonds said, "He runs the place, at least the investigative aspects. The chief himself will be here in a couple of minutes."

"He's sure got a lot of malarky. That son of a bitch almost made me cry."

Other policemen were now squeezing through the door.

After the second drink in less than as many minutes, McGarr decided he had better ease off, and thus at the public phone, which was a pay station hung on the wall near the jukebox, he placed a call to his office in Dublin.

Simonds had been right. A melodramatic tenor voice from the jukebox began lilting through "Danny Boy." A wiry policeman with a flame red face was punching the buttons. He selected "The Soldier's Song," "The Brave Colonial Boy," and "When Irish Eyes Are Smiling." The operator told McGarr it would be a few minutes before she could check on his credit-card number, put through the call, and get back to him.

McGarr's hand was weary by the time he got to the bar, and there in front of him he was faced with a half-dozen whiskeys. "Could you put these in a large tumbler with lots of ice?" he asked the bartender.

Through all the noises he could just barely hear the phone ringing.

A policeman picked it up, listened, then shouted, "I'll be god-damned if it ain't Dublin!"

On his way by, McGarr saw a policeman handing Paddy Sugrue a twenty-dollar bill. "For the army," he said.

McGarr stopped.

Sugrue said, "Unsolicited." He placed the bill in a large wallet. "Right?" he asked the policeman.

"Right. Anything I can do. I only wish I could afford more." He could see the question in McGarr's eyes. "It's for the people at home, ain't it? I mean, if we'd all pulled together a couple hundred years ago, I wouldn't have to be living here. Don't get me wrong," he added quickly. "This is the greatest nation in the world, but Queens—" His voice trailed off.

McGarr patted the man's arm and went for the phone. There was no use explaining that the I.R.A. and the Irish Republic were two different and often opposed political entities, but McGarr doubted the man had ever been "home." It could well be he was a second or third or even a more distant generation American, yet still he nurtured the feeling of being Irish. Perhaps it was a necessary identity here among two hundred and ten million people. Because of the diversity of the sprawling country—more a collection of many different countries than a single nation state—the term *American* really couldn't mean much. To say you were Irish was something else. Ireland had only four million Irishmen, England about the same if nothing but names were counted, and America perhaps eight or nine million whose ancestry was traceable to the olde sod. The twenty dollars had probably made the policeman feel very Irish indeed and was for him money well spent.

McGarr wished he could trace the transit of the money and

197

find out where and how it was spent. He didn't doubt that Paddy Sugrue was a fairly honest man or that the cause he represented was dedicated solely to the establishment of a united Ireland, but he wondered how that man would feel if he knew that his twenty dollars had been spent to purchase the explosive used to blow some innocent Londoner out of his seat in a restaurant five hundred miles distant from the trouble in the North. Would he then have thought twice? McGarr believed so.

In McGarr's mind the problem really didn't rest with the man who gave the twenty dollars alone but with the I.R.A. leaders who had chosen terror as a guerrilla tactic. McGarr himself longed for a united Ireland, but at what price—the labeling of the Irish for good and all as a people more savage than any in Europe? In that light the twenty dollars was wrong.

"Peter? Peter?" a voice was saying through the receiver. It was Bernie McKeon at McGarr's office in Dublin Castle, where it was three in the morning. "I've been waiting for your call. What gives over there? Sounds like a tinker's wedding or a free-for-all. Who's the bloke with the busted throat in the background?" He meant the music, but he didn't wait for McGarr to answer. "Got a full report on the pitchfork we found in Schwerr's trunk. It can't be the murder weapon. The prongs are spaced too far apart. They don't match the punctures on her chest nor the width of the scratches on the car. But we did find where it came from—the farm nearest the murder scene. Fellow named Cassidy owns the place. The one Schwerr stopped at to get help and where Fleming patched him up. Cassidy has a whole bunch of sons."

"So a whole bunch of pitchforks," said McGarr.

McKeon never heard him. "So a whole bunch of pitchforks."

"Did he keep them all in one place?" McGarr shouted into the phone.

"Usually, but they're haying out there now and so leave them wherever they stop."

McGarr thought back to the morning they'd found May Quirk in the pasture. He had seen men haying not far distant.

"So," McKeon concluded, "we're working with a cute one, we are. If Schwerr didn't do it himself, whoever did was trying to hang it on him."

"Then why wouldn't the murderer have placed the real weapon in the trunk?" McGarr asked.

Said McKeon, "Didn't catch that. Are you hearing me?"

"Yes!" McGarr roared.

McKeon asked nearly the same question as McGarr and answered it. "The only pitchforks with prongs like the murder weapon are ancient. They were last manufactured in the early thirties at a place in Leeds. Can't be many around. We're now rechecking the area. Everybody here is being helpful. We should know something by morning.

"We've arrested Scannell at the Provincial Bank for fraud. When we checked his books we found them irregular. The bank laid the charges. He's definitely I.R.A. But I don't think we can lay anything else against him.

"The tire tracks are still up for grabs. Nothing yet."

"Have you checked the wreck at the James Cleary farm?" McGarr roared.

He couldn't hear McKeon's reply.

"Well, do that. And check there for the pitchfork. Carefully. I want the whole farm covered."

"Commissioner Farrell has been calling on the hour. That's about it from this end. What are you doing, presiding over a revolution?"

McGarr shouted his thanks to McKeon and hung up. When he turned back to the crowd he saw a group of men clustered around Sugrue, who was relating a story of the Troubles in a loud voice. McKeon could not have known how well he had spoken.

Some other men with much gold braid on the visors of their uniform caps were pushing in through the door. The man in the middle wore a suit. McGarr suspected he was the police commissioner. McGarr turned, placed a call to the consulate, and left a message for Noreen that he'd be late. There was a vibrancy in the air that was festive and not un-Irish, that of men who needed the excuse McGarr had given them to vent their best emotions. Throughout the bar they were laughing.

The commissioner removed his hat and coat.

The bartender pushed past McGarr and phoned home for help.

Three of New York's finest were behind the bar handing out drinks and lifting sodden bills off the wet bar top.

McGarr took a drink from his tumbler and resigned himself to a long night.

12

SYNTHESIS

McGarr awoke without opening his eyes. A circle of pain at the very back of his head was the cause. His back felt little better. And then he heard a rustling about the room, the sound of a window being opened, and was treated to the welcome smells of a breakfast tray by the side of the bed. Flexing his toes, he could tell that the bed was immense, because he was lying across it prone, or so the fingers of his outstretched arms told him, yet he couldn't feel the other edge.

Now street sounds were keeping him awake, and he began to worry about the coffee on the tray. He preferred it piping hot, especially when he felt as he did this morning, after his bash with the N.Y.P.D. He pushed the pillow off his head, turned his face onto the other cheek.

On a small table was the game board of Potlatch, O'Connor's invention. It belonged to the consul's daughter. McGarr and Noreen had played it after his return from Queens, until he had felt he was sober enough to go to bed without disastrous consequences.

While they had played, Noreen had extolled the many virtues of New York: the galleries, theatres, concerts, museums. "It's the tenor of this place. Just look at what's going on here." She had thrust a copy of the *New York Times* at him. Her cheeks were flushed. "And it's not just that more is happening here, but it seems to be a whole different order of activity. Everything is bigger, more powerful. Just listen to this." She had advanced on the French windows, which opened onto the street. "Hear that roaring? You only hear that roaring in London or Paris or Rome, but here it's louder. It's the sound of—"

"A great beast," McGarr had said. He hadn't been able even to focus on the paper and had been having trouble enough concentrating on the game, which was interesting even to a man in his condition.

"No, it's the sound of the heart of a civilization. In Paris it's mild, just a gentle hush. In Rome it's brash. In London it's a steady, busy hum. But over here it sounds like—"

"A bloody, big dynamo roaring through my skull. Close it, will you, Noreen?" But McGarr felt bad about that. She was deflated. After a while he had said, "All right, what does it sound like?"

"Like a shredding machine, if you must know. One big enough to accommodate a pint-sized Dubliner with a rancid disposition."

Now McGarr rolled over and placed the pillow on his face again. He thought of O'Connor and how he had reacted to May Quirk's articles about him—seemingly without anger, only a kind of quiet disappointment. He had let her take her shots at him, and not once but twice. The tenor of the second article had been strident, as though she had become enraged over his and the country's seeming unconcern for her opinion of his work. Obviously, the articles had bothered him—he had then tried to write something with which, he had thought, she might be satisfied. And he had still cared very much about her. His reaction to the news of her death had seemed genuine enough. He also had somewhat of an alibi for the period of time during which she was murdered. He had remained in Griffin's pub at least until closing, certainly too long to have gotten to the scene before Schwerr and Hanly. But could he have followed May Quirk to Ireland and, if so, why? He had said not, but . . .

What had struck McGarr as most interesting was the similarity of O'Connor's and Fleming's approaches to New York. They had even both dwelt upon the odd word *potlatch*. McGarr wondered what a wealthy young man, a writer who seemed to have lost interest in his writing, would do with his time. O'Connor had told McGarr that he didn't care for the tactics of the I.R.A. Could he be believed? And if so, did that matter? Phil Dineen himself had admitted as much, and there Dineen was Galway CO and a major Provo tactician.

Nora Cleary: She had been in Ireland the night of May Quirk's death and had lied to him about it. Why? She knew how to use a gun, in fact, the very same type that May Quirk had had in her hand. How had she come by that knowledge?

Fleming: May Quirk had written two articles about him as well. In both, Fleming had tried to debate her. Here the issue wasn't personal; it was an assessment of the quality of life in two vastly different areas of the world. Whereas O'Connor had sidestepped her thrusts, Fleming had confronted her on every issue. She had found a sore spot and had kept probing. Fleming had no real alibi either; he was near the scene of the crime, and he was involved with both Hanly and Schwerr and the men who had tried to kill McGarr and Dineen. What was more, he had made no bones about his dislike of May Quirk even from the first interview. And then Sugrue had told McGarr to check Fleming's house carefully.

Who else?

Schwerr: McGarr didn't think he'd murder the woman he had

wanted to marry when, in fact, she had admitted to carrying his child. The very mention of abortion had set him off. That was his story, of course, but his statement of having knocked her around made McGarr believe him. He *would* abuse her some, but he wouldn't kill her.

And Hanly: He was beyond murder, McGarr believed, even a murder designed to implicate his young rival Schwerr. In fact, Hanly had probably been beyond design the night of May Quirk's death. McGarr had watched him closely that next morning. And if he had killed her, why hadn't he concealed the proper pitchfork, the one that had killed May Quirk, in the trunk of Schwerr's car and not some other that was dissimilar? In his shape, could he have been capable of such intrigue? But McGarr had been wrong before. And McAnulty had thought Hanly had been acting. That was important. McGarr had been doing so much acting himself that morning that he was probably beyond assessing the histrionic element in Hanly's answers.

The pitchfork itself was the crux of the case, McGarr believed. Whoever had killed May had in a panic tried to pin it on Schwerr. Whoever had killed her had probably heard them arguing, witnessed her shooting Schwerr, and then taken the opportunity that the wild, dark place afforded to creep close to her and jab her. After the deed had come the realization that the pitchfork could be traced back to him. And that was the reason a second pitchfork had been placed in Schwerr's trunk.

Also, May Quirk's work diary was central to the case. She had kept such diaries on every other assignment she had ever done. Where was the diary on the financing operations of the I.R.A? Perhaps she had found out too much, some hitherto unknown source of funding, or some of their plans.

Yes—McGarr sat up. That would be a credible reason why

she would be killed in a manner that would make it look like an ordinary murder of passion. That would be the reason McGarr and Dineen had nearly been killed and McGarr followed at Shannon. McGarr wondered how Hughie Ward was coming along with his search of the Quirk farmhouse.

He placed a call there.

"Nothing. I've just about finished. Not a word about the I.R.A."

McGarr hung up and groped for his coffee.

Who else was there?

James Cleary: Certainly he was desperate enough to do something mad like killing her. The tire tracks could have been his. The car McGarr had seen burning in front of his farmhouse was an ancient Triumph Herald, just the sort of car that would have a bald front tire through which the cord was showing. Could he have followed her, overheard her telling Schwerr she was pregnant and was going to abort the child? That would definitely have outraged his peasant and Catholic sensibilities.

And then it struck McGarr that his sister was right. He *would* have a pitchfork of the type McKeon had described. His farm was an inheritance, had been worked for centuries. That would be a weapon for a farmer. How curious it was that May Quirk, a creature who had spoken for the modern world of New York and had condemned the ethos of Clare, should be killed by such a crude instrument, one of the symbols of that barren, backward land.

The phone was ringing.

McGarr picked it up.

"Dublin calling, sir," said a pleasant female voice.

"Peter?" It was McKeon. "We found the murder weapon. You'll never guess who owns it."

"James Cleary," McGarr said without a pause. All he could hear was the crackling of static and the odd word of other conversations that intruded on the wire.

Then McKeon said, "How d'you know that? McAnulty call you?"

"Lucky guess."

"But do you know it's been wiped clean of prints?"

"No. How do you mean 'wiped clean'?"

"Just that. The rag used to wipe the handle was greasy. McAnulty says it's some sort of nitrate solution on it."

"Fertilizer?"

"Or gelignite. He's working on it himself right now. And you know those two gunmen you had Shannon lift?" McKeon didn't wait for McGarr to reply. "When they clammed up, we decided to do a thorough search of them. The linings of all of their pockets were coated with a fine film of cedar sawdust. We checked records. Neither of them has ever had anything to do with carpentry, lumberyards, wood cutting, and so forth. So we provided them with prison ordinaries and did an analysis of their clothes. I bet you can't guess what we found on the cuffs of their pants."

"Gelignite," McGarr said, again without hesitation, speaking of the gelatin dynamite made from an absorbent base of sodium nitrate or some other nitrate and sawdust.

McKeon was deflated no less. "Did you buy a bloody crystal ball over there?"

"Just guessing. You gave away all the hard parts."

"Then where the hell else do you think we found some of this particular gelignite that had cedar sawdust in it?"

"In the remains of the room in Salthill I got blown out of."

"Well I'll be goddamned! Are you pulling my leg? Have you been talking to McAnulty?" When McGarr didn't say anything,

McKeon went on. "Well, here's something nobody knows. In the offal of the outbuilding near where we found the pitchfork, which, incidentally, wasn't there two days ago when a guard checked, was a print of a shoe with a strange heel and sole. It's the kind hikers or mountain climbers wear; you know, full of little rubber blocks for traction. Where the prints were situated makes McAnulty believe they were left by whoever leaned the pitchfork against the wall.

"And listen to this—in the trunk of Hanly's car is a pair of them shoes. They're called Dunham treking boots and sold at Callaghan's on Dame Street."

"Hanly buy them?"

"Nobody else. Last spring."

"The proper size print?" McGarr, in spite of this evidence, still didn't believe Hanly had killed May Quirk. To begin with, Hanly had been in custody since the morning following the murder. "Has McAnulty checked those shoes?"

"Yup—I knew you'd ask that. The composition of the mud found between the treads of those shoes is far different and too dry for those shoes to have made the prints."

"But it's the proper size to have made the prints?"

"Yes."

"So—somebody's still trying to hang it on Hanly, and whoever it is, he's getting careless. Sounds like another coup for the Technical Bureau."

"And they need one, too. Farrell has discovered the little fib you told him about the first pitchfork."

"Me? A fib?" McGarr asked, as though smitten. "I only told him what was found."

"But not *where* it was found."

"That's not a fib. It was early in the morning. I was tired."

"Just the withholding of vital information."

"Vital for whom? Vital to what? The information was only vital to Farrell's curiosity. I want you to prefer a murder charge against Hanly."

McKeon paused, then asked, "What?"

"Just what I said. Tell all the papers. Make sure they blow it up big." McGarr wanted to make sure Fleming and O'Connor heard about it.

"But Hanly couldn't have killed her, could he have?"

"I don't know. I don't think so, but I want to make those other two think I do."

"Then O'Connor and Fleming did it?"

"Fleming, I think. He then tried to blame it on either Schwerr or Hanly. They used the two of them to confuse the issue and make us work for the arrest. Fleming's alibi isn't airtight. I talked to May Quirk's uncle. He's not a person who lives by the clock. O'Connor could have been up there on the cliffs himself. He said he had another pint and then, right about closing, left Griffin's.

"Also, I want you to have McAnulty's crew run a discreet check on Fleming's farmhouse."

"For sawdust and nitrate?"

"That's right. Maybe you can get one of them to go there to be treated for something."

"Distemper?" McKeon suggested.

McGarr was too engrossed in the problem to quip back, however. "I wonder if that boot is made here in the States?"

"You mean you wonder if Fleming or O'Connor might have a boot like that. O'Connor is out, of course. He's got gunboats, without a doubt. I was giving that some thought myself, since McAnulty's crew is sure it wasn't a planted footstep."

McGarr said, "And I remember Hanly had small feet for a man carrying his weight."

"Is Fleming a tall man?"

"No."

"Well, he didn't buy them at Callaghan's. We've checked. Hanly's was the only pair they sold in that size, and they're the sole distributor here."

"Telex me a photo of the print. Have it sent to Assistant Commissioner Sidney Simonds, Headquarters, New York Police Department. Put a rush on it.

"And then get me the addresses and names of the holders of these phone numbers." McGarr reached for his wallet, took out the slip of paper, and read to McKeon the numbers he had taken from Sugrue and Nora Cleary.

"Then place more guards on Phil Dineen's hospital room or, better, move him to a prison.

"Tell Hughie to leave off his search of the Quirk house, if he hasn't quit already, and find out where Fleming has put James Cleary. It's probably a hospital or rest home or mental institution. That's if he's still alive. Place guards on him and go through his effects."

"Me or Hughie?" McKeon asked.

"Hughie, of course."

"Oh." McKeon was dejected. He was always looking for an opportunity to get out of the office. That was a detail assignment that was just up his street. "He's a devil for work, that little nipper. Sometimes I think he's after me job. He can have it too, you know. Fecking solitary confinement, it is. I swear."

"Not too loudly," said McGarr. "This is an international wire. And it'll never happen."

"Why not?"

"All the questions he asks me I can never answer, and I enjoy feeling superior when I talk to you."

"You do, do you? Well, speaking of jobs, the *Times* is calling for yours. Says here—" McGarr could hear the rattle of a newspaper, "—you're running this place like David Nelligan, just another sort of Gestapo but more pernicious, since the way information has been suppressed about May Quirk's murder and the Salthill dance hall bombing makes it seem that McGarr is mounting his own pro–I.R.A. coverup. He wants Ireland to think of the consequences of having the police and the I.R.A. in cahoots. He asks what you and Dineen might have been discussing in the back room of the dance hall and why you didn't arrest Dineen straightaway."

"By *he* you mean Fogarty, of course."

"Who else? Sure and you're becoming his Mephistopheles."

"What does the *Press* say?"

"Front-page pictures of the Technical Bureau on the scene. 'Murder Weapon Recovered by Daring Police' and all that sort of rot."

"Inaccurate but nice," said McGarr.

"Fogarty wants to know where you are, why you're keeping yourself incommunicado, why Commissioner Farrell has yet to issue a statement about either case. I don't think the charge against Hanly will satisfy him, especially when we'll have to be withdrawing it in a little while. Perhaps it's time for the truth." McKeon's voice had changed. He was serious now.

"Farrell been calling?"

"On the hour."

"Then you can tell him I'll be back in Shannon later today with a full explanation of the murder. Just do what I've asked of you and things will work out fine."

"Really?"

"Count on it."

"What about Fogarty?"

"Call him and tell him to meet me at Shannon, if he's that interested. I'll drag him along. There could be something revealed that is much more important than the laying of a simple murder charge."

"More important than maybe a gelignite factory?"

"Yup."

"Well, what—"

"I've got to rush. The plane and so forth. See you soon, Bernie." Before he hung up he waited for McKeon's curse.

"God rot you, you—"

McGarr hung up.

He then tapped the yoke and had the switchboard operator ring Magowan's Pub in Lahinch. That was where Hanly had last stopped and Michael Daly drank.

While she put the call through, McGarr spiked his coffee with a hefty dollop of malt, drank half, and opened the linen leaves of the bread basket on the tray. Croissants, and piping hot! And they were the real crescent-shaped item made with lots of butter and basted with potato flour and boiled water. The croissant had originated in Budapest, or so McGarr had been told by a former Hungarian freedom fighter who now worked for Interpol. It seems that some bakers who were working through the night had heard the Turks, who were besieging the city, tunneling underground. They alerted the guard and the enemy was repulsed. To reward these heroic bakers, the king granted them alone the privilege of making a pastry in the shape of a crescent, the symbol on the Ottoman flag. The year was 1686.

McGarr spread a little butter and some ruby red jam on a bit of croissant. He bit into it. Hot, buttery dough and tangy preserve. What was it, this taste? McGarr had some more and still couldn't decide. He dipped his finger into the jam and tasted it without the croissant. Not citrus, nor grape nor berry, nor any fruit he had ever tasted.

He picked up the phone and asked to be connected to the kitchen. Rose hip jam. No wonder he hadn't recognized the taste; he had never tasted it before. But he made another mental note: Jack Daniels bourbon and rose hip jam.

The phone was ringing. McGarr picked it up.

"Magowan's, Lahinch, on the line."

"Peter McGarr here."

"Yes, Inspector," a voice roared into the phone, "but *where* are ya? The lady said something about New York calling. You were here only yesterday."

McGarr could imagine that every ear in the pub was listening to Magowan's voice. "It's a small world."

"For some it is. What can I do for you?"

"Michael Daly. Is he there?"

"Do you have to ask? Michael!" Magowan shouted.

When Daly came on, McGarr said, "I want you to think back to Friday night, Michael. Tell me what you saw before and after Hanly sped up the road toward the cliffs."

"I don't understand what you mean, Peter."

McGarr imagined that Daly's stock with the other bar patrons was soaring, talking to the chief inspector transatlantic and on a first-name basis. "Was there a lot of traffic?"

"Of course. It's summer, don't you know."

"But locals?"

"Let me see." Daly paused. "I was pretty much taken with your man," meaning Hanly, "but now that you mention it, Dr. Fleming's Renault was the next car up the road and then a bit behind that Jamie Cleary's old banger. You'd think the thing was burning turf, the way it was giving off fumes. Nearly choked me, it did."

McGarr thanked Daly and hung up.

He then called Columbia University and requested them to

212

ready copies of Dr. John Fleming's university transcripts, both the one from their university and the one they had received from U.C.D. The I.R.A. might have managed to tamper with the files of the sleepy academic institution in Mount Merrion, but he doubted they had breached the data bank of Columbia University.

In the Seventeenth Precinct two hours later, Nora Cleary had her lawyer with her. He was a short young man dressed in a three-piece suit. He had done something to the mass of his brown hair, which was shaggy à la mode. It neither moved nor quivered while he strode around an interrogation room saying, "You have no jurisdiction here, Mr. McGarr. My client tells me you broke and entered. You're an alien. You came to this country as a visitor. That is to say, without going through official police channels first. Since you are here as a private citizen and since it seems you acted alone," he flashed his eyes at Simonds, "Miss Cleary can have you arrested for any and all of those reasons." His voice was testy, nasal, and McGarr imagined it might shatter crystal if raised another octave. Simonds had briefed McGarr on the man. His name was Cauley. He was an I.R.A. lawyer in New York who got a lot of work in the Irish community because of his involvement with the cause.

Nora Cleary said, "He doesn't have a thing on me, anyhow. It's just Dublin braggadocio. Lots of lip, that's all." She was sitting at a table.

"Please, Miss Cleary. I'll do the talking," said Cauley.

McGarr was willing to bet Cauley was from Dublin too. He had the look of perpetual surprise—that the world had granted him a fiddle, the tunes from which lined his pockets with gold.

Simonds was on the other side of the table.

Another N.Y.P.D. officer was standing near the door.

"As I see it," Cauley continued, "we've got a test case for the Civil Liberties Union here. Lots of money behind it. Lots of publicity." He glanced at Simonds, then at McGarr.

The door opened and Paddy Sugrue stepped into the room. A police officer was behind him.

But McGarr never took his eyes off Nora Cleary. He removed a Woodbine from his nearly empty last packet and lit it. He said to her, "If you can keep his," he pointed to Cauley, "lip buttoned, I'll tell you why you're in big trouble and will be needing every little squeal he has in him."

Cauley went to object, but McGarr stared him down.

McGarr then placed copies of the passenger lists of two T.W.A. flights to Ireland in front of Nora Cleary. Simonds had had the N.Y.P.D. get them during the night. "You lied to me yesterday. You arrived at Shannon on the twelfth, you left on the thirteenth. May Quirk was murdered on the twelfth."

"No reason she should have to tell you anything, much less—"

Nora Cleary turned to Cauley. "Hush up, now. Let's hear the man out. Maybe we might learn what all of this is about."

McGarr laid another sheet on the table. "This is a ballistics report on your gun, this the report on the one May Quirk had in her hands when we found her. And this is the report on the slug taken from Max Schwerr. Your cohort Dr. Fleming dropped it in a basin and one of the Cassidy kids couldn't resist saving the souvenir from the wounded I.R.A. gunman. You shot Max Schwerr. There's only a bit of difference between the barrel markings that those guns make, but it's enough to charge you with assault."

"Perhaps, but in Ireland," said Cauley. "And you'll have to extradite for that. Miss Cleary is a U.S. citizen. Your chances aren't very good. And that's no mere ploy, that's fact."

"Paddy," McGarr said to Sugrue, "were you the one who told this woman what May was doing over in Ireland?"

Sugrue said nothing, just looked at his shoes.

She said, "Don't you think I would have known, living with her as I did?"

That was when Simonds spoke up. "We checked that too, ma'am. Nobody—the doorman, the garage attendant, the people who work in the deli, dry cleaners, beauty parlor, and grocery store in that building—nobody knows who you are. You set yourself up there the moment you got back from Ireland. A good job, I might add. You sure could have fooled me." He looked at McGarr.

He said, "And you, Nora, being the CO of the Provisional I.R.A. here in New York" (information McGarr had gotten from the commissioner of police himself at the bar in Queens), "were quite interested in the article May was writing for the *Daily News*. It was a threat. She was going right for the organization's jugular, wasn't she? And when Fleming called saying he believed May Quirk had gotten wise to what was going on in the new basement of his father's farmhouse, you decided you had to do something."

She looked up at him as though she hadn't understood a word he had said.

McGarr laid Fleming's U.C.D. record in front of her. "Gelignite is easy for a man with Fleming's background in chemistry to produce. He could probably make an atomic bomb, had he the materials."

The lawyer was pacing up and down now, wishing—McGarr supposed—he had some information to refute these charges one by one.

"You decided to go over there and handle it yourself. Fleming wasn't much at the assassination game, nor was O'Connor, who had only recently come over to your way of thinking and on philosophical grounds—all the hearts-and-sorrows jingoism that you people hand out.

"Your plane landed at Shannon at six fifty-eight on the twelfth. It hadn't gotten off the ground until just about midnight on the eleventh, then had gyrocompass problems and had to put in at Gander. Nobody there had the parts to fix it, so the captain decided to radionavigate to Shannon as soon as he could get permission from New York. That took five more hours. After that there was the cab ride to your brother's house." McGarr laid a copy of the bill in front of her. He had had a Telex copy of that sent from Shannon only a few minutes before.

"By the time you put the situation together, things were already happening. Hanly was drunk, Schwerr blinded by his love for May Quirk, and your brother Jamie had lost his grip on reality.

"You and he got into his car and followed Schwerr and May Quirk—that is, you followed Fleming, who was following Hanly, who was following them—but when you got to the pasture, the situation had deteriorated.

"Schwerr was beating May Quirk. He was roaring, cursing, and shouting. Hanly was staggering blindly toward them. Fleming had parked at the Cassidy farmhouse and was coming to the pasture on foot.

"And then your brother Jamie jumped out and got his pitchfork from the back seat. He started after Schwerr, but he and Hanly had a tussle. Either your brother or Schwerr knocked Hanly cold, but in the melee your brother dropped the pitchfork. You then shot Schwerr."

"Why would I do that?"

"He was raving like a madman. He's big, powerful. You couldn't reason with him.

"In the meantime, Fleming had come running. At the sound of the gunshot, he picked up the pitchfork, which he found near Hanly. He knew May Quirk carried a gun. He was the one who

216

had contacted you about her discovery of the lab in the basement of his house. She had just filed a damaging story about him that linked him to the I.R.A., and then there was her work diary, which contained all that damaging information she had obtained by pumping Max Schwerr." McGarr glanced at Nora Cleary.

She tried unsuccessfully to keep her eyes straight ahead of her.

"When May plunged her hand into her coat pocket, Fleming jabbed her.

"Your brother, who was just reviving, saw that and went stark raving mad.

"You figured it was best to get him in check because as a witness he had seen everything and Fleming, not just as a doctor alone, was the single most important person there, and so you went over to Jamie. He was bent over May Quirk, hugging her, crying, wailing, and so forth. You pulled him off her, but neither Fleming nor you could find her work diary." McGarr looked closely at her.

Her forehead had pulled back ever so slightly, but it was enough.

"This work diary." He pulled out a diary he had taken from May Quirk's apartment less than an hour ago. It was a shill, of course, and not based on the I.R.A. work.

She looked up at him, despair in her eyes.

"Hanly was out cold. So was Schwerr. What were your options? You could dump May Quirk over the cliffs, but that would make it look like an assassination. You knew we'd find out she was doing a piece on the I.R.A. You wanted to make it look like a crime of passion. That was why you got O'Connor to lead me to Schwerr the next day. Schwerr had blown his cover already, as had Hanly, whose usefulness was passed anyhow. And making

217

the crime somewhat complex would titillate us as well, make it seem like we had cracked one.

"The person you couldn't count on was your brother. And you couldn't stay around and help him, either.

"Do you know what my bet is?"

She said, "We may as well hear it. It can't be any wilder than these other fabrications."

"I bet your brother took the work diary off her there on the cliffs. She probably had it in the inside pocket of the coat. When he tried to see how bad she was hurt, either he found it or she, still alive, gave it to him. He had doubtless heard you talking about it. He took it, but not knowing what to do himself, appalled by what had happened, he raced across the pastures toward the cliffs. He had Hanly's bottle of Canadian Club in his hands. You and Fleming ran after him. You couldn't have him kill himself like that. It would confuse the picture a bit too much.

"But Jamie couldn't bring himself to jump. He had a bottle of booze in his hand, the very symbol of the only other social trouble he'd had in his life. He opened the top and dropped the cap where I found it, snagged in the gorse. He drank some, enough to make him drunk. He hadn't eaten anything for days. That pacified him and you got him back into the car.

"Fleming got another pitchfork from Cassidy's field and stuffed it in Schwerr's trunk, after making sure Hanly was out cold and running it down the side of Hanly's car.

"You took your brother home and, after believing you had talked him into going along with what had happened, you left the country."

"Why would I have to do that?"

"Because you knew sooner or later we'd find out who you were, what you did for the I.R.A. over here in the States.

"And then yesterday sometime, Fleming, thinking that we might be getting near him, replaced your brother's pitchfork in his shed. I found Fleming's phone number among the things you placed in May Quirk's apartment to make it look like you lived there while you went through her files. Somehow you were just too well acquainted with her files for a servant.

"And you went along with that, didn't you? Fleming had told you how disturbed your brother was, how he was even unable to speak anymore. Better to sacrifice him than Fleming and yourself. But Fleming—your man with all the brains—blew it.

"Not only did he wipe the handle clean with a rag that had traces of gelignite constituents on it, but he also stepped in the offal there with a very interesting style of boot."

He placed that report in front of her too. It said that Abercrombie & Fitch, the New York sporting goods store, had sold a pair of Dunham boots with Montagna block vibram soles to Dr. John Fleming four and a half years ago. The size, 9B, matched the track taken from the shed.

She pushed all the reports aside. "Interesting fable. Prove it."

"My sentiments exactly, gentlemen," said the lawyer.

"Can we hold her on the gun charge?" McGarr asked Simonds.

"Better—threatening an officer with a loaded weapon is a felony."

"We'll beat that," said Cauley.

Simonds was smiling now. He shook his head. "You might have when we were believing the lie that she lived there. But now—not a chance. *She* broke, *she* entered, *she* gave false information to a law enforcement officer. *She* is in big trouble. Here and abroad." He stood. "McGarr—you're a prince. I thought you were good last night, but the performance you've given this morning is unbeatable. I gotta admit I was worried earlier." He wrapped his arm around McGarr and began walking him out the door. "I'm rusty. Been in an office too long. I was hasty with her. Like you said, it was a matter of pride. But now," he looked back at Cauley, who was shaking his head, "it doesn't really matter, does it? Lunch? Wait until the boys hear about this one."

As the door closed, McGarr heard Cauley say to Nora Cleary, "You never told me about all these things. He wasn't blowing smoke, that mick. If this stuff all checks out, we're in a jam."

"*I'm* in a jam. You're fired," she said flatly. "I better get myself somebody who's tough."

McGarr begged off lunch. He thanked Simonds for everything and invited him to come see him at Dublin Castle. He said he had to get home right away. Whatever was in May Quirk's work diary must be quite important; he was convinced of it.

13

A COOPER, SOME SCOOPS, MACKEREL, AND A HORSE SHOW

As the Aer Lingus 707 shuddered down from its transatlantic route into a holding pattern over Clare it broke through the cloud cover suddenly, and McGarr and Noreen could see a quilt of fields bounded by hedgerows. Usually, anything growing was brilliant green, but because of the dry spell the colors had muted—a field of beige wheat, browning hay new mown, the delicate green of second-growth grass. The contour was irregular and soft, not the concrete gridwork laced by superhighways which from the air was Long Island and New York. Here lay large rocks that people had worked around instead of removing, farms and roads and boundaries that conformed to the movement of the land. In the fields cows, sheep, and donkeys grazed. The buildings seemed indistinguishable from the general vegetation below. A barn looked like a big brown bush, a house like a patch of grass or a garden plot on top of a lime rock.

McGarr, sipping a final malt whiskey over crushed ice, was moved to consider the dilemma of Dr. John Fleming: that such a young, vigorous, involved man should choose this gentle, archaic patchwork of homesteads instead of the bustle of the earth's most dynamic metropolis seemed an irreconcilable disjunction of expectations. Fleming had returned hoping to find the seeds of a new order, one that wasn't as brutal and mechanistic and unfeeling as that which he had experienced in New York. But after only a few short years he had become involved with an organization that represented the most vicious, atavistic aspects of the Celtic personality. Why? McGarr put it down to boredom. Fleming had had little to do. He had even tried his hand at veterinary medicine.

McGarr glanced down at the university transcripts in his lap. It had to be boredom. A man with a record like this—McGarr hefted the dossier—didn't support and actively engage in terrorist activities. At least he wouldn't stoop to the level of actually producing the bombs that ravaged politically innocent persons in cities far distant from the immediate problems in the Six Counties. Nor did he murder a long-time acquaintance with a pitchfork just to further the cause. But yet—he had. That was the truth of it.

McGarr opened the folder. The record was clear: First Honors with special distinction in chemistry from U.C.D., and then a concatenation of superlatives from Columbia Medical School, A pluses and phrases like "exemplary achievement, brilliant performance." His undergraduate thesis on T-jump measurements had been published by Cambridge University Press, and he had turned down a number of offers to go into biochemical research. Instead, he had become a surgeon specializing in internal medicine. Here too the record showed him to be extraordinary. There was a memo attached to the original transcript to the effect that if Fleming were to request to have his transcript forwarded, the dean of Columbia Medical School wanted to be put on notice, doubtless to make a counteroffer. Fleming was that good, McGarr had been told over the phone, that he could afford to spend a number of years back in Ireland without the system forgetting him. "Do you represent a research institute or hospital in Great Britain, Mr. McGarr?" the dean had asked.

"I'm afraid the most I can tell you is that I'm an officer of the Irish government."

"Is he being offered a post there?" There had been an edge to his voice. Columbia had the money and facilities, McGarr had not doubted, to better any Irish offer, and would have done so without hesitation.

"That's all I can say. You'll probably read about it in the papers." McGarr hung up.

Now, as the plane eased down toward the runway, Noreen read McGarr's thoughts. "Maybe you're wrong." But she knew that was not likely.

And then there was O'Connor, who was a much more usual Irish figure, the romantic, idealistic writer searching for a cause to support. The book he had explained to McGarr had been satirical, an attempt to point up the deficiencies of modern American life. McGarr didn't doubt that O'Connor's other books were in part social critiques. To take away something evil from the world rather than to add something good was a very Celtic point of view. O'Connor's disenchantment with his career had probably made him susceptible to Fleming's way of viewing the world. And the I.R.A. social program—if it could be dignified by such an expression—was vague enough to accommodate O'Connor's social preferences.

And then O'Connor was quite wealthy, too. Whatever it had been that had brought them together, Fleming and O'Connor would have been a very formidable team, a whole different order of leader from the common run of I.R.A. gunman and terrorist, had they not been scared off by McGarr's murder investigation and gone to ground, and McGarr had no reason to suspect that they had.

Liam O'Shaughnessy, who met them in the bus that transferred passengers from the plane to the terminal, was smiling slightly with a look he only assumed when the pieces of an investigation were fitting together with great facility. "The both of them," he said, meaning Fleming and O'Connor, "are moving about Lahinch as though they were above suspicion, as though they've believed every word we've released to the press about Hanly."

Noreen glanced at McGarr, who turned to O'Shaughnessy.

He said, "But just in case they're only feinting, waiting for the proper moment to take off, I've put details on the addresses of the phone numbers you gave Bernie." He pulled a small black memo book from an interior pocket of his gray summer suit. "Let me see. We've got Harry Greaves in charge of watching an old school in Dunquin that's owned by a former Englishman art dealer in Dublin who has I.R.A. sympathies."

"Not Trevor Towne?" Noreen asked.

"The same," said O'Shaughnessy, not looking up from the page.

"From the way he talks and acts, I would have thought he was a militant Unionist."

"He's a slippery one, so it seems. And I've got Sinclair covering the Brazen Head."

"That's another number?" McGarr was surprised. The Brazen Head was possibly Dublin's oldest public house. It was also a hotel. And then McGarr thought of Fleming's interest in the work of James Joyce, and O'Connor's literary persuasion. "Say no more." He knew where two men such as they would choose to go to ground, not in the picturesque West of Ireland that Fleming had often praised but in town, where O'Connor could get a good meal and both of them might engage in conversation and read current editions of the world's periodicals. There was a wide gap between the preferences Fleming claimed for himself and those he espoused.

"That's what I was thinking as well," said O'Shaughnessy, "although I've put teams on both other locations—a farmhouse outside Mullingar and a youth hostel in Glendalough."

But the expression on Dan O'Malley's face wasn't in any way sanguine. He was waiting for McGarr and Noreen in the terminal. He had Fogarty from the *Times* with him. The latter's face was as set and as hard as an irregular lump of Clare shale.

"Don't tell us," said Noreen. "Hughie has had no luck with James Cleary. Phil Dineen won't say a word and keeps asking for Peter."

O'Malley blinked. He took Noreen's hand as she stepped off the bus.

Fogarty said to McGarr, "You mean to say you tell her all your police business?"

"It's better than telling somebody like you, who'd plaster it all over the front page of that scandal sheet you work for." The *Times* was the most reputable paper in all of Ireland.

Fogarty stopped. "Are you starting again?"

McGarr stepped back and took Fogarty by the arm. "Don't take it to heart, Billy. We're a strange, unlikely people. What we say always sounds worse than it is. It's because we hate to be disappointed. I promised you a big story. Has Liam filled you in on what we've found so far?"

Fogarty nodded. He was wary of this new familiarity from McGarr.

"Is that a big enough scoop for you?"

Fogarty nodded again. His eyes were darting every which way. His brow was slightly furrowed. His old hatchet face was worried. He was wondering what machination McGarr was forming to dupe him.

"Then stick around. It's going to get bigger." McGarr could have added, "So big you won't be able to print it," but McGarr wanted to save the best for last. McGarr had decided to husband his *agon* with Fogarty. It made his public life interesting; and in no way would this old fossil fault him in the pages of the *Times*, since McGarr planned to tell and show him everything and put the onus of that responsibility squarely on Fogarty's shoulders for once.

When McGarr went out into the parking lot, however, he got a surprise. There alongside Dan O'Malley's Triumph Toledo that had a bullet hole in the right fender was a gleaming and new-looking Mini Cooper. It was exactly the same as the one that had been blown up on the beach at Black Head, right down to its dark green lacquer and number plates. And standing next to it was Fergus Farrell, his pocked face the color of liver.

"Jesus," said McGarr, like a child who had been presented a new toy. "Where'd you get that? They stopped making Coopers in 1971."

"It's a 1971." Farrell glanced in the car. "With about the same amount of mileage on it." He reset his tortoiseshell glasses on the bridge of his nose. "It was a little old lady from Ballybunion's before the Garda Soichana bought it to replace your own."

"You're codding. Is that right?" He turned to O'Shaughnessy, who was smiling now himself. "Cripes—that's gracious of you, Fergus." McGarr shook Farrell's hand and walked around the auto. His own Cooper had been a '65 and in only passable shape. "Not a scratch on her. Hardly run in." He looked up and saw O'Malley, who was staring at the bullet hole in the fender of his own new car.

McGarr said, "Of course, by the same token, we need to get a new fender for Dan's car."

"It's coming," said Farrell.

They got in the cars and McGarr told Farrell everything that had happened in New York. Farrell said they'd already begun extradition proceedings against Nora Cleary.

James Cleary was propped in the pillows of a bed in a large private room at the Saint Agnes Psychiatric Hospital near Kilrush. Hughie Ward was standing close by. A large spray of red-and-white carnations sat in one vase, yellow chrysanthemums in another.

McGarr examined the cards. The first was from John and Aggie Quirk—God bless them, McGarr thought—the second from Rory O'Connor.

Cleary had had a shave and a close haircut in the style that, McGarr had noticed, was making a comeback in New York. He had just enough hair to comb a part. This, somebody had formed with great precision. The hair was still wet.

Also, Cleary's face shined. The room smelled of the flowers, after-shave lotion, hair tonic, and talcum powder. In all, Cleary presented McGarr with an entirely different picture from that in which he had first seen the man, back at his farmhouse near Lahinch. Except for his eyes. They were the same—pale blue and glassy, the pupils mere pinpricks at the centers.

Ward whispered to McGarr, "The medical thinking is that he had a severe emotional shock recently, but also that he had taken or was given something else, too."

McGarr turned to Ward.

"Something like a hallucinogen. Something that disorients his perceptions. They've found traces of it in his blood."

McGarr thought back to the scene in the kitchen of the farmhouse where Fleming had given Cleary a shot to calm him. It had put the old farmer right out. "Has he said anything to you?"

"Not a word, although I've gotten the impression that he's been trying. He's slobbered a couple of times and he whimpered once after I put him a question about the Quirks."

McGarr advanced to the bed.

Cleary had an envelope in his hands. His left thumb was moving over the surface of it.

McGarr said, "I'm Peter McGarr, Jamie. I'm chief inspector of detectives at Dublin Castle. That's," he pointed to Farrell, "the commissioner of police himself, Fergus Farrell. And you know Dan O'Malley.

"I know you saw May Quirk murdered. Fleming did it, didn't he? With the pitchfork you brought with you when you drove Nora to the cliffs."

Cleary's appearance hadn't changed a bit. Still his thumb worked over the envelope.

"Don't you worry, we're going to get Fleming and make him pay. Sooner or later. And you can help us, too. When you bent over May up there on the cliffs to see how bad she'd been stuck, you found something that was falling out of her coat. Do you remember that?"

Still nothing. Still the thumb on the envelope.

"It was May's work diary. The one she made notes in for the story she was writing. You took that. It was smart of you. You'd heard Nora speak of it. She must have told you some lie about it to get you to drive her up there." McGarr watched Cleary closely once more.

Still nothing. Just the thumb.

"You decided they wouldn't get it after what they'd done to May. You slipped it under your belt. One of these—" McGarr turned to Fogarty. "Let me see yours, please, Billy."

"My what?" asked Fogarty.

"Your work diary."

"What's that?"

"The thing you take your notes in."

Fogarty looked away, out the window. "I've been in this business too long to take notes."

O'Shaughnessy glanced at Farrell, who then took a long look at Fogarty.

Ward handed McGarr his notebook.

"Like this, Jamie. It's just like this. If you can tell us where it is you can help us put Fleming in prison." He held it up to Cleary's eyes.

Still nothing.

That was when McGarr looked down at the thumb. It was still working over the surface of the envelope, and not any faster.

McGarr handed the notebook back to Ward, then reached for the envelope. "May I, Jamie?"

Cleary's hands released the envelope. It was as though he had wanted McGarr to take it from him all along.

It was the envelope which the card for the flowers from the Quirks had come in.

McGarr stepped back and thought for a moment. Cleary had come to the Quirks' door late at night and thrust the open bottle of Canadian Club at John Quirk. Why, then, hadn't he given him the work diary, if he had had it? Maybe because of something Nora, his sister, had said or Cleary had overheard. Maybe he hadn't thought old Quirk was the right man. Maybe May Quirk had been alive and had asked him to do something specific with it when he took it from her.

McGarr kept staring down at the envelope, kept running his own thumb over the surface.

Then it struck him. "Did you—" He stepped closer to the bed. "Did you put it in the postbox? Is that what you did with it—put it in Quirks' postbox?" The Quirks probably hadn't checked the mail since hearing of May.

Cleary opened his mouth and whimpered. An unsightly rope of saliva dropped from the corner of his mouth.

McGarr placed the envelope back in Cleary's hands. "Good. Thank you, Jamie."

McGarr picked up the call cord that lay on the pillow and pushed the button for a nurse, then started toward the door.

"Some scoop," said Fogarty.

McGarr wrapped his arm about Fogarty's shoulders. "Patience, old sod, patience. It's necessary to truly great gumshoeing of the kind both you and I do without notes."

McGarr drove his new Cooper, Noreen in the front seat, Farrell and Hughie Ward in the rear.

It was twilight again and McGarr let the little car course over the twisting stretch of coast road between Kilrush and Lahinch. He couldn't understand why British Leyland had stopped making the Cooper. It clung to the road like a crab and could accelerate as fast as any motorcycle. The one problem was tires. They were small and wore quickly, and McGarr had found he had to replace his about as often as some people changed the oil in their cars. But he was willing to put up with the expense for the sort of handling the Cooper provided.

Behind them Dan O'Malley had long since ceased trying to keep up with him.

McGarr cranked on northwest into a brilliant twilight sky. It was clear and cloudless, the sun like an orange globe on the horizon off toward Iceland. On the hills as they neared the sea, McGarr could pick out bobbing points of light that were fishing boats—some, huge ships; others, private craft that were trawling after mackerel. They would be running now. The water was azure in toward shore where the bottom was sandy, but black out in the deep.

Noreen, sensing McGarr's thoughts as he slowed on a cliff to look down into a small boat below them, said, "Broiled mackerel with mustard sauce."

McGarr turned his head to her. "With a chilled bottle of Pouilly. A '59." It was one of McGarr's favorite dishes.

"How's that?" asked Commissioner Farrell. He had removed his coat and tie and had not said a word when McGarr had stopped at a bar for a dozen bottles of Harp lager and produced a bottle of Jack Daniels from his bag. Farrell had drunk the beers and sipped the sour mash, all the while acting like a truant from hated duties, as though he were involved in a grand adventure—hurtling up the winding road after a work diary that might tip them off to something important about the I.R.A. He had talked incessantly, even sung a bit.

Noreen explained that there had been a restaurant called Le Conquet in Les Halles, the Paris marketplace that has been moved into an ugly concrete structure on the outskirts of Paris. But when McGarr was working for Criminal Justice, Le Conquet was situated in a crumbling gray building on the corner near the fish and seafood stalls and had been there so long it had two Utrillos in the main dining room and an exquisite Sisley over the bar. The family, who were Bretons, had taken the paintings in trade from the artists and at the time had considered the exchanges bad deals. One of the house specialties was broiled mackerel with mustard sauce.

"While the mackerel is broiling, the chef makes a paste of butter and flour, adds boiling white sauce, and then a mixture of egg yolks and whipping cream. He beats this over heat until it boils for about five seconds. Then it's seasoned to taste and fresh lemon juice is added."

"Oh, Jasus," said Farrell. "And that's put on the fish?"

"Not yet. He takes some strong Dijon mustard—you know the type, it's brown, not yellow, and has been made with wine and spices and wine vinegar—"

"Cripes," said Farrell. "I'm famished."

"—and some unsalted butter. He blends them together."

"Good God! You have to wonder how those Frogs ever get to thinking up all of that."

McGarr brought the Cooper down to a roll and turned onto a goat track that led from the highway down to the beach.

"And he beats the mustard sauce into the hot *sauce bâtarde*. This he then spoons over the freshly broiled mackerel. It's served with a dry white wine."

"Say no more," said Farrell. "I despised mackerel unawares. I've eaten in tens, possibly hundreds of fine restaurants. Why is it that I missed broiled mackerel with mustard sauce?"

"You won't tonight." McGarr got out of the Cooper. They were on the beach now. He leaned back and whistled once. The sound was shrill and the man in the boat turned to look shoreward. McGarr waved to him.

Noreen honked the horn.

Farrell got out of the car too. "What are you going to do?"

"Buy some mackerel."

"But what about May Quirk's work diary? What about Fleming and O'Connor? The I.R.A. is probably searching every nook and cranny for that thing right now. Shouldn't we—?"

"They're not searching the proper nooks and crannies. Specifically, they're not searching the Quirk mailbox. And we can lift Fleming and O'Connor anytime we want."

"Honestly, you amaze me. I thought in hiring you my worries were over and I could do a little office work and then go home and sleep at night."

"Are you dissatisfied with my results?"

"Oh, no. It's not the results that worry me, it's your methods. They're—" Farrell couldn't find the right word. Finally he said, "Cavalier."

The engine of the little open boat had started. The bow swung around and headed toward shore.

Farrell turned and looked out toward the open ocean, which

232

was calm, with only the occasional roller lazing over the rocks. "It's as though you think you're at some sort of party. One that ranges all over the goddamn world!" He took a pull from a lager bottle.

McGarr turned to him. "Just so. And why not, Fergus?" McGarr had the bourbon bottle in his right hand. He raised it to his lips. "What's the harm in my thinking I've been invited to one long bash at which, from time to time, I'm asked to perform a few small services to justify my presence?"

Farrell sighed. "What's New York like?"

"A good party town."

Farrell turned and walked back to the car.

The man in the small boat had not only mackerel but two large rock lobsters that he had snagged in his net.

McGarr paid him a fiver and what was left in the bottle for the lobsters and a dozen mackerel.

When McGarr got back in the car, Farrell said, "What the hell. Maybe for once I've been invited to the party too."

Up on the road, O'Malley's Triumph had caught up to them. "Since you've been fishing," said O'Shaughnessy, "we can take your catch over to my aunt's house in Kinvara." All O'Shaughnessy's people were fishermen, and the welcome they always laid out for Liam was extravagant. "After—" O'Shaughnessy added.

"Of course," said McGarr and he geared off.

Reaching for another lager, Farrell said, "I see you've got your men well trained, Peter."

"Party manners," said McGarr. "Don't let them turn your head."

Inside the Quirk farmhouse a wake was in progress. Cars were parked on both sides of the road and in every laneway.

The mauve light of dusk had cast a funereal pall over the house.

McGarr didn't look for a parking place. He rushed the Cooper up to the mailbox and applied the brakes.

Leaning on it was none other than Detective Sergeant Bernie McKeon, McGarr's detail man and second in command back at Dublin Castle.

McGarr and Farrell got out.

"Commissioner, Chief Inspector," said McKeon, "what took you so long?" He opened the mailbox and pulled out several letters and a small blue loose-leaf notebook. McKeon was a stocky man nearly fifty who had fine blond hair combed over his forehead. His eyes were small and playful. McKeon was seldom without a smile, and tonight it was mischievous.

"What are you doing here?" McGarr asked. "And what have you got in your hand?"

Said McKeon, "Day off. I got to thinking just what would a disturbed country man like James Cleary do with such an item with the I.R.A. after it and him not knowing who was in the army and who not, his own sister being one of their gunwomen. Sure, says I, he'd put it in the post if he was able, and since he wasn't he'd put it in a mailbox. His own or Quirks', since he was beyond getting to the Garda barracks. That would explain the car and burning furniture." He wiggled the notebook over his head.

McGarr could tell McKeon had been drinking.

John Quirk, standing by McKeon's side, was not sober.

In the house McGarr could hear singing, and in through the kitchen windows he could see people dancing.

"I thought I'd follow me hunch."

McGarr extended his hand.

McKeon gave him the notebook.

Quirk asked, "Have you caught the bastard, McGarr?"

"Not yet."

"Do you know who he is?"

"Yes."

"Anybody I know?"

"Yes indeed."

Quirk sipped from the glass of amber fluid in his left hand. "Say no more. I don't want to know." He turned and walked toward the house.

McGarr raised the book to the faint light from the falling sun. Farrell looked over his shoulder. Fogarty came up to them. They read:

August 8th: Went over to Dr. John Fleming's house to confirm my suspicion that I'm pregnant. Took him a long time to answer the door. In his office, which doubles as an emergency room, was a man with a gaping wound in his stomach that had obviously been made by the shrapnel of a bomb. John was all alone and having difficulty treating the man without an additional pair of hands. I scrubbed up and assisted him. Midway in the operation the man began to moan and thrash about. John sent me down to the basement for supplies of anaesthetic. As far as I could remember, this house had no cellar. There I found a complete laboratory equipt in what seemed a most modern way. The storeroom was chock full of all sorts of chemicals, but I noticed in particular several fifty-gallon drums of nitrates. Near the storeroom was a table with a map of Ireland under glass. The map was covered with markings of districts, commanding officers, and numbers of men. Fortunately, I was carrying my Minox in the pocket of my slacks and I snapped that. Then my eye caught something else. It was like a memo but had obviously come in code, and John had been busy trying to translate it when the man upstairs had interrupted him. All he had pieced out so far was, "All bets on horse show." I took a picture of that too and hustled back upstairs. Later John asked me if I had understood the sig-

nificance of the setup in the cellar. I told him I'm neither
dumb nor blind. Perhaps that was a mistake, but he's not
the sort of person who would have believed a lie from me.
He said nothing else, only looked at me. John has never
done anything halfway. Once he's decided, he becomes a
zealot. There was a certain cast to his eye. For some time
now we haven't been on the best of terms. This assignment
is becoming more snarled by the day. I seem to have become involved with these people—Max Schwerr and Fleming—on a personal basis, which can be fatal for a journalist.

How well she had written, she could not have known,
McGarr thought.

"The Dublin Horse Show?" Commissioner Farrell asked.
"Why, that begins in three days. Mother of Mercy—the queen
is planning to attend for the first time in ages. Her daughter is
riding for England. It's not since before independence that the
English regent has attended the show."

"There's more," said McKeon, with that same self-satisfied
smile on his face. He flipped a page.

August 10th: Tragedy has struck. I took the film out of
my Minox last night and put it on my bureau so in the
morning I could take it to Limerick, where I had arranged
to get the use of a photographer's darkroom. But my Da,
who gets up with the sun and can't be doing enough for
me, took the roll of film into the chemist's in Lahinch. His
name is Fitzgerald, and I know for a fact he's a Fenian. I
couldn't just rush to him and demand it back, because
they're watching me closely now and would know something was up. So I tried all day long to get it back from the
photo lab in Dublin, but it seems that's impossible.

August 11th: Film back today. Lightning service for Ireland. Perhaps we should consider putting the I.R.A. in
charge of the mails. The film, of course, was blank.
Fitzgerald was far too solicitous of my photographic tech-

niques. Said, "Those little spy-type cameras are no good at all. Sure only a criminal would use one anyhow." And so I've decided to begin carrying the weapon Paddy gave me in New York. Tomorrow I'm to pay Max $27,000, which the I.R.A. leadership has demanded as payment for their candor. It smacks of extortion, but if the "Horse Show" et al. means the Dublin Horse Show, then the tip could be worth every penny. The queen will be there. I've tried to put this notebook in a safe deposit box in the bank, but it was closed when I got there. I'm afraid to leave it at home. I'm causing my parents enough worry as it is with this assignment.

That was the last entry she had made.

Farrell asked, "Do you think she wouldn't have tipped us off, all the while knowing something was going to happen?"

McGarr turned to him. "Would you if you were a big-time newspaper person and had gotten a tip on a breaking story that would have enormous international significance?" McGarr then turned his head to Fogarty, who had been looking over his shoulder.

Fogarty scratched the ridge line of bone along his perfectly bald head. "After all, Commissioner, she wasn't a policewoman, and you fellows will be protecting the queen with tanks, I should think."

Farrell's eyes widened. He glared down on Fogarty. "It always helps to know."

"Oh, of course," Fogarty added quickly. "*We'd* tell you. The *Times.*"

McGarr said, "The day the queen arrived."

Farrell said, "And let me tell you something else, my friend from the fourth estate: what you're seeing here is state information. You'll have a telegram from the minister of justice about that within the hour. You've got to go on working with me and

Peter, so don't go making another dumb-ass mistake or you'll find yourself in the cooler quicker than you can say Adolf Hitler. Have ya got me right?"

Fogarty looked away and sighed.

14

THE DEVILS WE KNOW

McGarr and Farrell didn't stop at Kinvara with the others. They dropped Noreen and Hughie Ward off at O'Shaughnessy's aunt's house and drove on to Galway City and the hospital in which Phil Dineen was receiving care.

The hall of the third-floor wing was thick with Gardai. It was just midnight and the shifts watching Dineen were changing.

Dineen's wife, Bridie, was there as well. She rushed up to McGarr. "Peter—I knew you'd come. Can you tell me how much he'll get?" She meant jail, of course. She took McGarr's hand. She was a small woman whose mother had been Spanish-Irish from someplace out here in the West. Bridie's sallow complexion and dark eyes, ringed and sleepless, made her look haggard. She wore her hair, as always, in jet black ringlets. Women with Latin blood, McGarr had noted in the past, seemed to age more quickly, especially when they'd had children. Bridie Dineen had six children and one on the way.

McGarr bent and kissed her cheek. "That depends upon what he's done. And I know of nothing he's done that we're interested in, do you, Commissioner Farrell?"

The two policemen had talked about Dineen on the ride to the hospital: how Dineen could help them with the horse show lead they'd uncovered, how if he did they would refuse to prosecute him on other evidence of criminal activity they had against him. Dineen himself, McGarr imagined, understood his position with the Provos. For some reason, they had decided to get rid of him.

His wife said, "He caught a bit of the bomb in his left eye. But it was enough. They say he'll lose it. He went through Korea and Suez and Cyprus and Lebanon without so much as a scratch, and now this. And by the people he was supposed to be fighting for, too. But I guess he was lucky." And then, when she remembered, she added, "And you too, Peter. I almost forgot." She squeezed his hand again.

McGarr assured her everything would work out for the best and went in to Dineen.

Unlike Jamie Cleary's hospital room, Dineen's was dark, except for a small bluish light over the door.

"Saying your prayers?" McGarr asked.

"That's the only dependable guidance, they say." Dineen's head was swathed in bandages and both eyes were covered. He held out his hand.

McGarr shook it and introduced Farrell.

"All the big guns," said Dineen. "My nose, which has become quite perceptive of late, tells me there must be a deal in the air. If so, my prayers have been answered. Or are these voices I'm hearing from the lower world?"

Farrell looked at McGarr and smiled. "We don't have much time, Mr. Dineen. It's the horse show plans we're after."

"You mean they're going through with that foolishness?"

McGarr said, "So it seems."

"Christ. Then I'm glad they're through with me."

Said Farrell, "We can promise you this. Protection and a pardon."

Dineen hesitated.

McGarr said, "C'mon, Phil, we can't do any better than that."

Still Dineen said nothing. He fumbled on the nightstand, found his packet of cigarettes, and took out a smoke.

Farrell lit it.

McGarr took a chair by the bedside. "Don't tell me you want money?"

Dineen shook his head. "It's not that. I'll get by." He blew out the smoke. "It's that I've never been a fink. I spent seven months in a North Korean prison camp without giving more than my name and rank. It's hard to—" he drew again upon the cigarette, which glowed brightly in the darkness of the room. "—and then there's my family. I don't know if my kids would even begin to understand." He waved his hand. "You know, how I really had nothing to do with this situation."

McGarr said, "Well, when did the Provos ever even use you? Shit—it seems to me they kept you stuck way out here because they're afraid of your kind of fighting. When did they ever go at things your way? Face up to it—you made a mistake. They're just a pack of sneaks. Drop the bomb and run. They did it to us. They're planning to do it at the horse show, am I right?"

Dineen nodded.

Farrell pulled up a chair.

McGarr said, "The other day when we talked, you said you'd joined them because you'd made a decision about how things should be in this country and you were doing something about it. Okay. I accepted that. But your position has changed. The decision to blow up scores of people and maybe a queen has already been made too. It's just another affair that stinks. Now you know enough about these bastards that maybe the bunch of us working together can stop it from happening. But it's up to you. You've got to decide if it's right or wrong.

"Look—here's what we'll do: protection for your wife and kids. By that I mean we'll move them, someplace out here where your wife's mother is from. A new identity. A house." McGarr glanced over at Farrell.

He tilted his head, but then nodded.

"Aw, Peter—" Dineen began to say.

"Wait—hear me out. And a job for you."

Farrell reached over and touched McGarr's sleeve.

But McGarr continued, "We've been thinking of expanding our surveillance of the Provos and other I.R.A. activity. We'll consider this your first assignment." That much was true. Farrell and McGarr had gotten the minister of justice to agree to the proposal already. "Now that's a necessity. Who better to head that team but you, who know about them personally." McGarr turned to Farrell, who liked the idea only somewhat better.

Farrell said, "We'd have to get that through the minister himself."

"What rank and pay?" said Dineen. He added, "I'm only saying that for my kids."

McGarr turned to Farrell, who stood and said, "Let me call the minister. If I can clear the idea with him, then we can talk terms." He left the room.

Dineen thanked McGarr. "I was worried about what I'd do. Who the hell would think of hiring a one-eyed bandido with special disqualifications in this country, I was asking myself."

"Only the Garda Soichana," said McGarr. "What about Fleming?"

"A true believer. He was the one—"

McGarr knew what he was going to say. "Who killed May Quirk, who tried to kill us. What's he like as a tactician? What can we expect from him at the horse show?"

"Anything. He's unpredictable. And he's managed to put

242

together a large band of followers. They're like he is—total commitment. He's got a kind of zealot's charisma. He's bright, and he's got money."

"O'Connor's?"

"Not just his. Fleming's got other money. Funny money."

"From a foreign government?" No wonder they hadn't hesitated to blow up the packet of money McGarr had delivered to Dineen at the Salthill dance hall.

"I don't want to be hard about this, Peter. But let's see what your boss has to say. I'd prefer to have him legitimize my blabbing."

Twenty minutes later Farrell returned and said he had a carte blanche to quash whatever Fleming had in mind for the horse show and to put him behind bars.

Dineen was given a superintendent's pay with a written guarantee of a five-year tenure that was renewable. The three men talked until dawn. Then an angry doctor ejected the two policemen. Dineen's eye was infected and he needed rest.

For the first time in his career, McGarr had taken copious notes.

15

THE BASTARDS WHAT DONE IT

The Brazen Head was Dublin's oldest public house. To get to the bar, one had to walk through the cobblestone courtyard of the inn. The ceiling was low and a tall man had to stoop.

Out of the corner of his eye McGarr was watching for that. He was seated at a table with his head turned from the door. He was wearing a soft hat with a wide brim.

Fergus Farrell was standing at the end of the bar. There he had a Walther PPK concealed under a newspaper.

Bernie McKeon was seated on a stool on the low dais playing a fiddle with other amateur musicians, who had been recruited from the Garda Soichana as well.

Hughie Ward, dressed in a porter-stained frock, was pulling pints behind the bar.

Out in the courtyard, Harry Greaves was slouched into the corner of a wall. He looked like he was sleeping it off.

Paul Sinclair and Liam O'Shaughnessy were sitting in the back of a van parked outside. It also contained a one-way window, a radio, and three uniformed Gardai.

A similar van stood in the alley behind the Brazen Head.

O'Connor was the first to arrive. He came down the staircase from the guest accommodations upstairs.

McGarr turned his head away from him.

Hughie Ward bent as though to arrange the rows of bottles under the bar.

O'Connor took a seat in the far corner of the room. He kept his back to the wall.

Five minutes later Fleming appeared in the doorway. He looked around.

Ward pulled two pints of black and frothy Guinness for him and cashed a twenty-dollar American travelers check.

Fleming spoke with a Midwestern American twang when talking to him. The bar was too dark for O'Connor to recognize Ward from the distance.

Fleming carried the drinks to a table and sat.

A half hour later, when their pints had dwindled and they obviously had begun to feel comfortable in the room, Ward placed two more pints on the table.

Fleming looked up, surprised. "We didn't order these."

"From the gentleman sitting near the door." Ward withdrew from the table but did not go back to the bar.

O'Connor and Fleming looked around the room. All the other guests had left.

McGarr turned and faced the two young men from Clare. He had May Quirk's Mauser in his right hand.

The music stopped.

Farrell and Ward had their weapons drawn as well.

McGarr gestured with the gun and O'Connor and Fleming stood with their hands raised. O'Connor's head was touching the ceiling.

McGarr flicked the barrel of the gun again and they turned and faced the wall. McGarr stood and approached them. "I'd call it a strange setting for two revolutionaries in search of a new social order. But I suppose even Lenin quaffed the odd pint. He

245

was a killer too, but I wonder if he ever stooped to murdering a childhood friend or a lover."

O'Connor rested his forehead against the wall.

Fleming began to turn his head to McGarr.

"Keep your sly, foul eyes on the wall, Doctor." McGarr removed a Baretta special from Fleming's jacket, a large Colt pistol from under O'Connor's sweater. "I know two pensioners on the Kishanny road who wouldn't shed a tear if I were to plug two bastards like you."

A day later the queen arrived. Her daughter and son-in-law performed creditably, but Harvey Smith won the puissance.